THE
HUSBAND
BEFORE
YOU

BOOKS BY A J MCDINE

The Baby

The Photo

Everyone Has Secrets

When She Finds You

Should Have Known Better

No One I Knew

The Promise You Made

The Invite

A J MCDINE

THE HUSBAND BEFORE YOU

bookouture

Published by Bookouture in 2025

An imprint of Storyfire Ltd.
Carmelite House
50 Victoria Embankment
London EC4Y 0DZ

www.bookouture.com

The authorised representative in the EEA is Hachette Ireland
8 Castlecourt Centre
Dublin 15 D15 XTP3
Ireland
(email: info@hbgi.ie)

ISBN: 978-1-83525-938-2
eBook ISBN: 978-1-83525-937-5

To Sue McDine and Barbara Ward, with love

1

ALEX

NOW

I KNOW THE TRUTH.

The four words have been scrawled in capital letters across the crumpled piece of paper in my hand.

It's the same handwriting, the same message, as all the others that have been pushed through our letterbox in the last couple of weeks. Seven in total. Eight if you count the one my husband Carter tore into pieces and threw in the recycling, dismissing it as the work of a nutter. I've kept the rest as evidence. Evidence of what, I'm not sure, because it's not exactly a threat, is it? *I know the truth.* The truth about what?

I shiver, my spine tingling. I have the oddest sensation that I'm being watched, even though there's no way anyone could have crept into our bedroom while I was in the en suite. I spin round, scanning the room, but I'm alone. It's just me and the note and a feeling of unease that's hard to shake.

I exhale slowly, one hand on my diaphragm and my eyes closed, then slip the sheet of paper into the top drawer of my dressing table with the others. I refuse to let an anonymous message ruin tonight. Carter and I have a table booked at The Oak and Ivy, a Michelin-starred gastropub he's been dying to try for months. It's the fourth anniversary of our first date and my second husband is hot on anniversaries in a way that I still haven't got used to. My first husband Freddie and I rarely used to bother. But Carter has always been one for grand gestures.

Six foot four with dark-blond hair and piercing blue eyes, Carter's a consultant paediatrician and is treated like a demigod in the children's ward at Thornden Green Hospital. Patients, parents and staff all worship the ground he walks on. And why wouldn't they? The man saves kids' lives for a living, for goodness' sake. I still can't believe I'm married to him. He's a champagne and flowers kind of guy, an old-fashioned romantic. There aren't many men who'd whisk you to the Royal Opera House to see *La Traviata* on your first date.

I sweep my hair into my trademark updo, securing it with a handful of pins, then check my reflection in the mirror. Ruby-red lipstick to match the clingy dress Carter surprised me with this morning. Smoky eyes, heavy on the kohl, just as he likes it. Towering heels. Ditto. If I squint slightly and suck in my stomach, I could still pass for the woman he married, even though, objectively, I know my curves are getting out of hand and no amount of concealer can hide the bruise-like shadows under my eyes.

Sometimes, I wonder what Freddie would make of me now. It's been ten years since he disappeared, ten years of not knowing if he left us willingly or met some terrible fate. He was declared legally dead three years ago. Carter says it is time I moved on and maybe he's right. But the questions still haunt me, every single day. Where did he go? Why did he leave?

I turn my back to the mirror, shrug on my jacket and make my way along the landing to the nursery. Dylan is asleep, his breathing still a little snuffly after a recent cold. He is sucking his thumb and looks so adorable I want to smother him in kisses, but I resist the urge. It took the best part of an hour to settle him tonight and our table is booked for eight. I make do with smoothing his fine blond fringe from his face. He sighs in his sleep, his thumb falling out of his mouth.

The girls had dummies when they were babies but when Dylan was born almost two years ago Carter said there was no way his son would ever have a pacifier.

'They're breeding grounds for bacteria, never mind the fact that they'll ruin his teeth. Relying on pacifiers to soothe babies is lazy parenting, and we are not lazy parents,' he'd said, somewhat sanctimoniously, when I brought one home from the supermarket. Dylan was a month old and fractious with colic and I was getting desperate.

'The girls turned out fine,' I protested.

'Remind me, when is Erin's next appointment with the orthodontist?' he replied, then grinned as I batted his arm because he knew he'd won the argument. Fourteen-year-old Erin will be in train-track braces for the next two years, and the dentist reckons her ten-year-old sister, Megan, will follow suit.

Still, by choosing to suck his thumb, our son had the last laugh.

'Love you, Dyls,' I whisper, dropping a kiss on his cheek. It's only when I stop in the doorway and steal one final look at him do I realise that the lipstick smear I've left looks like he's been daubed with blood.

* * *

I find Erin and Megan in their onesies in the snug, their heads bent over my iPad.

'What are you two watching?' I ask, peering over Erin's shoulder.

'Just Taylor.' Megan grabs the tablet from her sister and

shows me the screen. Her idol, Taylor Swift, is in a recording booth, earphones on and guitar in hand. 'It's on YouTube.' Megan pronounces it YouToob, like Carter. Since when did she start picking up his Americanisms? I make a mental note to tell him over dinner. He'll be thrilled.

'Have you seen Carter?' I ask. 'We're supposed to be leaving in ten minutes.'

'I think he's in his study,' Megan says.

'Dad's study,' Erin mutters. Megan idolises Carter, but Erin has always been more resistant to his charms. Four when Freddie left, she still remembers her dad with the unwavering devotion of a disciple.

'What time's Auntie Gemma coming?' Megan asks.

'She was supposed to be here at seven. She's probably been held up at work.' My best friend is a staff nurse on the same paediatric ward as Carter, and, like him, she often works late. I feel bad that she's babysitting after a long shift but she did offer. Besides, finding a babysitter on a Saturday night round here is virtually impossible and I'm pretty sure Carter would turn his nose up at a takeaway for our anniversary. 'I'll call to see if she's on her way.'

Megan nods, her focus back on the iPad. I'm halfway across the room when she calls, 'Mum?'

'Yes, darling?'

'I forgot to say, you look pretty.'

I blow her a kiss and she pretends to catch it mid-air, then looks over my shoulder and giggles. Before I can work out why, sinewy arms clasp my waist and I stifle a shriek as I'm dragged into the unlit hallway. Carter nuzzles my neck, his hands roving over me.

'Megan's right,' he breathes into my ear. He smells of spearmint and Dior Sauvage, a heady mix that makes me weak at the knees. 'You look very pretty. Very pretty indeed. What say we scoot upstairs and take a proper look at that dress of yours? Off, preferably.'

'Shush,' I chide, holding my finger to my lips. 'The girls will hear. Anyway, Gemma's going to be here any minute.'

He pulls a face and releases me. It's cold without his arms around me, as though someone's left the back door open and a chill wind is whistling down the hallway. I stand on my tiptoes and kiss him lightly on the lips. 'Can it wait?'

A sigh. 'I suppose it'll have to. But I'm going to hold you to it. You can't keep a man hanging, Alex.'

'I won't.' I kiss him again. 'I promise.'

Appeased, he disappears in search of his shoes while I turn the oven on for the girls' pizzas and try calling Gemma. It goes straight to voicemail.

'Hey, Gem, I'm just checking everything's still OK for tonight, only our taxi is on its way and you're not here.' I pause, realising how peremptory I sound. 'Anyway, let me know your ETA and I'll have a glass of Sauvignon waiting for you.'

As I reach for a wine glass, Carter storms into the room waving a shoe, Fleming, our elderly Golden Retriever, on his heels.

'Look what your bloody mutt has done now,' Carter cries, thrusting the brogue into my hands. Toothmarks pierce the tan-coloured calf leather, and one end of the laces has been chewed right through.

'Oh, Fleming,' I say, and the dog looks up at me with soulful eyes as if he simply cannot fathom how one of Carter's hideously expensive shoes ended up in his mouth. Named after Sir Alexander Fleming, the physician who discovered penicillin, Fleming is twelve years old and has never outgrown the chewing-everything-in-sight phase.

I hand the shoe back to Carter. 'I thought you liked the vintage vibe.'

'This isn't vintage, it's wrecked.' He shoots Fleming a poisonous look. 'How am I supposed to wear them now?'

'Don't worry, I'll find you some new laces and the scratches will polish out. They'll be fine,' I soothe.

'Polish out?' Carter splutters. 'It's not a frigging car.'

I leave him grumbling in the kitchen and head back into the hallway to ferret through the top drawer of the beech console table where I'm pretty sure I saw a pack of brown laces the other day. I smile in satisfaction when I find what I'm looking for and I'm pushing the drawer closed when the doorbell rings. It'll be Gemma. She has a key but she's always leaving it at home or in her locker at work.

'Coming,' I call as I walk to the front door, my heels clicking on the parquet floor. 'Honestly, you'd forget your head if it wasn't screwed on,' I say, turning the latch. 'Where've you left your key this time, Gem?'

My words dry up as I stare at the man standing on the doorstep. He is gaunt, his eyes hooded in an angular face. He has a straggly beard and flint-grey hair in dire need of a wash.

Freddie.

My hand flies to my mouth and I stumble backwards. My mind must be playing tricks on me because it can't be him. Not after all this time. Not after *ten years.*

'Alex?' he says, taking a step towards me. His voice is gravelly, as if he hasn't used it in a while. Blood whooshes in my ears, sending my head spinning.

Freddie is back.

His face is panicked as he takes another step forward, his hands stretched towards me. His fingernails are caked in dirt.

It's the last thought I have before everything turns black and I crumple to the ground.

2

ALEX

NOW

I edge into consciousness, my senses slowly coming round. Sounds first. The thrum of my own heart. My name, whispered so quietly I wonder if I've imagined it. Smell next. The faint scent of lavender and eucalyptus from the potpourri in the hallway. Something else, something earthier, more masculine. Stale sweat and musty fabric. Then touch. Something, some*one*, is stroking my face, knuckles gently grazing my cheek.

I want to open my eyes, but I don't dare in case I'm dreaming. God knows, I used to dream about Freddie turning up on the doorstep just like this every night for years. Dreams in which he supplied plausible explanations for walking out of our lives. He'd suffered amnesia after hitting his head, or he'd got himself so deeply in debt he had no other option but to disappear. He'd been taken into witness protection after his evidence led to the conviction of an organised crime group. He was sorry and he wanted to come home.

Every morning, I would wake up to find his side of the bed

empty and my pillow damp with tears. Gradually, over the years, I dreamt about Freddie less, and the tears dried up.

Of course this isn't Freddie. It *can't* be him.

A hand clasps my wrist, a thumbprint on my radial artery, and I imagine the blood pulsing through the veins into the tips of my fingers. A normal resting pulse rate for adults is between sixty and a hundred beats per minute. It's the kind of fact you absorb by osmosis when you're married to a doctor.

'Alex, are you all right?' the voice says.

It's no good. I have to know. I prise my eyes open and a face swims into focus. Close up, it's almost cadaverous, and I shrink back, I can't help myself. But there is an aching familiarity to the heavy eyebrows, the almond-shaped eyes, the high cheekbones.

'Freddie?'

His eyes lock onto mine and when he gives me the ghost of a smile, I know I'm not dreaming. Freddie, my husband – I correct myself: my *first* husband – is back.

'What the fuck!' Carter roars and Freddie and I both start as he crashes into the hallway, grabs Freddie by the neck and hauls him to his feet before flinging him against the wall. 'Call the police!' he yells at me, then turns back to Freddie and tightens his grip on his neck.

Panic pumps a shot of adrenalin straight into my heart and I scramble up.

'Carter, no!' I cry, tugging ineffectually at his shoulder, but he shrugs me off. 'Can't you see?' I plead. 'It's Freddie!'

Carter's hands fall to his sides and he steps back as if he's been winded.

'Mate.' Freddie holds out a hand. 'Long time no see.'

Carter shakes his head as if he can't compute the fact that his old friend is back. I know how he feels. It's too much to take in. Carter was as devastated as I was when Freddie went missing. It took years of therapy back in the States to find closure. I glance at him. Emotions play across his face. Disbelief. Hope. Something else. Something *darker*.

He is angry. I get that too. I'm sure I'll be incandescent once the shock has worn off. A muscle twitches in his jaw. He looks as if he might punch Freddie's lights out or wrap him in a bear hug. It could go either way.

'Carter,' Freddie says, and maybe it's the ring of pleading in his scratchy voice, or his hollow cheeks and scruffy clothes but, after a moment's hesitation, the tension in Carter's shoulders eases and he grins and cries, 'Where the hell have you been, you bastard?' And the tears stream down my face as the two men embrace.

A movement catches my eye and I look round. Megan is hovering in the doorway of the kitchen wide-eyed, a bowl of popcorn in her hands. Her gaze tracks from Freddie to Carter and then she turns to me.

'Who's that man?'

For a moment I'm lost for words. Because how can I explain that her biological father, the man who walked out on her when she was a three-month-old baby, is back? Before I can find the words Erin appears behind her.

'Daddy?'

Freddie drops to his knees and holds out his arms. 'Hey, princess.'

A grin spreads across Erin's face, in stark contrast to her sister, who is rooted to the spot, staring at Freddie with an almost morbid horror as if he is a zombie returned from the dead. Which he may as well be, for we all thought we'd never see him again. Erin sidesteps Megan and runs down the hallway to her father only to be knocked flying by Fleming, who bowls in from the kitchen like a mini tornado and hurls himself at Freddie.

It is then that I hear a key in the lock and the front door opens.

'Sorry I'm so late,' Gemma says. 'There was a problem with a patient's PICC line which pushed the handover back...'

She appears round the door jamb and stops in her tracks as she takes in the scene. Fleming bouncing around the hallway like an overgrown puppy, barking joyfully. The girls' shell-shocked faces. Carter and I standing to one side, as frozen as mannequins. And, in the centre of everything, Freddie, who has walked back into our marital home almost as casually as he left it a decade ago.

Gemma's mouth falls open. 'Holy crap,' she says.

3

FREDDIE

TEN YEARS AGO

I walk through the double doors into the children's ward and past the colourful circus mural paid for by the local Rotary Club. I'd questioned the wisdom of including a clown among the trapeze artists and acrobats, the horses and the dancing dogs, when the artist painted it.

'A fear of clowns is one of the most common phobias in children,' I told my boss at the time, Eric Langsford. 'It'll give the kids nightmares.'

But Eric was weeks away from retirement, too focused on the motorhome in which he planned to tour Europe to care about his young patients, and so the clown stayed.

Only the other day a little boy with a stage four brain tumour asked me in a frightened whisper why the creepy clown was staring at him. I would have gone straight out to buy a tin of emulsion and painted over the bloody thing there and then, but there wasn't time. There was never any time.

Today is no different. The moment Simisola, the ward's senior staff nurse, sees me arrive, she beckons me into the cramped office where the night team are finishing their handover.

Carter, my best friend from med school and one of the registrars on Dolphin Ward, breaks off as I walk in, greeting me with a weary smile.

'Welcome to the madhouse, Freddie.'

I sip my takeaway coffee and listen as Carter brings the day shift up to speed. Every bed in the ward is full, as are the four bays in the children's assessment unit and the three beds in the high-dependency unit. As if it can't get any worse, Simi announces that two of her nursing team and a healthcare assistant have phoned in sick after succumbing to a particularly nasty strain of flu that's doing the rounds.

I run a hand through my hair and try to keep my rising sense of panic under control. The trick, I've discovered, is to pretend everything is fine and sometimes – not always, but sometimes – you can convince yourself it is.

The stress is unrelenting. Every day I'm responsible for life-and-death decisions. Every day I and my equally exhausted colleagues work under increasing pressure, a legacy of decades of underinvestment in the health service. Sixty-hour weeks are the norm, and hardly a weekend goes by when I'm not on call. At least two of my med school cohort have been signed off with long-term stress after suffering burnout.

I tune back into the handover, hoping I haven't missed anything. My mind is already racing as I mentally prioritise my patients. Top of the list is Bertie, a four-year-old with complex needs who came in yesterday with a kidney infection and needs a CT scan and bloods done ASAP.

'Sorry I'm late. The bloody bus drove right past my stop.' Gemma flies into the office, her cheeks flushed pink, shooting an apologetic look at me and avoiding the gaze of Simi, who runs a tight ship and doesn't tolerate tardiness. As Gemma unwinds the woollen scarf Alex knitted for her last Christmas, I catch the faintest whiff of cigarette smoke and feel a pang of longing. I gave up smoking in my third year at med school but right now I would kill for a fag.

'Can't be helped.' I turn to Carter, who looks grey with exhaustion. 'Are we done?'

Carter nods. 'We are.'

A phone rings, and Simi answers. 'Dolphin Ward, Sister Adebayo speaking.' She pauses, her eyes trained on me. 'He's about to start his ward rounds. I see. Right, I'll pass you over.' She covers the receiver with her palm. 'It's Helen Fairchild. Says she needs to talk to you urgently.'

My heart sinks as I take the phone. Fairchild is the trust's new clinical director and is keen to make her mark on the organisation after rising through the nursing ranks.

'Morning, Helen.' I attempt to inject warmth into my voice and fail miserably. 'What can I do for you?'

'We've just been notified of an upcoming inspection by the CQC and they're focusing on Dolphin Ward.'

The contents of my stomach lurch sickeningly and I slump onto the nearest chair. Why the hell is the Care Quality Commission, the healthcare watchdog, suddenly inspecting us?

'Concerns about staffing levels have been raised by parents,' Helen continues, reading my thoughts.

'Probably because they're inadequate,' I begin, but the clinical director cuts across me.

'I need you to prepare a full report on staffing patterns and patient outcomes for the last six months.'

'Of course.' My old boss Eric would have pushed back, but I feel too young in post to argue. 'When do you need it?' I ask, thinking of Bertie and all the other children on the ward. They need me more than a bunch of box-ticking inspectors.

'Yesterday,' Helen says crisply and the line goes dead.

'What's up, bud?' Carter asks from the other side of the office.

'A CQC inspection. Helen needs me to pull together some stats. I'll have to do it tonight.' I swear as I remember Alex's parting words as I left the house.

'Something wrong?'

I rub my face. 'Alex will kill me if I'm late again. She... she isn't coping too well.'

'With the baby?'

I nod. 'Nothing too serious, just a touch of the baby blues. Megan isn't feeding well, and Erin is flexing her muscles.'

'Poor Erin. She's probably feeling a bit sidelined,' Carter says sympathetically.

'Something like that,' I agree. 'But it's stressing Alex out.' When I kissed her goodbye this morning she burst into tears and begged me not to go to work, but what choice do I have? I can't let my patients down.

'Tell you what, I'll stay on and do ward rounds while you put together your report for the CQC,' Carter says.

'But you've just worked a twelve-hour shift.'

'And you've probably been up half the night with the baby,' he points out.

He's right. I slept for about four hours last night. Alex tries not to wake me when she gets up to feed Megan, but with the baby in a cot in our room it's impossible to sleep through her piercing wails and it seems disloyal to decamp to the spare bedroom.

I could weep with gratitude. 'Are you sure?'

'Course I'm sure.' Carter loops his stethoscope back round his neck. 'That's what friends are for.'

Perhaps I should feel disloyal for implying that Alex is barely holding it together, but I don't. Instead, I feel relief that Carter is here for me, when she's not.

Alex and I can't go on like this. Something has to give. The question is, what? And even if I figure it out, will it be in time to save us?

4

ALEX

NOW

My heart still thumping, I take charge, ushering everyone into the kitchen, then retreating to the living room to cancel our cab and table because it's clear that Carter and I will not be going out for a meal to celebrate our anniversary tonight.

My head is all over the place. It is, as the girls would say, totes awks, though that might be the understatement of the year. It is beyond awkward, it's... actually I don't know what it is. All I do know is that the man I married fifteen years ago has absolutely no idea that I walked down the aisle with his best friend twelve years later.

There's a tap at the door and Gemma appears, a sympathetic expression on her face.

'I thought I might find you in here.'

'I was just cancelling the cab.'

'And laying low,' she says, one eyebrow raised.

I hold up a hand. 'Guilty, M'lud.'

Gemma perches next to me and lays a comforting hand on my knee. She's been my best friend since our first day at secondary school. We've been through everything together. Bad haircuts, spots, teenage crushes. First dates, first jobs, first heartbreaks. We're closer than sisters. Sometimes I think she knows me better than I know myself.

In some ways, we're chalk and cheese. I'm five foot four and curvy with a mass of walnut-brown hair. Gemma is blonde, a good six inches taller, with the lean build of a long-distance runner and legs up to her armpits. While I'll do anything to avoid a confrontation, Gem has a kick-ass attitude that leaves me in awe; she's never afraid to stand her ground, especially when she feels wronged. At times I wish I could be a little less Alex and a little more Gemma.

'How are you feeling?' she asks.

I groan. 'I don't know. All those years of waiting, of wondering where Freddie was. And he turns up on the doorstep just like that! I should be elated, but I just feel...' I shake my head. 'Numb.'

'It's the shock,' Gemma soothes. 'It's bound to take a while to process.'

'We need to tell the police, the presumption of death people.' My voice is rising. 'What about Alan and Mary?' Freddie's elderly parents are on a six-week cruise in the Caribbean. 'I should try to call them to let them know he's all right.'

'Slow down,' Gemma says. 'One step at a time. Anyway, I think it's up to Freddie to tell his parents he's back, don't you?'

'And the girls. What the hell must they be thinking?'

'Erin looks like Christmas came early.'

'What about Megan?' I ask.

Gemma won't look me in the eye and my stomach swoops. While Erin can remember her father, as far as Megan's concerned, Carter is her dad. Who can blame her? He's the one who comes with me to parents' evenings and school sports days. He takes her swimming and he taught her to play basketball. He is her dad in all but name.

'Megan will be fine, she just needs to get used to the idea, like the rest of us. Come on,' Gemma says, jumping up from the sofa and heading for the door.

I follow her on leaden legs.

* * *

Carter is standing by the sink with his hands in his pockets, staring out into the dark. Freddie is sitting at the kitchen table, a pot of tea and a packet of chocolate digestives in front of him.

'Where are the girls?' I ask.

'Looking for photo albums to show their father.' There's a hard edge to Carter's voice and I glance at Freddie to see if he's noticed too, but he is working his way through the biscuits as if he hasn't eaten for a week.

'I'll go and find them,' Gemma says, ignoring my pleading look.

Once she's gone, Carter turns round to face Freddie. 'So, you're back.'

'I am,' Freddie says evenly.

'Where the hell have you been?'

Freddie tugs his beard. 'Do we have to do this right now?'

'Yes, we bloody well do!' I cry. 'I went through hell when you walked out. Hell! You knew I was struggling. Did you not stop for one minute to wonder how I would cope on my own?' My voice cracks. '*If* I would cope on my own?'

Freddie's gaze drops.

'And what about Erin and Megan? They've had to grow up without their dad because of... because of what? Please tell me, because I'm all ears.'

He still can't meet my eye. My heart crashes in my chest. I've suppressed so many emotions for so long in a desperate attempt to shield the girls that this rage is cathartic.

'I'm sorry, I—' he begins.

'You're sorry? And that makes it all right? That's how this works, is it? You apologise, I forgive you, and we can all go back to playing happy families like the last ten years never happened?'

'No, but I was hoping—'

'If you think you can breeze in here like everything is hunky-dory, you've got another think coming. And why come back now?'

'I... I thought it was time.'

Carter exhales and turns back to the window. Freddie pushes the packet of biscuits away. My own stomach churns, my rage giving way to apprehension. At what point do I tell Freddie that Carter and I are married? That we have a child together? I glance around the room. There are clues every-where. The baby monitor next to the toaster; the photos of Dylan and the girls on the mantel above the range cooker; the blue sleepsuits airing on the radiator.

The stand-off is broken by Erin, appearing with a stack of photo albums.

'Look, Dad,' she says, 'Mum and I did them for you. One for every year so we could show you what you'd missed when you came home.' She pushes the teapot to one side and sets the albums on the table. 'The first one's when Megan's still a baby. They go right up to last year when—'

'I'm not sure your dad wants to look at them right now, sweetheart,' I begin, but Erin ignores me. Soon they are leafing through the albums together, and even though it was my idea to do them for Freddie in the first place, I feel as though I'm under a microscope, my life being judged, and it makes my skin crawl.

Looking for a distraction, I remember the girls still haven't had their tea so I put a couple of pizzas and some garlic bread in the oven. By the time I've cut up some cherry tomatoes and cucumber and set the table, Gemma and Megan have appeared.

Freddie looks up from one of the albums and addresses

Carter. 'Thank you, mate. You obviously took your job as Erin's godfather seriously while I was away.'

I freeze, one hand on the oven door.

Gemma looks horrified. 'OMG, you haven't told him, have you?'

'Told me what?'

Feeling the heat of Freddie's gaze, I glance at Carter. His expression is unreadable.

'We're married,' I say at last.

'I know we are,' Freddie says equably.

'Not us,' I say, shaking my head. 'Carter and I. We're married.'

5

FREDDIE

TEN YEARS AGO

I brace myself as I unlock the front door. The days when I used to look forward to coming home seem a long time ago. Our four-bedroom, late-Victorian villa in a tree-lined street near the park used to be a haven, a refuge from work, where I could forget all about the demands of my high-pressured job. OK, maybe not forget, but at least put to the back of my mind. But lately our home has become a battleground, and I've started to dread putting my key in the lock, never sure which version of my wife I'll find inside.

Despite what I told Carter this morning, I know the tears and the low moods, the anxiety and the feelings of hopelessness are more than the baby blues. But whenever I try to broach the subject, Alex either flies off the handle or storms off in a flood of tears.

This evening, the house is silent, and a tiny flicker of hope flares deep in my belly. I could do without having to jolly Alex out of her despair for a change. I've had the day from hell. After pulling together the report for Helen Fairchild, I sent Carter home and got on with the day-to-day business of reviewing patients, writing discharge summaries and ordering blood tests and scans. In the afternoon, I had a clinic which, as usual, over-ran, and then it was back to the ward for the handover to the late team. At least I'm not on call tonight. Small mercies.

'I'm home,' I call into the empty hallway, frowning when there's no answer. It's gone seven. Normally Alex is in the throes of bath and bedtime by now. And where's Fleming? The retriever has the hearing of a bat and a seemingly innate sense of when I'm about to come through the door, waiting to greet me with excited woofs and a thumping tail.

Perhaps they've decamped to my parents'. My mum knows Alex is struggling and tries to pop by every couple of days to take Erin to the park or to prepare our dinner. Alex's own parents moved to North Cornwall when they retired and, apart from a flying visit when Megan was born, aren't much help.

I drape my coat over the newel post and heel off my shoes. Erin's toys are scattered on the parquet floor like fallen leaves and the hallway smells faintly of vomit. I pull out my phone, about to call my mum, when I hear a muffled sobbing, carrying through the stillness of the house. I hurry into the kitchen to find Alex, still in her pyjamas, huddled in the corner by the washing machine, her shoulders juddering and her face wet with tears. Megan thrashes in the Winnie-the-Pooh bouncy chair on the other side of the room, her little face puckered and puce. I spin on my heels, searching for Erin, relief washing over me when I spy our eldest daughter, wearing only a T-shirt and pants, curled up on the sofa by the bay window, fast asleep. The kitchen looks like a bomb's hit it: dishes piled high in the sink, dribbles of spilled milk on the worktops, empty cereal packets spewing out of the overflowing recycling bin.

I scoop the baby up and hold her close, shushing her gently as I sway from side to side. Underpinning my relief is a spark of anger, a spark fanned by the pent-up frustrations of the day, my lack of sleep and the exhaustion of having to deal with Alex's new Jekyll-and-Hyde personality on top of everything else. All she has to do is keep the three of them alive while I go to work, for Christ's sake. Is it too much to ask?

Megan is rooting against my neck. 'Have you fed her?' I ask Alex.

She uncoils like a cobra, her tear-stained face twisted in fury. 'Have I fed her?' she spits. 'I've been feeding her for the last eight hours. I have done nothing but feed her and still she won't stop crying.'

On the sofa, Erin stirs at the sound of Alex's voice, lifts her head and starts grizzling.

'Oh, for Christ's sake,' Alex cries. 'Not you as well!'

'Alex,' I say warningly, cradling Megan's head as I cross the room to Erin. 'Hello, angel. Have you had your tea?'

Erin shakes her head, her round eyes solemn.

'What d'you fancy, some spaghetti on toast?' It isn't exactly nutritious, but at this point I'm past caring.

'Alphabet spaghetti?' Erin checks.

'Of course.' I smile. 'Why don't I get you some veggie straws while I fix it?' I rummage through the cupboard where we keep Erin's snacks, finding an old packet of veggie straws behind a couple of cartons of formula left over from when she was a baby. My hand hovers over the cartons. Alex was eaten up with guilt when she couldn't breastfeed the first time around. The other mums at our antenatal class seemed to find it so easy, and although Alex persevered, after two bouts of mastitis even the district midwife advised her to switch to formula. She's been determined to make it work with Megan, but our daughter struggles to latch on, and Alex's milk has been slow coming through.

I rip the packet of veggie straws open with my teeth, give them to Erin, then reach a decision, taking one of the cartons of formula from the cupboard.

'What are you doing?' Alex snaps. 'I'm supposed to be breastfeeding, remember? It's better for the baby.'

'I know, but you're exhausted, and she's not getting enough milk.'

'What kind of a mother am I if I can't even feed my own baby?' Alex wails, flipping from vengeful to woebegone with a speed that makes my head spin.

'You are feeding her. We're just going to use a bit of formula to top it up. There's no shame in that.'

'But—' Alex begins, then her body sags. 'Oh, whatever. Do what you like. I don't care.'

I sweep aside a pile of clutter on the kitchen table, lift Megan's bouncy chair onto it and strap her in so she can watch while I find the bottle steriliser and pop it in the microwave. While I wait for it to ping, I pour Erin a beaker of milk and sit her on her booster seat. 'I'm going to give your sister her bottle, then I'll do your spaghetti, OK?'

Erin nods. 'OK, Daddy.'

I test the temperature of the milk on my wrist, then settle Megan in the crook of my arm, gently brushing the teat of the bottle against her lips. The tension leaves her face as her mouth closes over the teat and she starts to feed. Alex hauls herself up from the floor and begins making Erin's tea, her movements so slow as she opens the tin of spaghetti and pops two slices of bread in the toaster, they are almost robotic.

The smell of the bread toasting makes my stomach rumble. I didn't have time for lunch, existing on a handful of chocolates from a tin of Quality Street given to the nursing staff by a grateful parent. I don't dare ask Alex what we're having for dinner, not in the mood she's in. It isn't worth the aggro. I'll have to order takeout. Again.

Something occurs to me as I sit Megan on my knee and rub her back. 'Where's Fleming?'

Alex looks up from the toast she's buttering, her brow furrowed.

'The dog,' I add patiently. 'You know, that big, yellow four-legged doofball that wags his tail and barks a lot?'

Her face pales. 'Oh, God, I let him out for a wee after lunch.'

'He's been outside since then? But it's freezing out there.' I hand her Megan, who promptly starts wailing, and march over to the back door. Unlocking it, I whistle, and the retriever shoots out from behind the shed and bounds across the lawn towards me. I reach down and bury my face in his fur. As I breathe in his familiar doggy smell, the weight of everything hits me like a ton of bricks. The relentless demands of my job, the lack of sleep, the fact that Alex seems to have checked out of our marriage. I feel suffocated by it all: the pressure to be a good doctor, a good father, a good husband, is overwhelming.

For a fleeting, terrifying second, I realise I can walk away from it all, anytime I like. I can grab my coat and leave. I can't seem to do anything right, so who would miss me? Then, just as quickly as the thought appears, I push it away, common sense and a deeply ingrained sense of duty taking over. I love Alex and the girls and can't imagine a life without them. They're everything to me. This is just a rough patch and I need to try to get us all through it. I give Fleming's ear a final tweak, straighten stiffly, and shuffle back to the table to rejoin my wife and daughters.

6

ALEX

NOW

Freddie's eyes narrow.

'You're married? My wife and my best friend. Wow.' The colour drains from his face as he stares at us in disbelief.

Gemma looks pointedly at the girls, who are watching the exchange with a kind of fascinated terror. 'Hey, chicks, shall we watch some Swiftie in the snug while we wait for your pizzas?'

I shoot her a grateful look as she shepherds Erin and Megan out of the kitchen, then I turn back to Freddie.

'You have no right to judge me, Freddie Harris. You weren't here. What was I supposed to do, live like a bloody nun for the rest of my life, bringing up the kids you abandoned for me to raise on my own?'

'But you're still married to me.'

'Actually, the marriage was dissolved when you were legally presumed dead three years ago, mate,' Carter says.

Freddie frowns. 'You killed me off too?'

'I was in limbo,' I cry. 'Of course I didn't want to think you were dead, but you'd been missing for *seven years*. There'd been no activity on your bank accounts, no trace of you anywhere. It was as if you'd disappeared off the face of the earth. I had to apply for the presumption of death certificate to sort out our finances. I didn't have a choice.'

He seems to crumple before us, the anger gone.

'I'm sorry. You're right.'

'I think we could all use a drink.' Carter walks across the kitchen to the fridge, pulls out two bottles of beer and hands one to Freddie before pouring me a large glass of Sauvignon.

He takes a long draught and then tips his bottle towards Freddie. 'You know, it might help if you explained where you've been.'

'And why you left.' I'm trying hard to keep the emotion from my voice, but it's impossible. The words dip and tremble as they tumble out of me.

Freddie rubs the back of his neck, then shakes his head. 'No.'

I gape at him. 'What d'you mean, "no"? I think I deserve an explanation, Freddie.'

'We both do, mate.' Carter crosses the room to stand beside me. As a play, it's as subtle as a sledgehammer, and I'm not surprised when Freddie bristles. He's always had a stubborn streak and ganging up on him won't work. He'll just dig his heels in.

'I mean, I can't do this right now,' he says quietly. 'I need a bit of time.'

My lip curls. 'Ten years not long enough for you?'

'Please, Alex.'

I've been desperate for answers for so long that it's almost unbearable to know that they're almost within my grasp, but I've waited ten years. I suppose one more day isn't going to make a difference.

I sigh. 'Have it your way. Where are you staying?'

'I... I hadn't really thought that far ahead.'

I blink. Surely he didn't think I would welcome him back into the marital bed?

'There's a hotel up the road,' Carter says. 'I'll book you a room.'

Freddie shifts in his seat. 'Thing is, I don't really have the money for a hotel.'

'Not a problem. I'll cover it.'

'That's very kind, but I can't let you do that.'

'So where will you go?' I press.

'Don't worry, I'll find something.'

I close my eyes briefly. Freddie could have spent the last ten years living on the streets for all I know. He could be an addict, anything. Before he left I would've trusted him with my life but that doesn't mean I should let him stay under our roof now.

My mind spirals. What if I send him away and he disappears as abruptly as he arrived? He'd break the girls' hearts. If they discovered I'd kicked him out they'd never forgive me. Underpinning everything is the need to know where the hell he's been. If he walks away now, I might never find out.

I reach a decision. 'It's OK, you can stay here for the night.'

'I don't want to put you to any trouble, but if the spare room's free that would be amazing.'

Carter and I exchange a look. What used to be the spare room when Freddie and I were married is now the nursery. Freddie didn't exactly take the news that we were married well, so what will he say when he finds out we have a toddler?

'Would it be all right if I took a shower?' Freddie asks.

'Of course, mate,' Carter says. 'Where's your bag, in your car?'

'I left it in the hall. I don't have a car.'

'How did you get here?'

'Hitchhiked.'

'You? Hitchhiked? Pull the other one,' Carter says.

Freddie shrugs then disappears into the hall, returning with a tatty grey rucksack.

'Is that it?'

'Yup.'

Carter drains his beer and wipes his mouth with the back of his hand. 'You want me to lend you some stuff so we can put your clothes through the wash?'

Freddie grimaces. 'Is that a polite way of telling me I reek?'

'You stink to high heaven,' I say briskly, placing my glass on the table. 'Come on, I'll find you a towel.'

* * *

I leave Freddie to it and poke my head around the door of the snug. Gemma is sitting in the middle of the sofa, her arm round Megan, with Erin's feet in her lap. On the TV, Taylor Swift is strutting across a concert stage in a silver tailcoat, glittering bustier and matching briefs. I feel a rush of gratitude towards Gemma, who is always there for my kids. They are all so absorbed I decide to leave them to it, but just as I'm about to slip away Gemma looks round.

'Hey, how's it going?'

I let out a self-conscious laugh. 'Oh, you know. Not your average Saturday night.'

'Where's Dad?' Erin asks. Her heart-shaped face is tight and my throat constricts.

'He's in the shower, sweetheart. He's going to stay here tonight.'

She gives a quick nod.

'I explained to the girls that they need to give their dad a bit of space, at least for tonight,' Gemma says.

'Thanks.'

'There'll be plenty of time to get to know him again, won't there?' She ruffles Megan's hair.

'Of course there will,' I say, even though I have no idea how long Freddie is planning to stick around. I don't know anything about him any more. Where he's been. Why he's back. What he wants.

But I'm damn well going to find out.

7

FREDDIE

TEN YEARS AGO

I know in my bones that the inspection by the Care Quality Commission has not gone well. My team and I spent two days answering questions, sharing protocols and procedures and being observed by the blank-faced inspecting team. We were microbes under a microscope, every decision, every action ready to be dissected – and likely censured – at a later date.

The report isn't due for several months, but that hasn't stopped a twitchy Helen Fairchild summoning me to her office to address the shortfall in staffing ahead of its publication.

'There is no more money,' she tells me bluntly. 'You need to think outside the box.'

I roll my shoulders. How the hell am I supposed to magic up more nurses without the funds to pay for them? The hospital spends an obscene amount of its staffing budget on agency and bank staff because its retention rates are so poor. And the reason nurses and doctors are leaving in their droves is because of the burnout they face due to staff shortages. It's a vicious circle.

I leave Fairchild's office, glancing at my watch as I hurry

down the stairs, wondering if I have time to duck into the staff restaurant and grab a coffee. The broad arrow hands of my Omega Seamaster 300 show it's almost half three.

I bought the watch with my first pay packet on Carter's recommendation.

'Not only is a great watch a status symbol, it's also a sound investment,' Carter said, rolling up his sleeve to admire his own vintage Rolex. 'It sends everyone a subtle message that you're successful as fuck, and that's what we're aiming for, right?'

'Fake it till you make it?' I said.

Carter had grinned. 'Damn right.'

He'd been spot-on. The admiring glances from my fellow medics and members of the hospital trust made the watch worth every penny of its £1,250 price tag. And when I checked its value the other day, I was amazed to see similar watches fetching more than four grand.

My bleeper pings. It's a message from Carter. Two words. *Call me.* I pull my mobile from my pocket.

'What's up, mate?'

'We have a problem.' Carter sounds breathless, which is out of character. He's usually so unflappable. I feel a pulse of disquiet.

'Go on.'

'You know the girl in bay ten? Sapphire Kelly?'

I try to remember. The morning handover was cut short when Bertie, the little boy with complex needs who came in at the beginning of the week with a kidney infection, pulled out his IV line and had a meltdown when Gemma tried to put it back in.

'The one who came up from A&E last night,' Carter says. 'Suspected pneumonia.'

'Oh, yes.' According to her records, Sapphire was admitted with typical pneumonia symptoms – a cough, high temperature and vomiting. I haven't had a chance to examine her yet, but she's in capable hands with Carter. 'What's happened?'

'Her mother's kicking off,' Carter says. 'Wants her moved to PICU.'

'PICU?' The hospital's paediatric intensive care unit cares for critically ill children, and although Sapphire is clearly unwell, I'm confident the infection is nothing a strong dose of intravenous antibiotics won't fix. I haven't spoken to the child's mother, but I can picture her. Tall, with a severe bob and a strident voice, she made her presence known the moment she arrived on the ward. 'Why?'

'Says the kid's not herself.' Carter gives a derisive snort. 'Of course she's not. She has pneumonia.'

'You've asked for bloods?' I check. I'm passing the men's toilets and badly need to pee. I meant to go before I saw Fairchild but was in such a rush I clean forgot. Now my bladder is aching uncomfortably. I shoulder the door open, the phone still pressed to my ear.

'Of course I asked for bloods. Gem's about to do them,' Carter says.

'Good. Look, I need to go. I'll have a word with Sapphire's mum as soon as I get back,' I promise, ending the call and wondering how long I can hide in the toilet cubicle before someone sends out a search party.

It's almost five o'clock before I have a chance to speak to Ingrid Kelly. I find her perched on the chair next to her daughter's bed, reading her a story. Sapphire smiles weakly at me. Ingrid looks me up and down appraisingly, then gives a curt nod. I introduce myself, then draw the curtains around the cubicle to give us some privacy.

'As you're aware, we're waiting for the results of Sapphire's blood tests to come back, but in the meantime we are treating her with fluids and—'

'I thought they were antibiotics,' Ingrid Kelly says sharply, waving a hand at the IV drip behind her daughter's bed.

'We're waiting to see what kind of infection we're dealing with before we administer antibiotics. They'd be pointless if Sapphire has a viral infection.'

'Can't you give them to her just in case?' The woman's querulous tone grates on my already frayed nerves. I'm the one who completed years of medical training, yet the parents of my young patients invariably know best. But hitting up Dr Google doesn't make them the experts.

I skirt around the question, instead saying, 'I can assure you Sapphire's in the best possible hands. We're monitoring her closely. You have nothing to worry about, Mrs Kelly.'

'It's not Mrs. It's Ms,' she says.

'My apologies. Ms Kelly.' Most of the parents urge me to call them by their first names. Not *Ms* Kelly, apparently.

'She's going to be absolutely fine.' I summon a reassuring smile, and then, for some inexplicable reason, I give a small bow before pulling back the curtains and walking the length of the ward, feeling Ingrid Kelly's sharp, knowing eyes on my back with every step.

It's as if she can see straight through me, knows I'm struggling to hold it all together. That my efforts to balance the demands of work and my family are floundering. That sooner or later, everything will start falling through the cracks. And what will happen then?

8

ALEX

NOW

My two husbands are circling each other like boxers in a ring and, once the girls have eaten their pizzas and reluctantly headed to bed, I follow them upstairs, glad of an excuse to leave the claustrophobic kitchen.

I find Erin sitting cross-legged on her bedroom floor rifling through the box of mementos she's been keeping since the day Freddie left. It was my idea; I wanted her to feel connected to her father, to realise that he was and always would be part of her life, no matter where he was. I wanted to make sure her memories weren't all tinged with sadness, to remember the happy times we had before he left.

I sit next to her and peer into the box. It's a jumble of disparate items: a photo of Freddie holding Erin in hospital when she was a few hours old; a lock of her wispy baby hair; her first tooth; a Lego figure of a dark-haired man; her first school report; her recorder; her primary school tie; a shell from the beach near my parents' bungalow in Cornwall; a tatty copy of *The Gruffalo*, one of Erin's favourite books when she was tiny;

the Father's Day cards she insisted on making every single year even though she had no one to give them to.

I take out the school report and skim-read it. *Erin is a diligent, thoughtful little girl who always tries her best and is a pleasure to have in the classroom.*

'You OK?' I ask her.

Her eyes shine. 'Dad's come home. Of course I'm OK. It feels like my birthday' – she scrunches up her face – 'or the first day of the summer holidays. Or, I don't know, I've just been made captain of the netball team.' She grins. 'And you know how lame I am at netball.'

Her delight should be infectious, but it makes me sad. I fold the report carefully and replace it in the box. 'Still, it's a lot to take in.' I pause. 'It's OK to be angry with him too, Erin.'

She looks at me as if I'm mad. 'Why would I be angry?'

Because he walked out on us when you were four and your sister was a baby, I think. *Because he left me to cope on my own when he knew I was struggling. Because he has the nerve to waltz back into our lives and expect to pick up where he left off.*

I don't say any of these things, of course. I kiss her goodnight, tell her not to stay up too late and leave her to her box of keepsakes.

Megan's room is a vision of pink. Candy-pink walls, hot-pink bedding, blush-pink curtains and a pale-pink carpet. Carter is always threatening to paint over the walls with the same elegant Farrow & Ball French Gray Erin chose for her room. I have expressly forbidden him. It's Megan's room and she gets to choose.

She's curled up in bed reading my childhood copy of *The Lion, the Witch and the Wardrobe*. It's her go-to comfort read when she's worried about something.

I perch on her bed and tuck a strand of hair behind her ear. 'Where've you got to?'

'The bit where they meet Aslan at the stone table.'

'Why don't you leave it there for tonight?' I suggest. Even though she must have read the book a dozen times, Megan always cries when Aslan is killed by the White Witch, even though she knows he comes back from the dead, and today has been emotional enough.

She nods, slotting her most prized possession – her ticket to Taylor Swift's Eras Tour concert – between the pages and setting the book on her bedside table.

Carter spent four hours in an online queue, refreshing his browser every few seconds, trying to bag tickets for one of the London shows only to discover they'd completely sold out just as he reached the front of the queue. Most people would have given up there. Not Carter. He set the two Edinburgh concerts in his sights, and when he couldn't get tickets for them either, he tried Dublin. Third time lucky. Megan had actually cried.

'Mum? Are you pleased Daddy's home?'

I smile. 'Of course I am. Aren't you?'

She bites her bottom lip. 'The thing is, are you absolutely sure it's him?'

I frown. 'What makes you say that?'

'He doesn't look like Daddy.'

Megan may have been a baby when Freddie left but there are photos of him dotted all over the house. I insisted on it, even after Carter and I married. Carter used to complain that with Freddie constantly staring down at him it felt like there were three of us in the marriage. Once, I even caught him drawing a silly moustache and devil's horns on a holiday snap of Freddie. I'd been livid and Carter, instantly contrite, had never moaned about the pictures again.

But Megan's right. The gaunt, stooped man with the straggly beard who turned up on our doorstep tonight looks nothing like the smiling, handsome man Freddie once was.

'He looks like a homeless person,' Megan says. 'And he smells funny.'

I take her hand and give it a squeeze. 'I know, darling. But he's taking a shower right now, so that'll solve one problem. And Carter's going to lend him some clothes, so when you see him tomorrow he's going to look a whole lot better.'

'I suppose,' Megan says, but I can tell by the way she won't meet my eye that something else is bothering her.

'What is it, Megs?'

'He left when I was a baby, didn't he?'

I nod, wondering where this is going. 'You were three months old. Why?'

She looks up at me, tears brimming. 'Was it something I did?'

'What d'you mean?'

'Did he leave because of me?'

Anger rises in my chest so swiftly it takes me by surprise. Ten years may have passed since Freddie disappeared and, outwardly, the girls and I have moved on. But it's clear that while the wounds may have healed, we'll always bear the scars.

'Of course not. He just... he just had to get away. His work was very stressful at the time.'

'At the hospital?'

'That's right. It all got a bit too much for him and I guess he couldn't handle the pressure. It absolutely wasn't because of you.'

She nods, and some of the tension leaves her face. I feel sick with guilt. I had no idea she blamed herself for Freddie leaving. Not a clue. Megan is such a sensitive child. How much damage have I caused by keeping this from her?

I check the Barbie-pink digital clock on her bedside table. 'Come on, it's gone half nine. You need to get some sleep.'

She stifles a yawn. 'Night, Mum.'

'Night night, Megs. Sleep tight.' I kiss her goodnight and am about to let myself out of the room when she calls me.

'Mum?'

'Yes, sweetheart?'

'Now Dad's back, will I have to choose between him and Carter?'

'Don't be silly, of course you won't. They both love you. You're allowed to love them both back.' I force myself to laugh. It sounds brittle, even to my own ears. I turn out the light and the room is plunged into darkness.

At least Megan won't see my tears.

9

FREDDIE

My irritation levels soar when I walk into Dolphin Ward's cramped office to find Carter perched on the edge of Gemma's desk, his head bent towards her as he whispers something in her ear. Gemma throws her head back in laughter, exposing the pale skin of her neck. At the sound of my footsteps, Carter coughs, and they both look over, Gemma with a look of guilt and Carter with a smirk.

The three of us have been friends since university. Carter and I were third-year medics when we met Gemma, a second-year nursing student who lived in the house next door. It was through Gemma that I met Alex, her best friend since secondary school.

We went on a couple of double dates, but it quickly became clear that while Alex and I were serious about each other, Carter – much to Gemma's frustration – continued to play the field. These days, Gemma's always falling for some guy or other, often, I suspect, to make Carter jealous. If only she realised she's fighting a losing battle. He isn't the type to settle down.

Even so, I'm pretty sure they still hook up occasionally, though Gemma treats the hook-ups as more than the booty calls Carter views them as.

'Have Sapphire Kelly's bloods come back yet?' I say curtly.

'I'll check.' Gemma sits up straight, glances at Carter, then starts tapping away at her keyboard. 'Um, no, not yet.'

'Chase them, will you?'

Gemma raises an eyebrow, then tugs an imaginary forelock, making Carter hoot with laughter. I let it go. I'd wondered how the power dynamic would pan out when I became the consultant on Dolphin Ward two years ago. Gemma has worked here ever since she finished her nurse training, and Carter had been the ward's registrar for almost a year, his eye on the top job. I'd worried how my best friend would react when I was offered the role, but Carter was nothing but supportive, assuring me his time would come. The occasional piss-taking is a small price to pay. At the end of the day, I know they both have my back.

I check my watch again, horrified to see it's already half past six. I promised to help Alex with bath and bedtime.

I address Carter. 'I need to go. What time do you knock off?'

'Eight. Why?'

'Will you check Sapphire Kelly before you leave? I'm on call tonight. Bleep me if you have any concerns.'

'Sure.' Carter stands and stretches. I hurry to the car, swearing under my breath at the queue waiting to exit the staff car park. I briefly consider calling Alex to warn her I'm running late but think better of it. It'll slow me down and I need to get back. I don't like leaving her on her own for too long.

The closer I drive towards home, the more anxious I feel. I can't tell if it's the prospect of facing Alex and her mood swings or the gut feeling I've missed something crucial at work, but the nagging sense of unease will not go away.

* * *

Expecting to be yelled at for being late, I'm surprised when Alex barely registers my arrival. I find her in Erin's bedroom folding laundry, Megan strapped to her chest in a baby sling.

'Daddy!' Erin cries, jumping out of bed and flinging her arms around my legs. 'Will you weed my story?'

'Of course I will.' Alex is worried Erin might have a speech impediment but I secretly love the fact that she still has trouble pronouncing her Rs because she sounds so damn cute. I pick her up and she clings to me like a monkey as I drop a kiss on my wife's cheek.

'Good day?' I ask.

'Your mother came round. She stayed with the children while I went to the supermarket.' She glares at me. 'She said she was surprised we'd started bottle-feeding the baby.'

'You should have told her it was none of her bloody business,' I retort. I love my mother, but she does have the tendency to offer her opinion where it isn't wanted.

Erin presses a finger to my lips, her eyes wide. 'No swearwing, Daddy.'

'You're right, pumpkin. Daddy's very naughty. Why don't you choose a story while I get changed?'

Obediently, she slips down to the ground and darts over to her bookshelf. I follow Alex into our bedroom. Like the rest of the house, it looks like it's been ransacked by burglars. Piles of clothes on every surface, drawers half opened, books and newspapers stacked on the floor and over everything a thick layer of dust. I know we should think about getting a cleaner, but what with the crippling mortgage and Alex not working we have to watch every penny.

'I thought we could go out for the day on Saturday. Maybe try that new petting zoo?' I say, as I change into jeans and an old sweatshirt. 'Or I could take Erin swimming, if you like?' I feel sure this will win me Brownie points. Alex is a poor swimmer and hates visits to the local pool.

'Up to you,' she says. I glance at her. Her expression is neither sad nor angry, just blank, which I find even more disconcerting than the depression or the rage. It's as if her curiosity, her personality, has been sucked dry by motherhood. I'm sure the laughing, vivacious girl I married is in there somewhere, hiding behind the armour she has constructed around herself. But I haven't a clue how I can tease the old Alex out.

'OK, well, maybe I could take both girls out somewhere, give you the day off.' I try a smile. 'At least that's one of the benefits of bottle-feeding.' When Alex doesn't answer, I admit defeat and go to read Erin her story.

Sitting in Erin's bed, my eldest daughter snuggled up against me, my mood lifts. This is a phase and, like everything, it will pass. I'll find Alex help. We'll get through this together. After all, we're blessed. We have two beautiful, healthy children and a roof over our heads. It's more than a lot of people have.

As I read *The Gruffalo* to Erin, the smell of Johnson's baby shampoo and strawberry bubble bath filling my nostrils, my thoughts drift to Sapphire and Ingrid Kelly. Hopefully Sapphire's blood results are back and Carter has decided on a course of treatment. I consider texting him to check, then change my mind. He might think his competence is being questioned. No, he's an experienced registrar and knows what he's doing. He can always page me if he needs advice.

I close the book and kiss Erin goodnight. Hopefully, when I arrive for work in the morning, Sapphire will have turned a corner; might even be well enough to be sent home.

The thought should reassure me, so why is that knot of anxiety still there, writhing in my gut like a nest of vipers?

10

ALEX

NOW

Carter is already in bed reading this week's copy of his favourite medical journal when I finally turn in for the night. He closes it and watches as I sit at my dressing table and take off the make-up I applied so carefully just a few hours ago.

I reach for a pot of moisturiser. 'I'm sorry we never got to celebrate our anniversary.'

'Not your fault.'

'I know, but you've been looking forward to trying out The Oak and Ivy for weeks.'

'We can go another time.'

I meet his eye in the mirror. 'You seem remarkably relaxed about the fact that my first husband just showed up on our doorstep.'

'He was my best friend long before he was your husband,' Carter points out. 'And yes, it's thrown me for a loop, but I'm stoked to see him when we all thought he was dead. Why, aren't you?'

I wait a beat before I answer, choosing my words carefully. While I don't have to tiptoe around Carter, I know his ego is fragile, despite his outward confidence, and I don't want to upset him, especially tonight. If I tell him Freddie coming home is the thing I've been dreaming of for the last ten years he will be immeasurably hurt, and how can I blame him? I'd feel the same if Carter's ex-wife, Elizabeth, turned up and announced their divorce had been a terrible mistake and she wanted him back.

'Of course I'm glad to see him. But I'll never forgive him for what he did to us.'

'He was under immense stress at work.'

'So were you, but you handled it.'

'That's because I'm a psychopath hiding in plain sight,' Carter jokes, and despite everything, I find myself laughing.

I massage the moisturiser into my skin, then pull the pins from my hair so it tumbles to my shoulders. I reach back to unzip my dress, tutting when the zipper sticks.

Carter props himself up against the pillows. 'Come here,' he says, patting the bed beside him. I sit next to him, and he eases the zipper down before pulling me close.

'I haven't cleaned my teeth.'

'I don't care,' he growls. He laces his fingers in my hair, his lips finding mine. I kiss him back, shivering as his hand slides inside my dress. His touch electrifies me; it always has. Sex with Freddie was intimate, comfortable, familiar. Sex with Carter is intense, passionate, erotic. I drop my head and kiss his neck and he groans in pleasure.

I break away, pulling the dress over my head and flinging it onto the carpet where it pools in rippling waves of red satin. Carter watches, his pupils black with desire and his mouth curved into a smile.

'Come here, beautiful.'

I straddle him, my hands on his chest as he unfastens my

bra. He reaches into the drawer of his bedside cabinet for a condom. The action sparks a memory that replays in my mind before I can block it. A memory of the day Freddie and I moved into the house fifteen years ago. We'd tumbled into bed, ready to christen it, when Freddie, reaching for a condom, had paused, smiled that easy smile of his and said, 'Shall we make some babies?'

I'd gazed back at him, my heart crashing in my chest. We'd only been married a month and had decided to hold off starting a family for a couple of years while we concentrated on our careers. Freddie was a paediatric registrar with ambitions to become a consultant. I was about to take my final accountancy exams and qualify as a chartered accountant. But in that moment, I couldn't think of anything I wanted more than to have Freddie's children. A month later, Erin was conceived.

And now, Freddie is asleep on the sofa, and I am here with Carter, his best friend. I pull away.

Carter frowns. 'What's wrong?'

'I can't, not with Freddie here. It doesn't seem right.'

His expression darkens. 'You're my wife now, Alex.'

'I know that. Just, not tonight, OK?' Without giving him the chance to answer, I scoot off the bed and head for the en suite, where I yank off my pants and grab my nightdress from the hook on the back of the door.

By the time I've cleaned my teeth and peed, Carter has turned off his bedside lamp and curled onto his side. If he's not asleep already, he will be very soon. Perhaps it's the years of shiftwork or something in his genetic make-up, but he's always been able to fall asleep at the drop of a hat. It infuriates me, the lightest of sleepers, that he nods off the moment his head touches the pillow. He can sleep anywhere. On a train, in the car, at the theatre. Once, he fell asleep in the dentist's chair while he was having a filling. He sleeps like the dead, too, not even stirring if Dylan wakes in the night.

Dylan. I swear softly under my breath. I've left the baby monitor in the kitchen. He normally sleeps through but his recent cold has unsettled him and he's been waking up crying the past few nights.

I pull on my dressing gown and creep downstairs, pausing outside the living room door. On the other side is Freddie. Not the Freddie I remember: the sweet, fun-loving man I married. The man who was occasionally impulsive but always kind. This man, this new Freddie, is an interloper. A dried-up, husk-like, haunted version. I lean against the door, press my ear to the wood and listen, wondering if I'll hear him breathing. But there is only silence, so I step away.

The kitchen is in darkness bar the red light on the baby monitor and a set of ghostly blue numbers on the range cooker clock, but my eyes have grown accustomed to the dark and I don't bother to switch the light on. I head to the sink, take an upturned glass from the draining board and fill it with water. One glass of Sauvignon turned into three and I'll need a clear head in the morning. I drain the glass, deposit it in the washing-up bowl and reach for the monitor.

'Alex.'

'Jesus!' I cry, jumping a foot in the air. I whip round. Freddie is sitting at the kitchen table, perfectly still.

'What are you doing in here? I thought you were asleep.'

'I don't sleep much these days.' He gestures at the monitor clasped in my hand. 'You forgot to mention you and Carter had a baby.'

'How did you—?'

'I saw the photos in the living room.'

Damn. I should have thought to move them. I stare at the monitor as I scramble together a response. Freddie always wanted a son. Not that he didn't love the girls, but he didn't have the best of relationships with his own father and I suppose he wanted a clean slate so he could finally get things right, in a way he never could with his dad.

'I... I was going to tell you in the morning.'

'What's his name?'

'Dylan.'

'Dylan? That's a bit ghoulish, isn't it? Giving your son the same name as your dead brother?'

'I thought it was a lovely thing to do, actually,' I say tightly, even though I'd taken some convincing when Carter announced he wanted to name Dylan after his brother, who died of acute lymphoblastic leukaemia when he was ten. It was why seven-year-old Carter decided he wanted to become a doctor. Looking back, I can't think why I had misgivings. My only defence is that my hormones were screwed.

Freddie is watching me with something like pity in his eyes.

'Why are you looking at me like that?'

'Like what?' he says, immediately rearranging his expression.

'If you've got something to say, just say it.'

He is silent for a moment, then shakes his head.

'Freddie, for God's sake, just spit it out!'

He scratches his chin, then exhales. 'I think you should be careful, that's all.'

'Careful of what?'

He looks around the kitchen, at the familiar detritus of family life. 'It's all very cosy, isn't it, Carter moving in the moment my back was turned?'

A cold fury is building inside me. How dare Freddie judge Carter when he was the one who walked out on us? Accusations and recriminations bubble in my chest, but before I can form the words, Freddie speaks again.

'I've known Carter a lot longer than you, Alex. He's a—'

'No!' I cry, cutting across him. 'I know what you're trying to do, and it won't work. Carter was here for us when you weren't. He has done nothing but love us.'

Freddie's chair scrapes the floor as he hauls himself to his feet. 'All I'm saying is that you'd be a fool to trust him.'

Without another word, he walks towards the hallway.

'Where are you going?' I call after him.

'To see your son,' he says. 'I want to see Dylan.'

11

FREDDIE

TEN YEARS AGO

A wave of exhaustion hits me as I lock the car and stride towards the hospital's main entrance. On the drive to work I calculated how much sleep I had last night, immediately wishing I hadn't.

Four hours and twenty minutes. Not nearly enough to function properly, let alone run a busy children's ward where every decision could be the difference between life and death.

Megan was running a slight temperature and woke, grizzling, every two hours on the dot, and at four o'clock Erin crawled into our bed after having a nightmare. I administered Calpol and cuddles, then lay staring, hollow-eyed, at the ceiling while Alex and the girls went back to sleep.

I left them all dozing, trying to ignore the resentment simmering inside me as I headed out of the house. It was all right for Alex, who could lounge around in her pyjamas all day if she wanted. I had to bring my A-game to work every single day.

There's a reason sleep deprivation is used as a form of

torture, I think, as I order a takeaway double espresso from the café in the foyer and make my weary way to Dolphin Ward. Our sleep was disrupted when Erin was born, but this is another level of tiredness. It leaves my brain fuzzy and my bones leaden. I nod at colleagues on autopilot as I pass them in the corridors.

Carter is already on the ward, looking as fresh as a daisy.

'Wow, you look knackered,' he says by way of a greeting. 'Rough night?'

I nod. Carter sounds so concerned that to my horror my eyes well with tears.

'Oh, mate. Things that bad?'

The urge to offload is overpowering, but Gemma's approaching and I clamp my mouth shut. Even though she's Alex's best friend, I have no idea if she knows quite how badly Alex is struggling. Lately, I've sensed an undercurrent of rivalry between the two women, and I'm not about to break my wife's confidence.

'No, it's all good. Nothing eight hours' uninterrupted sleep wouldn't solve, anyway.'

'You should stay over at mine at the weekend. We could hit the pub, have a few cheeky beers, then veg out in front of the TV with a takeaway. A proper boys' night, just like old times.'

The carefree, indulgent picture Carter paints is so far removed from my current life that I can hardly believe it was the norm when we were at med school. It amazes me that this is how some people – people without kids – still spend their weekends. Lucky bastards.

I can just imagine Alex's reaction if I waltzed in and announced I was staying over at Carter's for a boozy evening. I sigh. 'Tempting though it is, I'm going to have to decline your kind invitation on this occasion.'

Carter claps me on the back and laughs. 'Don't worry, only another eighteen years before they're off your hands.'

'Thanks for that.' I roll my eyes, then switch my foggy brain to work mode. 'Anything of note on the handover?'

Carter gives a brief rundown of every patient on the ward and a couple of children currently in A&E who might need to be admitted.

'What about Sapphire Kelly?'

'Stable. Her blood results still weren't in when I left last night so I asked the evening team to give her intravenous amoxicillin as a precaution and I've requested a chest X-ray this morning.'

It's a good call – and perhaps one I should have made. If the X-ray confirms Sapphire has pneumonia, the antibiotics will already be getting to work. If it isn't pneumonia, we can rethink.

'Her mother says she's developed a rash,' Gemma says, overhearing.

'Delayed reaction to the amoxicillin,' Carter tells her.

'You sure it's not hives?' I check. If it is, it could indicate that Sapphire is allergic to penicillin, in which case there's a risk she could develop life-threatening anaphylaxis.

Carter compresses his lips. 'It's not hives.'

'OK,' I say, about to take a look myself when Simi bustles into the office.

'Ah, there you are. Two things. I need you to sign off Rosie Green's meds before you start your rounds, and have you done Bertie's discharge summary?'

And so it begins, just another crazy-busy day on Dolphin Ward. It's almost two o'clock before I see Sapphire, and the moment I approach her bed her mother jumps up from her chair.

'Can I have a word?' she says tightly. 'Somewhere private?'

'Of course.' I swallow, the knot of dread back in my stomach. 'I'll see if the relatives' room is free.'

She follows me along the corridor to the small box-shaped

room where parents can make tea and escape the ward for a while. I pull up a chair and motion for her to take a seat.

'It's Sapphire,' Ingrid Kelly says. 'She's getting worse, not better.'

'As I think Sister Adebayo explained to you before lunch, both Sapphire's blood tests and this morning's chest X-ray confirmed our initial diagnosis of pneumonia. What she may not have mentioned is that the antibiotics can take up to forty-eight hours to start working.' I give the woman a reassuring smile and repeat the same words I said to her before. 'She's in the best possible hands.'

Ingrid Kelly's eyes narrow. 'That's the thing. I'm not sure she is.' Her gaze drifts to my shirt and I glance down to see what's caught her attention, only to realise it's buttoned up wrong. *Shit.* I got dressed in the dark so I didn't wake Alex and the girls, and now this woman is staring at me in distaste, no doubt wondering how she can trust a man who can't even dress himself properly to look after her daughter. 'I'd like a second opinion,' she adds.

'Obviously, I absolutely respect your right to ask, but I must warn you that it could cause a delay in Sapphire's treatment and might even involve moving her to another hospital.' As the senior clinician on Dolphin Ward, it's my decision whether or not to veto her request, and I'm minded not to. Why dump more work on one of my colleagues when I have every confidence in Sapphire's diagnosis and treatment plan?

'You're giving me the brush-off?'

'Absolutely not.' I massage the bridge of my nose. My head's pounding. It feels as if it's caught in a clamp and someone is turning the screw. I'm desperate for another hit of caffeine, but I didn't even have time to slurp down the polystyrene cup of tea one of the nursing auxiliaries poured me a couple of hours ago. 'We'll continue to monitor Sapphire. Meanwhile, why don't you try to get some rest? It's important you look after yourself too.' I pat Ingrid Kelly's hand in what I hope is a fatherly manner. She pulls it back as if she's been electrocuted.

'I know in my gut she's not right,' she says stubbornly. 'I googled her symptoms and I think it might be—'

My already frayed patience finally snaps. I rise to my full height, my expression flinty. 'Ms Kelly, I have to go. I have patients to see. Including your daughter. So if you don't mind—'

As I sweep from the room, Gemma rushes down the corridor, her face as white as chalk.

'Freddie... I mean, Doctor Harris. You need to come quickly. There's something wrong with Sapphire.'

12

ALEX

NOW

My grip on the baby monitor tightens as I stare at Freddie's retreating back with mounting unease. 'You want to see Dylan now?'

He stops in the doorway and turns and smiles. It doesn't reach his eyes. 'No time like the present.'

'It's late. We should wait until the morning.'

'Nonsense.' He disappears through the door. 'I assume he's in the spare room, and that's why I'm having to doss on the sofa?' Not waiting for an answer, he takes the stairs two at a time. I have no choice but to follow.

On the landing, I hold my fingers to my lips and ease Dylan's door open. The night-light Erin and Megan clubbed together to buy him for his first birthday projects fish across the walls and ceiling, turning the room into an underwater world. Dylan is lying on his back with his arms at perfect right angles. His nostrils flare as he breathes out and Freddie frowns.

'He's getting over a cold,' I whisper.

'He looks like Erin.'

'A bit,' I agree. 'But he's also the spit of Carter when he was a baby.'

'What do the girls think about their baby brother?'

'They adore him. They were such a help when he was born. It's just as well. Carter only took a couple of weeks' paternity leave.'

Freddie reaches into the cot and strokes Dylan's palm with the back of his forefinger. Instinctively, the toddler's hand curls around his finger, gripping it tightly.

'And how were you, you know, afterwards?' Freddie asks.

'Fine. Why wouldn't I be?'

He glances at me, his eyes full of compassion. I shake my head. I refuse to go there, not tonight. I'm not the one on trial here.

'Why did you go, Freddie?'

His gaze wavers. In his cot bed, Dylan stirs. Freddie gently prises his finger free and Dylan's thumb finds his mouth.

'You know why.'

'But I don't! I know things were difficult, but marriages weather worse storms. We made a promise to each other. Till death do us part.'

He gives a hollow laugh. 'How did that go for you?'

'Don't you dare lay this on me. You're the one who walked out. Have you any idea what that first Christmas was like without you? All Erin wanted was her daddy, the one thing I couldn't give her. It broke my heart. *You* broke my heart.' I'm on a roll, the recriminations pouring out of me like water from a burst dam. 'Where were you when Erin broke her arm and Megan had whooping cough? When Erin was being bullied at school and Megan was teething? I had to cope on my own. Every. Single. Time. You didn't even have the decency to let me know you were all right. Did we really mean so little to you?'

I sling each whispered accusation at him as if I'm firing arrows from a bow across the ramparts of the cot. He flinches, as if one of my arrows has struck home. But when he finally looks me in the eye, his expression is impassive. The shutters have come down and I know I won't get anything from him tonight.

I turn and walk from the room, beckoning him to follow. At the top of the stairs, I'm gripped by fatigue. 'I need to get some sleep. I'll see you in the morning, all right?'

He looks as if he's about to say something, then gives a quick nod. I wait, clutching the banister, as he climbs stiffly down the stairs. Only when I hear the living room door open and close do I make my way to my own bedroom and Carter. My sleeping husband doesn't even stir as I slip into bed beside him.

* * *

Carter is still out for the count when I wake the next morning, groggy and dry-mouthed. To my surprise, I slept like the dead, despite yesterday's dramas. I picture Freddie asleep on the sofa a few feet below us, his feet poking out of the single duvet and his hand tucked under his chin. Where has he been sleeping for the last ten years? Perhaps today is the day I finally find out.

I glance at the alarm clock, surprised to see it's just gone seven. Dylan usually wakes anywhere between six and half past. He must be catching up on his sleep too. I prop myself on one elbow and watch Carter. Sunday is the only morning he allows himself a lie-in. Every other day of the week he's up at six and is setting off on a five-mile run by ten past. I don't know how he does it. It takes me a shower and two cups of coffee before I even begin to feel human.

I leave Carter sleeping, pull on my dressing gown and pad out of the room. I stop at the top of the stairs and cock my head. I can hear the faint strains of the television coming from the kitchen. Erin and Megan must be up already. Dylan's door is ajar. Perhaps he's up too. With any luck, Erin, who takes her duties as oldest sibling very seriously, has given him breakfast.

I push the door open and peer into Dylan's room. The cot bed is empty and there's a pile of books and Binky, Dylan's treasured stuffed rabbit, on the carpet. I bend down to pick the rabbit up by its ear and head downstairs.

Freddie is sitting at the kitchen table, still in Carter's T-shirt and boxers, slicing a banana for Dylan, who is banging the tray of his highchair with his fists and chanting, ''Nana! 'Nana! 'Nana!' Erin is by the sink, carefully spreading butter onto some toast. Megan is lying on the sofa on her tummy, her chin cupped in her hands, watching the Disney Channel. I linger just outside the door, not wanting to intrude.

Freddie must sense my presence because he turns and smiles.

'Morning, sleepyhead. We didn't wake you, did we?'

I shake my head and cross the kitchen, not sure I can trust myself to speak. Freddie's warning from last night hangs in the air between us, as glaring as a neon sign. *You'd be a fool to trust Carter.*

What did he mean? Perhaps I should have demanded an explanation, but I didn't want to give him the satisfaction. He thinks if he can drive a wedge between me and Carter, he can slink back into his old life like he never left.

To halt my racing thoughts, I focus on filling the kettle, measuring coffee into the cafetière and finding mugs and milk.

Freddie gives Dylan the bowl of chopped banana and swivels in his seat to watch me. The heat of his gaze is like sunburn and I tug a hand through my hair self-consciously, wishing I'd showered and cleaned my teeth.

Erin sets the plate of toast and a glass of orange juice in front of her father, then passes him one of our best linen napkins.

I finally find my voice. 'You're getting the VIP treatment this morning, I see.'

Freddie smiles. 'I am.' He winks at Erin, who blushes. 'The children are a credit to you, Alex.'

I bite back a retort. I suppose I should be flattered, but I didn't have much choice. I had to be both mother and father to the girls throughout their formative years. Yes, Freddie's parents helped where they could, and Gemma has been a pillar of strength, but at the end of the day I was on my own. That Erin and Megan ended up as well-adjusted as they have is, frankly, a miracle.

I push a mug of coffee across the table to Freddie then retreat to the other side of the kitchen, keen to put as much distance as I can between us. There's so much I need to get off my chest, but I can't, not in front of the kids. It will have to wait until tomorrow when they're at school and Carter's at work. I catch myself. I'm assuming Freddie will still be here then. Before I can ask how long he's intending to stay, Fleming lifts his head from his bed in the corner and woofs twice. A moment later the flap on the letterbox rattles and Megan looks up from the TV and yells, 'Post!'

'But it's Sunday,' I mutter, setting my mug on the countertop and going to investigate.

The envelope lying on the doormat is the same as all the others. Cheap, flimsy paper, the kind you'd pay a couple of quid for a pack of twenty in a pound shop. Just the sight of it makes my heart miss a beat. I stoop down and stuff it into the pocket of my dressing gown without opening it.

It is only as I straighten and turn around that I see Freddie leaning against the door to the kitchen, watching me, his arms laced across his chest and his features giving nothing away. Questions buzz around my head, like mosquitoes trapped in a jam jar. What secrets are you keeping, Freddie? And why are you back?

13

FREDDIE

TEN YEARS AGO

I stride back onto the ward, Gemma and Ingrid Kelly on my heels. The curtains are pulled around Sapphire's bed and I pause outside.

'Gemma, I'd like you to take Ms Kelly back to the parents' room while we check on Sapphire.' I turn to Ingrid Kelly. 'I'll let you know the moment you can see her,' I say in a voice that leaves no room for argument.

Gemma takes the woman's elbow and guides her back through the ward. Parents at their children's bedsides stop what they're doing to watch. I can see what they're thinking as clearly as if there are cartoon-style thought bubbles above their heads, though they would never admit it.

Don't let us be so unlucky.

Sapphire's eyes are closed, her skinny chest rising and falling in shallow, rapid breaths. Simi looks up from adjusting the IV line on the back of Sapphire's hand. Blood has oozed through the see-through dressing and bandage. 'Her blood pressure's dropping.' Simi's normally gentle lilting voice is clipped, the words falling like stones on corrugated iron.

'How long has she been like this?'

Simi consults the clipboard at the end of Sapphire's bed. 'Her blood pressure was low when it was last taken two hours ago, but nothing out of the ordinary.'

I barely hear her answer, my gaze on the mottled skin on the six-year-old's neck. I lift the bed sheet. The angry red rash has spread across her torso and legs.

'How long has her rash been like this?'

Simi inhales sharply. 'That's new. She had a slight rash yesterday, which Doctor Petersen put down to a reaction to the antibiotics, but it was nowhere near as bad as this.'

I nod numbly. I remember Carter blaming the penicillin. I was more concerned about anaphylaxis. Now one word plays on a loop inside my head and I can't for the life of me fathom how I missed the signs.

'Sepsis,' I mutter. 'We need to test her for sepsis.' I watch Simi take more bloods, my mind racing. 'What time did she start on the amoxicillin?'

'Six this morning.'

'This morning?' I don't bother to hide my frustration. 'Carter said he told the evening team to sort it.'

'They were short and it was manic.'

I grunt. I know better than anyone that oversights happen when teams are up against it. It's easy to blame my colleagues but this is my mistake. I lost focus and now a little girl is gravely ill. The weight of my error presses down on my sternum, making it hard to breathe.

'Are you OK?' Simi says.

I force the rising panic down. I can't afford to fall apart now.

'Of course I am,' I say, sharper than intended. I pull out my phone. 'I'm going to see if there's a bed in intensive care.'

She nods, and I drum my fingers on the steel frame of the

hospital bed as I wait for the call to connect. I'm explaining the situation to the intensive care consultant when the curtains around the bed open and Ingrid appears, closely followed by a terrified-looking Gemma, who mouths, 'Sorry, I couldn't stop her.'

'Oh, baby,' Ingrid cries. 'I'm here. I'm here, my darling.'

Sapphire's eyelids flutter open at the sound of her mother's voice.

'Thirsty,' she gasps. Ingrid is there in an instant, holding a beaker to her daughter's cracked lips. She feels Sapphire's forehead and turns to Simi. 'She's burning up.'

I end the call. 'The team from the paediatric intensive care unit are on their way.'

Ingrid looks up sharply. 'Intensive care?'

'They have the equipment to help Sapphire breathe. They're best placed to care for her right now.'

Sapphire's eyes are closing again and the blood pressure monitor bleeps frantically.

'Her oxygen levels are dropping,' Simi says. 'Should we intubate?'

The question hangs in the air unanswered as I'm gripped by paralysis, all my years of medical training forgotten in an instant.

'Doctor Harris,' Simi says urgently. 'Should we intubate?'

'Yes, yes, of course.' My hands shake as I prepare for the procedure. It's like working underwater, every movement in slow motion. I push the tube down Sapphire's throat, wincing as she gags.

Suddenly the cubicle is filled with PICU staff, and I stand back, my hands shaking, as they take over, as perfectly in sync as a well-oiled machine, which only heightens my own sense of failure.

I've let Sapphire down. I wish with all my heart that I could turn back the clock. I should have realised there was a risk of sepsis when she was admitted onto the ward with suspected pneumonia. It's rare, but sometimes a patient's response to an infection spirals out of control, and the immune system, instead of trying to fight the infection, ends up attacking the patient's own organs.

If only I'd prescribed antibiotics when she was first admitted, or chased her blood results, or had her transferred to intensive care the moment Gemma mentioned the rash. So many chances to alter the course of Sapphire's future. But I took my eye off the ball and as a result there's a very real chance she won't make it.

I force myself to look at my young patient. The strong sedatives administered by the PICU team have kicked in and her face is slack now she's slipped into drug-induced unconsciousness.

'Please make her better,' Ingrid cries as she clutches her daughter's limp hand. I turn and walk away, knowing the sound of Ingrid's raw, choking sobs will haunt me till the day I die. Knowing I'll never forgive myself for what I've done.

14

ALEX

NOW

The envelope crackles in my pocket, and I ball it in my fist. Maybe if I squeeze hard enough it'll turn to dust and disappear. Fat chance.

'Is something wrong?' Freddie asks.

I glance down, unable to meet his eye.

'Look, Alex, I know my turning up like this is unexpected—'

'Unexpected?' I let out a bark of laughter. 'That's one word for it.'

He runs a hand over his scalp. 'I knew I should have called or written first.' His gaze flickers to my dressing gown pocket as if he can see through the towelling to the screwed-up envelope tucked inside. 'I'm sorry.'

'What for? Walking out on me ten years ago? Or turning up on the doorstep last night?' My eyes narrow. 'Perhaps you'd like to apologise for telling me I shouldn't trust my husband?'

'*I'm* your husband,' he says.

I shake my head. 'You gave up all rights to me the day you left, Freddie Harris.'

He doesn't reply.

'Perhaps if you told me where you went, I might understand.'

'I—'

'Mum?'

We both spin round to see Erin standing in the doorway holding Dylan's hand. 'He's done a poo.'

'Oh, right.' Erin's duties as oldest sibling stop short of changing her brother's nappy. I hold out my arms, frustrated that once again my attempts to find out where Freddie has spent the last decade have been interrupted. But it's not a conversation I'm prepared to have in front of the children. It'll have to wait.

'C'mon, stinky,' I tell Dylan. 'Let's get you cleaned up, shall we?'

'Bye-bye,' Dylan says to Freddie, opening and closing his pudgy hand as I carry him upstairs. 'Bye-bye.'

* * *

Once I've changed Dylan's nappy and cleaned his teeth, I sit him by his box of Duplo, pull the crumpled letter from my pocket and smooth it out on the carpet. Just as with the others, there is no name on the envelope, and the flap has been tucked inside rather than licked and fastened. Was it because the sender didn't want to leave any trace of their DNA? I slide my finger through the gap, open it and unfold the note inside. The scrawl is the same, and, like before, the letters have scored the thin, lined paper, but the message is different this time.

THE TRUTH WILL OUT.

Once again, I experience a frisson of fear. The kind of stomach-swooping sensation I felt when Carter and I took the kids to

THE HUSBAND BEFORE YOU

the Sky Garden in London and I stepped out onto the viewing deck five hundred feet above the city, just a thick sheet of toughened glass between me and the pavements below.

I stare at the message, trying to make sense of it. What truth? I have nothing to hide. Unless... Beads of sweat break out across my forehead. But Gemma's the only one who knows about that awful morning when I so nearly cracked under the pressure, and my secret's safe with her.

I shake the memories away, screw the paper back into a ball and thrust it deep into my pocket. Carter's right, it's just some random nutjob trying to put the wind up us. I need to forget all about it. I have more important things to worry about, like finding out where my first husband has been hiding for the last ten years. And why he has decided to come back now...

* * *

I walk into the kitchen, Dylan on my hip. Freddie and the girls have disappeared and Carter is sitting at the table nursing a cup of coffee and a scowl.

'Where is everyone?' I ask.

'The girls are in the snug, and Freddie's taking a shower.'

I set Dylan down and he scampers over to his dad. Dylan is a pint-sized replica of Carter, from his blond hair to his denim-blue eyes.

'Hey, little man. How's it hanging?' Carter scoops Dylan onto his knee with one fluid movement, ruffles his hair, then blows a raspberry on his neck, making Dylan squeal with laughter.

I gather flour and eggs, then pull a carton of milk from the fridge.

Carter's head jerks up. 'What are you doing?' he asks suspiciously.

'I thought I'd make pancakes.'

The scowl deepens. 'Pancakes for the prodigal husband? You never make them for me.'

I roll my eyes. 'How old are you – ten? I'm making them for everyone, not just Freddie. I've got a couple of eggs that need using up.'

'Yeah, right,' Carter mutters.

Making pancakes used to be Freddie's Sunday morning ritual. He'd whip up a mountain of them, and we'd smear them with honey or chocolate spread and eat them with our fingers. One morning, not long after he left, I asked Erin what she wanted for breakfast. 'Daddy's pancakes,' she lisped. That was the first time I felt real anger towards Freddie. Until then, I'd fluctuated between grief and worry, but Erin's simple request ignited something in me, like molten rock churning beneath the earth's surface. It was bad enough that Freddie had walked out on me, but abandoning the girls was unforgivable.

The anger yanked me out of the depression I'd slipped into after Megan was born. I had no choice but to carry on. The girls needed me.

And I made damn sure I learnt how to make pancakes.

Even though I haven't made them for years, muscle memory kicks in as I crack eggs into flour and begin to whisk. When the batter is the colour of butter and the consistency of single cream, I find the pancake pan and set plates, honey and a jar of chocolate spread on the table.

I heat the pan and wipe it with a square of oiled kitchen roll. 'Can you fetch the girls?' I ask Carter over my shoulder as I ladle a scoop of batter into the pan.

There's a sigh, the scrape of a chair and he's gone. I let the batter sizzle for a moment, watching as it bubbles and sets. But when I try to ease the palette knife under the pancake to flip it, it sticks to the pan.

'Damn it.'

'Here, let me try,' a voice says softly.

Startled, I drop the palette knife with a clatter. Freddie rescues it, takes the pan from me and works at the edges of the pancake until it loosens. With an economical flick of his wrist, he flips it over just before it starts to burn.

'Don't worry. The first one's always the worst,' he says.

'I know,' I reply tightly. 'I've got it from here, thanks.'

He hands me the palette knife. It's only then that I really look at him. I can't hide my shock.

The beard has gone.

In an instant, the years melt away and I'm staring at the man I fell in love with – the one who once came to my rescue at a student party, who worked two jobs in the holidays just to afford the train fare to see me. The man who proposed to me on a windy hilltop in Wales the summer he graduated. The man I married. The father of my daughters. My first love.

Just as quickly, my thoughts darken and I'm replaying the days after he walked out; the endless struggle to keep it all together. The lonely nights. So many lonely nights. My grip on the palette knife tightens.

'I said, I've got it.' My voice is flint-sharp and he immediately takes a step back, a look of hurt on his face. 'Could you find some knives and forks?' I nod towards the cutlery drawer.

'But we always use our fingers.'

'We may have once. Not any more.' I turn back to the stove, my heart thudding uncomfortably in my chest. I need to remember I'm married to Carter now. If Freddie thinks he can drive a steamroller through our marriage he has another think coming.

15

FREDDIE

TEN YEARS AGO

I drive home in a daze. I've screwed up, there's no getting away from it. When other people screw up at work it might mean a lost contract or an unfulfilled order, but if I do it, children's lives are at risk.

The crippling exhaustion is no excuse. I could have asked for help, but I didn't. I soldiered on, because Dolphin Ward is my little kingdom and I was too proud to admit I couldn't cope.

I've wanted to be a doctor ever since my nan and grandad bought me a doctor's outfit, complete with medicine bag and toy stethoscope, for my fourth birthday. A grade-A student, I breezed through the admissions process into one of the top med schools in the country. The workload at university was insane, but I'd found my calling and had flown, leaving after five years with a first-class honours under my belt and a hunger to embark on the next stage of my career. Qualifying as a consultant took another nine long years, but I didn't mind. My job defines me; has made me the man I am. When I meet people for the first time and the conversation strays, inevitably, to what everyone does for a living, I'm proud to tell them I'm a paediatric consultant. Although self-deprecation is my default setting, I nonetheless feel a tiny thrill knowing they're impressed by my choice of career.

At the hospital I'm top of the pecking order. Not quite godlike, but a commanding presence. Admired by staff and revered by patients and their families who have an almost blind faith in my abilities to make people better. Not Ingrid Kelly. The look she gave me as Sapphire was wheeled from the ward was one of pure hatred. I feel certain that Sapphire is going to die, and I have signed her death warrant. I'm supposed to save the lives of the children in my care, not kill them. It's inconceivable. Unforgivable.

I pull up outside our house, the journey a complete blank. I unclip my seat belt and am about to heave my weary bones out of the car when I falter. I'm not ready to see Alex and the girls, not yet. How can I wrap Erin in a hug or snuggle Megan into the crook of my arm while Sapphire clings to life by the barest of threads in her intensive care cot?

I reach a decision, lock the car and head down the road on foot. The Swan is a quiet boozer a twenty-minute walk away that's about as far removed from a gastropub as you could hope to get. Sticky tables, tacky carpets, sullen bar staff and the faint smell of tobacco, even though the cigarette ban has been in force for almost a decade. It's the perfect place to drown my sorrows.

I order a pint of bitter with a whisky chaser, then another. Three pints later, the sharp edges of the day are beginning to blur and I'm sliding into a well of self-pity. I consider texting Carter to see if he wants to join me. Getting pissed together is how we survived the ups and downs of med school and, later, foundation and medical training.

I pull my phone out of my pocket, bemused to see four missed calls from Alex. I didn't hear it ringing. But I wouldn't, would I? I always have it on silent for work. I should phone her back and tell her I'm running late, but I can't stomach the thought of her screeching down the phone at me or – worse – the reproachful silence. Fuck it. Fuck her.

I stare at the screen, typing out a text to Carter with one finger.

> *Mate, I'm in The Swan. Fancy joining me? Could use a shoulder to cry on.*

Two blue ticks pop up and I wait for Carter's reply. And wait. And wait. When, after fifteen minutes, he still hasn't replied, I bang my fist on the table. 'Fuck him too. Fuck the lot of 'em,' I announce to the empty pub. I stand unsteadily, stumble over to the bar and order another pint.

* * *

It's gone nine when I finally leave The Swan, hoping the walk home might clear my head. Because there's no getting away from it. Eight pints and six whisky chasers on an empty stomach and I'm as drunk as a lord. Off my face, in fact. Med school primes your liver for breaking down copious amounts of alcohol, but I don't drink much at all these days. Hangovers are no fun with a four-year-old, a newborn baby and an angry wife.

I pat my pockets as I walk down the street. Phone, wallet, keys. All there, present and correct. Carter hasn't texted back. Probably screwing some pretty young nurse. My eyes widen. Maybe even Gemma. It's clear to me, even in my inebriated state, that Gemma still holds a torch for Carter. She has a tendency to monopolise him with a possessiveness that borders on ownership. Shame for her that Carter is a player and always will be.

My head's spinning as I totter up the path to the front door and it takes several attempts before I manage to turn the key in the lock.

Fleming patters down the hallway and throws himself at me as if he hasn't seen me for a week. 'Steady on, old boy,' I slur, clutching the banister for support as the dog presses against my legs. I become aware of the weight of someone's gaze on me, and I look up slowly, the hallway shifting to one side then the other. Christ, I really am pissed.

'Sorry I'm late,' I say, only the words run into each other. *SorryI'mlate.* I try again. 'Something came up.' I wince as I'm gripped by nausea. The only thing about to come up is a stomachful of beer and the half-digested egg and mayonnaise sandwich Simi bought me from the staff canteen this morning, another lifetime ago.

Alex watches me from the top of the stairs. 'You're drunk.' Her voice is as sharp as a surgeon's knife.

'Maybe a little.'

'Brilliant.' Somewhere behind her, Megan starts wailing. 'Oh, for fuck's sake.' She turns on her heels and stomps across the landing and out of sight.

I take a deep breath and follow her.

16

ALEX

NOW

The pancakes are a hit. Even Carter, who watches his carb intake like a hawk, has four. I wipe the chocolate spread from Dylan's face and he toddles off to the snug to watch cartoons with Freddie and the girls, while Carter helps me clear the dishes.

It would be the perfect picture of domesticity if it wasn't so twisted. One wife, three kids, two husbands. It's like something from a down-market reality TV show.

As if reading my mind, Carter says, 'What happens next, Al? Freddie can't stay here forever.'

My hands are covered in soapy suds and I rinse them and pat them dry on my jeans. 'I know. It's just that I don't think he has anywhere else to go.'

'Why has he come back now? Is he expecting to pick up his life where he left it? Walk back into his job? His marriage?'

There is an edge to Carter's voice, and although objectively I can't blame him, a tiny part of me wants to call him out because that's effectively what he did, isn't it? He stepped right into Freddie's shoes when he took Freddie's job and married me.

But it's not fair to blame Carter, because none of it would have happened if Freddie hadn't fled his old life, leaving both his job and his family there for the taking.

'You think he wants his old job on the children's ward back?' I ask, surprised.

Soon after he left, Freddie was the subject of an investigation by the General Medical Council after the mother of one of his young patients reported him for negligence. Ingrid Kelly claimed he'd missed several opportunities to treat her daughter Sapphire's sepsis. Following the investigation, which went ahead in his absence, he was given a formal warning, even though there were some who thought he'd got off lightly and should have been struck off. But the GMC took into account his overall competence, his exemplary track record and the pressures he was under at the time, and decided the mistake was a one-off error, not part of a pattern.

'Even if he does, he can't return to clinical practice just like that, assuming he hasn't been working as a doctor wherever the hell he's been,' Carter says. 'There are hoops to jump through. He'd need to revalidate his licence to practise, for a start. There'd be training and supervision to make sure his skills were up to date. A lot changes in ten years.'

I raise an eyebrow. 'Doesn't it just.'

Carter finally smiles and holds out his arms. 'Come here, wife,' he commands. He is like a terrier, marking his territory, but I don't mind. His arms are strong around me and I sigh with pleasure as he nuzzles my neck. 'Come upstairs with me,' he whispers, his voice thick with desire as he slips a hand up my top.

For a second, I waver, but then I remember that the kids and Freddie are just down the hallway and Gemma said she'd pop round for a coffee later and...

I pull away, shaking my head. 'I can't.'

'Why not?'

I straighten my top. 'You know why not.'

He scowls. 'I'm beginning to think you don't want to.' His eyes narrow. 'Unless it's me you don't want.'

'Don't be silly. But we can't just disappear upstairs with a houseful of people.'

'With Freddie here, you mean,' he says sullenly. 'Your other husband.'

'I'll tell him he needs to find somewhere else to stay, OK?'

'When?'

'Today.'

'Promise?'

'I promise.' I stand on my tiptoes and kiss him lightly on the lips. 'Don't be cross. I'll fix it.' I say it with more conviction than I feel, because Freddie needs to be here if he's to build a relationship with Erin and Megan. Besides, I have to keep him close if I'm ever going to discover where he's been and why he left. I'm stuck between a rock and a hard place. How am I supposed to keep both husbands happy? I'm not sure it's possible.

Carter disappears into his study, leaving me alone in the kitchen. Freddie's words come back to me as I put a wash on and make myself a cup of tea. *I think you should be careful. People don't change. You'd be a fool to trust him.*

I let out a sigh of frustration. What the hell did he mean?

Everything was so simple when we were younger. Our roles were clearly defined. Freddie and I were going steady, our futures mapped out. A house, marriage, kids. Gemma and Carter were friends with benefits, though Gemma always craved more than Carter was prepared to give.

A memory creeps into my mind, unbidden. We were at a club, celebrating Gemma's graduation. She was on a high, the life and soul of the party, flirting outrageously with every man who crossed her path. Carter had been in a strange mood all night, knocking back shots like they were going out of fashion. Freddie and I had sat either side of him, keeping him company, while Gemma twirled and spun on the dance floor.

Freddie went to get drinks, leaving me alone with Carter.

'Hey, you know she only does it to make you jealous.' I nodded at Gemma, who was chatting up some guy at the bar.

Carter shrugged. 'She can do what she likes. She's a free agent.'

'D'you think you two will ever get together? Properly, I mean? It's all she ever talks about.'

He shook his head. 'She knows that's not what I want.'

'What *do* you want?' I asked, curious.

His face crumpled. 'I want what you and Freddie have. I want someone I'm crazy in love with, who loves me right back. Someone I can grow old with. I want the picket fence, the kids, the dog, the lot. You might not believe it, but I'm sick of playing the field.' He looked deep into my eyes and I felt a frisson of... of what? Understanding? Compassion? Connection? 'I know everyone thinks I'm a player, but I'm not, Al. I'm an old romantic at heart, looking for my soulmate.' He studied his hands, clasped in his lap, while I tried to ignore my racing pulse.

'Those things you want,' I said carefully. 'That's what Gemma wants too. More than anything.'

'Maybe, but it's never going to happen. I just don't feel that way about her.' He gazed at me again. 'I'm sorry. I know how neat it would be if we both coupled up.'

'It's OK.' I smiled to show it really was.

'Al?' he said softly, his eyes still fixed on mine. 'D'you think—?'

'Who's for a Jägerbomb?' Freddie said, slamming four glasses on the table with a triumphant grin and taking his seat next to Carter. He studied our faces. 'Who died?'

'No one.' Carter reached for a glass. 'Al was just helping me with some relationship advice. You want to look after her, mate. She's a keeper.'

'Don't worry,' Freddie replied with a grin. 'I intend to.'

As I sit at the kitchen table with my tea and my memories, it all seems so long ago. We are different people now. Older, wiser. All that youthful optimism whittled away by the vagaries of life. Somewhere along the way I realised that happy endings weren't a given, that life could – and would – throw curveballs when you least expected them.

I realised that all you could do was hope for the best while preparing for the worst.

There's another thing, too, because Freddie's warning has me questioning everything. Back in that nightclub all those years ago, Carter told me he wanted everything Freddie and I had. Then, when Freddie disappeared, he slid seamlessly into his place as husband, father, provider.

My heart skips a beat as I grasp the implications.

Was he waiting in the wings, or did he engineer it all?

17

ALEX

TWENTY YEARS AGO

'How do I look?' Gemma twirls in her black dress, the silky material clinging to her perfect figure. Her wavy blonde hair skims her bare shoulders, her highlights catching the last of the sun's rays in her shabby student digs. It's a rhetorical question – she looks amazing – but I know my best friend well enough to understand when she needs a little reassurance.

'Hot,' I say, making a sizzling sound.

Gemma blows me a kiss. 'Love ya.'

'Love you too.' I pull my new red jersey dress over my head and zip up my boots. 'Remind me who you've got your eye on?'

'So there's this American guy. Carter. Oh my God, Al, he's divine.' Gemma pretends to swoon, making me laugh. 'He's so out of my league, but it's got to be worth a shot, right? And if it doesn't pan out, he has a cute friend called Freddie.'

'And they're both medics?'

Gemma nods. 'Third year. And they both want to work in paediatrics, which is weird, isn't it? Almost like it was meant to be.' Gemma knew she wanted to become a paediatric nurse a year into her degree. I have a feeling she knew she wanted to marry a doctor way before then.

'Serendipitous,' I agree. 'So it's divine Carter or cute Freddie?'

'Or both.' Gemma winks lasciviously and we dissolve into giggles.

We grab our jackets and the bottles of vodka and Coke we bought from the corner shop and leave Gemma's room.

'Tom was cool with you coming?' Gemma asks.

Tom and I have been going steady since the start of sixth form, and despite heading to universities on opposite sides of the country – me in London and Tom in Exeter – we promised each other we'd make it work.

'Of course.' I shrug, then add – rather pompously, probably, 'We trust each other.'

Gemma looks like she's about to say something, then presses her lips together. She stops in front of the mirror in the hallway, runs her fingers through her hair, then blows herself a kiss. The dull thud of bass reverberates through the thin walls from next door.

She offers me her arm. 'C'mon, girl,' she says with a grin. 'Let's go partay!'

* * *

The house is the mirror image of Gemma's, though even more unkempt, if that's possible. Like all student houses, the living room has been converted into a fifth bedroom and the garage into a cramped communal area with a couple of tatty sofas and a threadbare carpet. Tacked onto the side of the long galley kitchen is a conservatory, in the middle of which is a scuffed pine table loaded with booze, crisps and paper plates and cups.

The air is thick with cigarette smoke and students are

crammed into every nook and cranny, leaning against walls, perched on the stairs or slouching on the mismatched furniture.

Gemma sets the bottles on the table, picks up a couple of paper cups and pours us both generous measures of vodka, topping each up with an inch of Coke. She hands one to me then scans the room.

'That's Carter,' she whispers in my ear. 'Lush, or what?'

I follow Gemma's gaze, spotting a tall guy with broad shoulders on the far side of the room, surrounded by a gaggle of people. My eyes widen a fraction. Gemma's right, he's gorgeous.

'Definitely a ten,' I say approvingly. We have a private scoring system for boys. You wouldn't touch a one if he was the last guy on earth. Fives are OK if you're desperate, but tens are, well, tens are usually out of our league. Even Tom is only an eight. 'Which one is Freddie?'

'The one with the floppy brown hair to Carter's right. The original wingman. A six and a half.'

I stand on tiptoes to get a better look. 'Bit harsh. Look at that smile. He's an eight, like Tom.' I chew my lip.

Gemma frowns. 'What's up?'

'Tom hasn't replied to any of my texts. He was going on a bike ride with a couple of friends this afternoon. What if he's had an accident?'

'I'm sure he's fine,' Gemma soothes. 'You can try calling him later. But first, get that down your neck.' She gestures to my drink before draining her own. I follow suit. The vodka gives me an instant buzz, though it could be the music or the second-hand smoke.

Gemma pours more drinks. We knock them back and she pours some more. Carter is still at the centre of his group of admirers. They remind me of close protection bodyguards shielding a president. Gemma tugs at my arm, pulling me closer.

Carter is leaning against the fridge, a mischievous grin on his face, clearly halfway through an anecdote.

'—I was in charge of prepping the cadavers for an anatomy practical and there was this one guy who was the spit of Johnny Depp, and I slipped a pair of sunglasses on his face and a lit fag in his mouth just before the professor and the rest of the class walked in.'

There's a ripple of laughter and Gemma breaks away from me, clearly impatient to find out what happened next.

'So the professor takes one look at Johnny Depp and says, "Looks like Captain Jack didn't get the memo about this being a smoke-free area." And he takes the fag from the cadaver's mouth and grinds it out with the heel of his shoe, cool as a cucumber. But the first years? Man, they were losing it. Couldn't keep a straight face. You shoulda seen it.'

As his fan club titters, Carter gives them a mock salute and announces he needs another drink. They part like the Red Sea and suddenly he's beside Gemma, helping himself to a bottle of beer.

'Hey,' he says, looking Gemma up and down approvingly. 'Have we met?'

She flashes him a wide smile. 'I live next door. Rob invited me. I'm Gemma.' She clinks her paper cup against his bottle. 'Cheers. Oh, and this is my bestie, Alex. She's studying accountancy at Middlesex.'

'Cheers,' he says, barely glancing at me. 'I'm Carter.'

Gemma holds his gaze. 'Oh, I know exactly who you are.'

18

ALEX

NOW

The door to Carter's study slams, pulling me out of my reverie. I push myself to my feet and carry my mug over to the sink. As I rinse it out there's a crash followed by a grunt and a string of expletives. Carter hobbles in, clutching his knee, his face apoplectic.

'That's it. I've had enough.'

'Whatever's happened?'

'I tripped over Freddie's rucksack, which he'd just abandoned in the hallway for someone else to pick up. What does he think this place is, a frigging hotel?'

'Shush, keep your voice down. He'll hear you.'

'I don't care if he does hear me. In fact, I want him to hear.' Carter disappears back into the hallway, calling, 'Freddie, can I have a word?'

After a moment or two, Freddie ambles into the kitchen. I tense like a vole caught in a kestrel's beady gaze, but Freddie seems unaware of the anger radiating off Carter.

'What's up?' he says.

Carter holds the tatty grey rucksack up by a frayed strap, his mouth a moue of distaste.

'Can you not leave your belongings all over the goddamn floor? I tripped over this and almost knocked myself out. It's not good enough. You're here as a guest. Please treat the place with some respect.'

Wordlessly, Freddie holds out a hand for his bag, but Carter's not done yet.

'We don't have to let you stay here, you know. Most people would have flung you out on your ear after what you did. But we are reasonable people. Is it too much to expect you to show a bit more consideration?' His voice has taken on the hectoring, overbearing tone that always puts my back up and, judging by Freddie's expression, it's having the same effect on him.

'What's really bugging you, Carter? That I'm here, or that Alex hasn't kicked me out yet?'

Carter's face darkens and a muscle twitches in his jaw. 'Don't kid yourself. She's only letting you stay because she feels sorry for you.'

'Carter, that's not—' I begin.

He holds up a hand and I fall silent. The atmosphere in the room crackles with tension as the two men square up to each other. I gaze from one to the other, my heart pitter-pattering in my chest. Carter's hands are fists at his sides. Freddie's whole body is as tense as a coiled spring.

'You think you can walk back in here and pretend the last ten years never happened, but it doesn't work like that,' Carter growls. 'Like it or not, everything's changed. This is my house now. Alex is my wife. And the sooner you realise it, the better.'

'God forbid anything messes up your perfect little world.' Freddie swipes his rucksack from Carter's grip. 'I'll go then, shall I?'

Carter shrugs. 'Probably for the best.'

'Fine. You can explain to the girls why you've chucked me out.'

'Suits me.'

'Just don't say I didn't try.'

'Enough!' I cry, stepping towards them. They both turn to me as if they've forgotten I exist.

'What d'you think the girls would say if they could hear you now?'

'He started it,' Freddie says sulkily.

'Well, if you hadn't left your bag on the floor—'

'Seriously?' I can't hide my exasperation. 'Will you take a look at yourselves?' I clench my own hands until my fingernails bite into my palms. 'I will not have you acting like spoilt brats under my roof. So I suggest you back off or... or you can *both* leave!'

Carter rubs the back of his neck and stares at his feet. Freddie drops his rucksack onto the floor and plunges his hands into his pockets. The door to the snug clicks open and Megan's voice floats down the hallway.

'Mum? Can I have a snack?'

I look at my two husbands, my fingers flexing, resisting the urge to bang their heads together.

'I would like you to apologise to each other,' I tell them as Megan's footsteps grow louder. 'Now.'

There's a long pause and I hold my breath, willing them to call a truce. Finally, Freddie clears his throat, glances up at the ceiling then back at Carter. He pulls his hands from his pockets and holds them up in surrender. 'Sorry, mate. Your house, your rules. It won't happen again.'

After a moment's hesitation, Carter nods stiffly before turning on his heels and marching from the room. I exhale slowly as I pluck Megan a satsuma from the fruit bowl.

It seems it's the best I can hope for. But I can't help wondering how long this fragile peace will last...

19

ALEX

TWENTY YEARS AGO

I sit on a low wall staring up at the back of the grotty student house, wishing I hadn't come to the bloody party. Gemma abandoned me the moment Carter showed an interest. The last time I saw her, he was leading her up the stairs. You should have seen the expression on her face. She looked like the cat that got the cream.

Meanwhile, my mood is plummeting.

I texted Tom a second time but he still hasn't answered. Images of him lying on the verge unconscious, his limbs splayed at awkward angles and his bike on its side next to him, its wheels still spinning, play over and over in my head. It's barely eight o'clock but it's already so cold my breath curls in vapours and the straggly grass on the poor excuse for a lawn sparkles with frost. What if no one finds him? He'll get hypothermia and probably die. He might even be dead already. I check my phone again. Nothing.

I consider calling the police down in Exeter but I can just imagine how the conversation would play out.

'I think my boyfriend has been knocked off his bike.'

'You *think* he's been knocked off his bike?'

'Well, he's not replying to my texts and when I ring it goes straight to voicemail.'

I'd be laughed off the line.

I take another slug of my vodka and Coke, so lost in my thoughts that I don't notice someone has joined me until he speaks.

'Everything OK?'

I look up with a start. Carter's friend, Freddie, is peering at me with concern, his thick eyebrows knotted. 'Only you look like someone's pinched your last Malteser.'

'What? Oh, no, I'm fine. I'm just worried about my boyfriend.' Is it my imagination or does a look of disappointment cross his face? 'He's in Exeter. I think he might have fallen off his bike which is why he's not answering my calls.' I pull a face. 'It's probably my phone playing up again.'

'Want to try mine?' Freddie takes the latest Nokia from his pocket and offers it to me.

'I guess. Thanks.' My fingers fly over the keypad and I press the phone to one ear, sticking a finger in the other in an attempt to drown out the noise of the thumping music as the call connects.

'Hello?' Tom says, and I slump in relief.

'You're all right!'

'Who is this?' he asks, and for a moment I'm confused, because music is playing on the other end of the line too. Which is weird, because he didn't say he was going out. In fact, he made a big thing about staying in to finish an essay after his bike ride.

'It's me, Tom. Alex.'

'Sorry. Terrible line. You're going to have to shout.'

A girl's voice cuts across him. 'Tom! Put that phone away and come and dance. It's our song!' As her words sink in, I recognise the opening chords of 'Thank You' by Dido and I almost drop the phone in shock, because that's *our* song.

'Tom!' the girl exclaims again. 'Come *on*. Promise I'll make it worth your while.' She gives a tinkle of laughter, and the sound is like shards of glass piercing my heart.

'Who is that?' I bark. Beside me, Freddie's eyes widen. In my ear, Tom says, 'Oh, shit, is that you, Al?'

'That's right,' I spit. 'Alex, your *girlfriend*. And who the hell is *that*?'

'She's... oh God... she's no one. I can explain, OK?' Tom swears under his breath and I screw my eyes tight shut.

'Don't bother!' I stab the end call button savagely, then burst into tears.

I sense a shift in the air next to me and when I look up Freddie has disappeared and I'm on my own bar a couple of lads sharing a spliff by the back door. My heart feels like it's breaking in two. To think I was worried Tom had fallen off his bike. Bastard.

I wipe my face and am about to pull myself to my feet to find Gemma and tell her I'm going back to hers when Freddie reappears, holding a blanket, two paper cups and a half-bottle of cooking brandy.

He wraps the blanket around my shoulders, sloshes brandy into the cups and offers me one.

'It's supposed to be good for shock,' he says.

I laugh, despite myself. 'Three years at med school teach you that, did it?'

He laughs too. 'No, but it's what they give heroines suffering from the vapours in books, isn't it? Got to be worth a try.'

I take a sip. The brandy burns the back of my throat and I splutter.

'Steady on,' he says. 'You don't want me to have to give you mouth-to-mouth, do you?'

'Certainly not!' I say primly, then fall silent. 'I suppose you got the gist of that call?'

He nods. 'Have you been together long?'

'Three years.'

'Ouch.'

'I know. It's shit.' I glare at him. 'Why can't men keep it in their trousers longer than five minutes?'

'Some men. Don't tar us all with the same brush.'

'All right,' I concede. 'Some men.'

'I don't know.' Freddie swirls the brandy in his cup, takes a swig, then wipes his mouth with the back of his hand. He has nice hands, I notice. Long, elegant fingers and neat nails.

'The really annoying thing is, Tom was the one who wanted us to stay together when we went to university.' I take another sip of brandy. This time it slips down my throat with ease.

'If you don't mind me saying, it sounds like your ego has taken a bigger battering than your heart.'

I consider this. Either the alcohol has anaesthetised me against the pain or Freddie is right.

'He still shouldn't have cheated on me. It was a really shitty thing to do.'

'Agreed, one hundred per cent.' Freddie places my cup on the grass, then takes my hands. 'You're freezing. Want to go inside?'

I shake my head. 'I'm going to go back to Gem's.'

'Is Gem the blonde girl from next door?'

'Yep. She's got the hots for your flatmate. It's the only reason we came tonight.' I make a show of looking over my shoulder to check no one's in earshot. 'She wants to bag herself a doctor.' I know I'm being a bitch but it serves Gemma right. She shouldn't have abandoned me.

'She won't get far with Carter. He's commitment-phobic.'

'That's your clinical diagnosis, is it, Doctor?' I pull myself to my feet, then sway as the blood rushes to my head. Freddie is by my side in an instant.

'Steady,' he says, gripping my elbow. I gaze into his eyes. They are brown and crinkled at the edges. Maybe I won't go back to Gemma's poky room quite yet. 'Nine,' I say to myself.

'Nine what?' Freddie asks. 'Ladies dancing? Cats' lives?'

'Nine out of ten.' My heart patters in my chest as I cling to this kind, sexy boy who swept in just when I needed someone. 'Maybe even a ten,' I whisper, snaking my arms around his neck and kissing him.

I was smitten. I thought I'd found my forever.

How wrong I was.

20

ALEX

NOW

Carter, still scowling, emerges from his study and paces the house restlessly.

'Why don't you take your bike out for an hour?' I suggest, when my patience begins to fray.

'Are you trying to get rid of me?'

'Of course not,' I say, though it's not entirely true. All I can think about are the endless questions circling my head. Where has Freddie been? Why is he back? And what did he mean when he said I shouldn't trust Carter? Even though a part of me dreads the answers, I need to know. And Freddie's more likely to open up with Carter out of the way.

I touch Carter's arm lightly. 'It'll do you good. And you know how turned on I get by middle-aged men in Lycra.'

He eye-rolls but the scowl disappears and he heads upstairs to get changed. Once he's gone, I check the kids are happy hanging out in the snug and go in search of Freddie. He's at the kitchen table, flicking through Erin's photo albums.

My pulse quickens as I pull up a chair. It's the perfect opportunity to quiz him. I clear my throat.

'Freddie?'

'Mmm?' he says, without looking up.

'While we're on our own I thought you could—' I'm interrupted by the doorbell. 'Oh, for pity's sake, who can that be?' I swallow a growl of frustration, then turn back to Freddie, trying my best to ignore it, but the doorbell rings again, shrill and insistent. It's as if the universe is conspiring to keep me in the dark. I stomp over to the front door and fling it open.

'Sorry, hon, I left my key at work,' Gemma says, dropping a kiss on my cheek and sauntering into the kitchen, completely unaware she's just barged in on my interrogation. 'D'you have time for a coffee?'

I want to tell her that, no, I don't have time for a coffee, because I'm finally about to discover what the hell Freddie's been up to, but I can just imagine her reaction. She'd rub her hands with glee and pull up a chair.

'Of course,' I say, admitting defeat – for now at least. The questions will have to wait. I sigh. 'I'll stick the kettle on. Freddie?'

'No, thanks. I'll leave you two to it.' He closes the album with a snap.

'Don't go on my account,' Gemma says. She's wearing a fitted leather jacket I haven't seen before with skinny jeans and black biker boots. Her blonde hair is falling in glossy waves around her shoulders and her lips are painted their trademark cherry red. She looks amazing. I touch my hair self-consciously and wish I'd spent less time making pancakes and more time on my appearance.

Freddie grunts something about going for a walk. My stomach twists in fear.

'How long will you be?' I ask, trying to keep my voice steady while searching his face for reassurance that he's not about to disappear again.

He gives me a brief smile. 'An hour? Two, tops.'

The moment we hear the front door close, Gemma turns to me and asks eagerly, 'Give us the low-down, then. How's the whole, "having two husbands" thing going?'

I know she's trying to make light of the situation so I pull a face. 'Bigamy's overrated, if you ask me.' I spoon coffee into two mugs. 'I'm joking. I'm not a bigamist. Not by choice, anyway.'

'Right. It was just an oversight, was it? Marrying two guys?' Gemma's voice is teasing.

'You know it wasn't.'

'So you say.' Gemma shrugs off her leather jacket, hangs it from the back of the nearest chair then checks her reflection on the oven door.

'New coat?' I ask, keen to change the subject.

'Had a third off in the sales.' She grins. 'It would've been rude not to.' She cups her chin in her hands and watches me. I fight the urge to squirm under her penetrating gaze.

She breaks eye contact to stir her coffee. 'Can I ask you something?'

'Fire away.'

'Did you think Freddie was still alive?'

I take a sip of coffee while I consider how to answer. It's a conversation we've been careful to avoid since the day he went missing. 'At first, I'm not sure I did. I assumed he'd been involved in some kind of accident. Been run over, or fallen in the canal, something like that.'

'Or killed himself,' Gemma says bluntly.

'Or that,' I admit. 'Anyway, I thought we would find his body.' I pause, remembering the dread I'd felt every time the phone rang or the doorbell sounded. The pure unadulterated terror that this was the time I'd be asked to go to the morgue to identify my husband's corpse.

Gemma is still watching me intently. 'It sounds like there's a but?'

I stare into my coffee cup. 'You'll think I'm being silly.'

She holds her hand to her heart. 'I won't, I promise.'

'I thought I would know if he was dead. I thought I'd sense it, and I never did.'

She frowns, creases deepening between her eyebrows, as if she's struggling to understand. It occurs to me that we haven't talked this frankly about anything for years.

'Why did you marry Carter if you thought Freddie was out there somewhere, still alive?'

'Freddie obviously didn't want to be married to me or he'd have come home, wouldn't he?' If Gemma's finding it hard to understand, I'm finding it even harder to explain. 'I suppose I felt, after all that time, we were divorced in all but name. The presumption of death thing made it formal. I was a free agent again.'

Gemma sips her coffee in silence. I push myself to my feet, find the biscuit barrel and carry it over to the table. She shakes her head but I help myself to a couple of chocolate digestives. I need the sugar hit.

'Has Freddie told you where he's been living?' she asks.

'No.'

'How long's he staying?'

'What's this, twenty questions?' I smile to take the sting out of my words and reach for another biscuit. 'Carter wants him gone today.'

'Two's company, three's a crowd?' she says, flicking her hair off her face.

I sigh. 'Something like that. Though why Carter's jealous of Freddie, I'll never know.'

Gemma makes a non-committal noise and we finish our coffee in silence, the atmosphere noticeably strained. Or maybe it's fine, and I'm being paranoid. Gemma would never judge me, she's my biggest supporter; was by my side through my darkest days, helping me with the girls, listening to my woes, proving herself indispensable. She's my best friend.

The doorbell rings again. This time I'm glad of the distraction and set my cup in the sink and hurry from the room.

A woman in her early thirties is standing on the doorstep, an expectant smile on her face. Everything about her is unremarkable, from her mousy, flyaway hair to her nondescript black trouser suit, and at first I wonder if she's a detective come to talk to Freddie.

'Can I help?' I ask, pasting a smile on my face.

She has come to talk to Freddie, it transpires, but she's not a detective.

'Morning, Mrs Petersen,' she says, her smile so wide she reminds me of a crocodile. 'Tess Brown from the *Daily Post*. We heard your husband – or should I say your *first* husband – is back from the dead. Any chance I can come in for a chat?'

21

FREDDIE

TEN YEARS AGO

I push open the door to Megan's room. Alex is jiggling from side to side, the baby in her arms. She sees me and scowls.

'Make yourself useful and get her a bottle, will you?' she says through her teeth. 'There are three in the fridge already made up.'

I nod, glad to help. I stagger back down the stairs and into the kitchen, take a bottle out of the fridge and am about to flick on the kettle when I pause, cocking my head. Megan's cries are getting louder. She'll wake Erin in a minute. Surely heating the bottle in the microwave won't hurt this once? I whack it in and am turning the timer clockwise when my phone beeps.

It's Carter.

Sorry, mate. Only just saw your message. Liar, I think. *Bit tied up tonight.* 'I bet you are,' I mutter. *Heard what happened to the Kelly kid. You mustn't blame yourself. These things happen. Talk tomorrow, yeah?*

I have a sudden flashback to Sapphire's expressionless face as she was wheeled out of Dolphin Ward, and my stomach lurches. I stagger out of the kitchen, making it to the downstairs loo just in time. Afterwards, I splash my face with water, rinse my mouth out and gaze bleakly at my reflection in the mirror above the sink. I look as rough as fuck.

'Freddie!' Alex hisses down the stairs. 'Have you got the baby's milk, or do I have to do that myself too?'

'Just coming.' I retrace my steps into the kitchen, take the bottle out of the microwave and give it a good shake to get rid of any hot spots. I trot back upstairs and give the bottle to Alex.

She hands Megan to me, thumbs the lid off the bottle and squirts a jet of milk onto the inside of her wrist.

'Ker-rist!' she cries, her face contorting in shock. 'It's boiling! Oh my God, Freddie. Did you put it in the microwave?'

'Just for thirty seconds.' I quail under her fierce gaze. 'Then Carter texted me so, I don't know, it might have been in there for a minute or two.'

'Jesus. I ask you to do one thing, one sodding thing, and you can't even get that right. She could have been burned, Freddie. Burned! Give her to me.'

'What?'

Alex holds out her hands. 'Give the baby to me.' Her voice is a growl. Obediently, I hand Megan over. My skin feels chill without her warm little body pressed against me.

'I'm sorry—' I begin.

Alex shakes her head, pushing past me to the door and thumping down the stairs. My legs buckle and I slide down the wall to the floor, cradling my head in my hands. What's wrong with me? If Alex hadn't tested the temperature of the milk we could have been phoning for an ambulance, our three-month-old daughter rushed to hospital with first-degree burns. The same hospital where just this afternoon I watched a girl who had her whole life ahead of her slip into a coma from which she's unlikely to recover.

It's as if everything I touch turns to shit, because I'm the common denominator. I'm the one making Alex miserable; the one who almost burned Megan's throat; the one who didn't spot Sapphire's sepsis until it was too late.

I start to weep. The last time I cried was when Erin was born. They'd been tears of happiness. These are born of despair and I swipe at them with the back of my hand. I have no right to cry, no right to wallow in self-pity. Then, through the tears, I have a moment of clarity. It's as if I'm seeing things clearly for the first time in weeks.

Alex, the girls, the children on Dolphin Ward. They would all be better off without me.

* * *

I have no idea how long I've been sitting on the floor in the corner of Megan's room, my hands clasping my knees and my head bowed. I must have fallen asleep at some point because suddenly something soft hits me, jerking me awake.

Alex looms over me, a rolled-up sleeping bag tucked under one arm, a pillow under the other. I gaze blearily round the room. There's a second pillow by my feet. Megan is asleep in her cot.

Alex drops the sleeping bag on the carpet. 'You can sleep on the sofa tonight,' she says in a flat voice. 'I'm done.'

I'm done? What does she mean? Done with me, with our marriage? I'm about to ask but am silenced by a single glance at her face. She's wearing that closed-off expression I'm coming to recognise. Pure, impenetrable granite.

A wave of despair rolls over me as she turns on her heels and marches from the room. I know things are bad, but it's clear Alex has decided our marriage is beyond salvaging. Has she forgotten how good we are together? Memories sweep in, one after the other. Our wedding, such a joyous day; our honey-moon at a small, whitewashed hotel yards from the beach in

Ibiza; the day we found out Alex was pregnant with Erin. High days and holidays, birthdays and Christmases. And the ordinary days, too. Those unremarkable, run-of-the-mill days that were memorable because I spent them with the woman I loved.

It seems they counted for nothing.

I haul myself to my feet with the painful, deliberate movements of a man twice my age. I bend over my youngest daughter's cot, kissing her forehead. She sighs in her sleep, her lips puckered. I stagger across the landing to Erin's room. She stirs when I kiss her and squints up at me.

'It's only Daddy, sweetheart. You go back to sleep, there's a good girl.'

She closes her eyes obediently and, when I'm sure she's asleep, I whisper an apology in her ear. 'I'm so sorry, baby. Sorry for running away.'

My resolve hardens as I shuffle down the stairs. I pull on my shoes and take my coat from the peg. I could leave a note, but what's the point? Alex has made it perfectly clear our marriage is over.

I open the door, step into the cold night and start walking.

22

ALEX

NOW

I go first hot, then cold. The journalist takes a step towards me, but I hold my ground. How the hell does she know Freddie's back? Someone must have tipped her off. Perhaps one of the neighbours saw him on the doorstep last night. How they recognised him I'm not sure, when I barely recognised him myself.

Another possibility occurs to me. Freddie insinuated he's broke. Maybe he called this Tess Brown woman himself, planning to sell his story? The missing doctor who walked out of his life with just the clothes on his back returns ten years later to find his wife has married his best friend. A cold weight settles in my chest.

'Mrs Petersen?' she repeats, peering around me down the hallway. 'Is Doctor Harris at home?'

'No, he isn't,' I say, holding the door tightly. There's no way I'm letting her barge her way in. I know from bitter experience what tabloid journalists are like. They'd trample on their own grandmother to get a story. 'So, if you'll excuse me—'

A tall man with a camera swoops in front of her and has

taken my photo before I can react. 'Please, go. I don't want this,' I stutter. I step back, about to close the door in his face, when Gemma joins me.

'What's going on?'

'They're from the *Daily Post*. They want to talk to me about Freddie.'

'Who told you he was back?' Gemma demands.

The journalist's smile is wider than ever. 'I would never normally reveal my sources but, on this occasion, I don't have to. It was an anonymous tip-off. I thought it had to be worth checking out.' She is holding her phone in her right hand, I realise. She's been recording the entire exchange in which both Gemma and I have unwittingly confirmed her tip-off was correct and Freddie is indeed back.

'Mrs Petersen has told you she has nothing to say and, as you're on private property, may I very politely suggest you piss off back down whichever hole you crawled out of,' Gemma says.

Far from being offended, Tess Brown seems to find her outburst amusing. Chuckling to herself, she asks her photographer if he has everything he needs and when he nods, she pulls out a business card and presses it into my hand.

'Nice to meet you, Mrs Petersen. If you change your mind, give me a call. It would be good to hear your side of the story.' With that, she turns on her heels and strides down the path to the road, the photographer checking the back of his camera as he follows in her wake.

I press the door closed and lean against it, while Gemma peers out of the small porch window.

'Have they gone?' I ask.

'They're getting into their car. Wait, they're not moving. Looks like they're settling in. Yup, they both have takeaway coffees. They're obviously waiting for your two husbands to show up.' She grins at me, but I look away, lips pursed. I know she's trying to make light of the situation, but there's nothing funny about the fact that a journalist has turned up on my doorstep asking about my private life.

'You should phone and warn them both,' she adds.

'I can't. I don't know Freddie's number and Carter never picks up when he's on his bike. God, what a nightmare. You don't think they'll run a story, do you?'

I want her to reassure me, to tell me that of course they won't, that our private drama is of no interest to anyone else, but she would be lying. Of course they're going to run a story. Who doesn't love a juicy tale of bigamy and betrayal? Tess bloody Brown is probably on the phone dictating her copy to her news desk as we speak.

'Your guess is as good as mine,' Gemma says. She takes one final look out of the window. 'But it was inevitable they'd find out sooner or later. Perhaps it's better to rip off the plaster now.'

'What did she mean, it would be good to hear "my side of the story"?' I ask. 'She made it sound like I'd done something wrong.'

'It's just a turn of phrase. Don't worry about it.' Gemma checks her watch. 'I need to make a move. I'm meeting the girls at twelve. We're going to try that new wine bar in town.'

'That sounds nice,' I say, trying not to sound too pathetic. What I would give to spend the afternoon drinking and gossiping with my girlfriends. My right arm? A kidney? But I can't, because a) I have to stay with the children, and b) I don't have any girlfriends other than Gemma. It sounds like a crappy meme, but friendships are like plants: they take time and effort to nurture if they are to flourish, and when Freddie left I didn't have the time or the energy. Besides, Gemma was always there for me. I didn't need anyone else.

Lately, though, I've found myself wishing I'd kept up the friendships I'd made at university and made more effort with the other mums at the school gates. It would be so nice to meet girlfriends in town for a drink or a film, or to be able to pick up the phone and call someone for a heart-to-heart. Not that I don't love Gemma, but sometimes spending so much time with her makes me feel a little... claustrophobic.

Gemma, on the other hand, has a close circle of friends – most of them nurses at the hospital – and is always out socialising. But then she's never had to worry about anyone other than herself. She doesn't have to spin the plates I do, every day a merry-go-round of shopping, cooking, cleaning and washing. Playdates to organise, school trips to remember, arguments to referee. She doesn't know how lucky she is.

She trots off down the hall to say goodbye to the kids, and I take another look out of the window. Tess Brown and her photographer are sitting in the front seats of a navy saloon. As I watch, the photographer points to something outside and they set down their takeaway coffees in unison and scramble out of the car.

I watch, warily, as they scoot up the pavement and stop behind a parked van. A passing cyclist slows, the rider unclipping his shoes. It's only as Brown and her sidekick jump out at him that I realise with horror that the man they are virtually accosting in the street is Carter.

I yell for Gemma, hoping we can nip outside and cause a diversion, but I'm too late. The front door swings open, and Carter stalks in.

'What the fuck is a reporter from the *Daily Post* doing here?' he growls.

23

FREDDIE

TEN YEARS AGO

I walk through the empty streets, my head tucked into my chest and my mind in overdrive. It's clear our marriage is over. Alex doesn't love me any more. Worse than that. She despises me. It's obvious when I think about it; the signs are all there, have been for months. She flinches when I touch her. Turns her head away if I try to kiss her. She barely looks me in the eye and when she does, her gaze is devoid of all emotion. Those dancing, laughing eyes that gazed into mine with such love on our wedding day are cold now. Indifferent.

I'm not a fool; I know passion doesn't last forever. Look at my parents. They've been married for nearly forty years. The romance and grand gestures have been replaced with affection and everyday acts of kindness. The cup of tea Dad makes Mum every morning. The hours of Formula One she endures because she knows he loves it. Their marriage is solid as a rock. Whereas my own wife can't even stand to be in the same room as me.

I stop to catch my bearings. It's started to rain, a light drizzle that gums my eyelids together and plasters my hair to my head.

I'm on the far side of town, close to Carter's flat. I consider heading there and blagging a night on his sofa, but I'm not sure he'd appreciate me turning up on the doorstep unannounced, three sheets to the wind and dripping puddles on his expensive travertine tiles, especially if he has a woman over.

I remember a bench on the bank of the canal. I used to take Erin there to watch the narrowboats when Alex needed a break. Tucked beneath the branches of a towering oak tree, the bench will at least afford me some shelter from the rain while I decide what to do.

I'm about to turn into the narrow, cobbled street that leads to the canal when I become aware of footsteps behind me. I glance over my shoulder. A slight figure in trackie bottoms and a hoodie is treading lightly along the pavement a dozen paces behind me. My stomach clenches and I quicken my pace.

I step in a puddle, water sloshing into my shoe. Is it my imagination, or are the footsteps getting closer? I try to tell myself the hoodie doesn't make the man a criminal. It's raining, for Chrissakes. Of course he's pulled his hood up. I would too, if I had one. As it is, rain drips in an icy trickle down the back of my neck. Or maybe it's fear, I can't be sure. My thoughts are all over the place.

''Xcuse me, mister,' a voice says, and for a moment I'm nonplussed, because it's not the voice of a man, as I'd expected, but of someone much younger. Without thinking, I stop and turn around.

'Can I use your phone?' The kid – for he can't be any older than sixteen – appears agitated, his movements jerky.

'No.' I wasn't born yesterday. There's no way I'm handing my phone over. But something about the boy claws at my conscience. Perhaps it's the slightness of his shoulders, or the hint of pleading in his voice. 'I can make a call for you, if you like.' I pat my pockets before remembering I've left my phone at home. 'God, I'm sorry. I don't have it with me.'

The boy's eyes are fixed on my wrist as he clocks the Omega Seamaster peeking out from the sleeve of my coat.

'Gimme your watch.'

'What?'

'I said, give me your watch.' The boy thrusts his hand in the pocket of his joggers and when he pulls it out something glints in the light of the street lamp. My legs threaten to buckle and I hold out a placatory hand, but this only seems to antagonise the boy, who surges forward and waves the knife in my face.

'Give me the fucking watch or I'll cut your fucking hand off!' he yells.

My gaze darts up and down the street. Old industrial units line both sides. The nearest house is a good fifty metres away. If the boy stabs me I'll bleed out on the cobbles, probably won't be found until the morning. Not that Alex will care. But Erin and Megan need me. I unbuckle the watch and hold it out gingerly. The boy whips it from my hand and runs off, his trainers pounding the rain-slicked pavements. In seconds, I'm alone again. I feel winded, even though he didn't touch me. A bitterness rises in me like bile. This is what happens when you trust someone. They let you down, every single time.

I turn up the collar of my coat and step back into the night.

24

ALEX

NOW

Carter pulls off his cycling helmet and shoves it into my hands. 'The reporter's just asked me how I feel about my wife's first husband coming back from the dead.'

I swallow. I can feel the anger coming off him in waves. 'They came to the house too. Someone tipped them off that Freddie's home.'

'First, please tell me you didn't speak to them, and second, how many times do I have to remind you, Alex? This isn't Freddie's home any more. It's my name on the deeds, and I'm the one who pays the freaking mortgage.'

'I know,' I soothe. 'And of course I didn't talk to them.'

'We told them to bugger off,' Gemma says, appearing from the kitchen with her jacket on and her bag over her shoulder.

'Good.' Carter unclips his cycling shoes. 'I'm going to take a shower, and then I'm going to call that woman's editor and tell him exactly where he can stick his poor excuse for a rag.'

Once he's safely out of earshot, Gemma turns to me with a deadpan look. 'Consultants and their God complexes, eh? Also, why must he assume the woman's boss is a man?' She whistles through her teeth. 'I don't know how you put up with him.'

I weigh the cycling helmet in my hands. Carter's confidence is his superpower and his Achilles heel. It both attracts and repels me. I love the way he commands a room and takes charge of any crisis, but when his confidence tips into arrogance he can be hard to live with.

I'd assumed it was a rhetorical question, but Gemma's waiting for an answer. I force a laugh. 'Just taking one for the team.'

She leaves with a promise to call round after her shift tomorrow. I watch her go from the safety of the porch window, my eyes widening when she strolls up to the photographer's car and taps on the passenger window. She has a short conversation with Tessa Brown, then ambles towards town.

I thumb a text. *Fraternising with the enemy? WTF?*

She replies in seconds. *I was telling her to piss off, actually. You're welcome.* The text ends with a raised-eyebrow emoji and immediately, I'm contrite.

Sorry, Gem. Ignore me. All this drama's making me paranoid. Thanks for coming over. I don't know what I'd do without you. Have a lovely, boozy lunch with your friends and see you tomorrow xx

I stare at my phone for an age. Just when I'm about to give up, she sends a blowing-a-kiss emoji. It seems I'm forgiven. One small consolation in a nightmare that's fast spiralling out of control: Freddie's shock return, the anonymous notes and the looming threat of tabloid headlines all conspiring to send my anxiety spiking through the roof.

I shuffle back to the kitchen to make a start on lunch. I usually do a roast on a Sunday, but I've left it too late, so I take the sausages I was planning to cook tomorrow and sling them in the oven, then start peeling a small mountain of potatoes. Carter, who has become a devotee of the roast dinner since he's lived in the UK, will have to do without today. Sausages and mash it is.

While the potatoes boil, I check on the kids. Erin is helping Dylan make a Duplo tower and Megan's watching Taylor Swift on YouTube. 'Lunch won't be long,' I tell them, before knocking softly on the door to Carter's study.

'I can't get hold of the editor, so I've lodged a formal complaint via the website,' he says, leaning back in his chair, his hands laced behind his head. His blond hair is still damp from the shower and his white T-shirt stretches tightly across his chest. A rush of longing hits me with such force it's all I can do not to drag him upstairs.

Oblivious, Carter tips the chair forward and pulls his MacBook closer. 'That woman has breached at least three clauses in the Editors' Code of Practice. I checked. It says they're not allowed to engage in intimidation, harassment or persistent pursuit, and everyone is entitled to respect for their private and family life. She's going to wish she never knocked on my door.'

Pushing aside all thoughts of bed, I swivel the laptop round and skim-read the code. A paragraph near the end catches my eye. *There may be exceptions to the clauses where they can be demonstrated to be in the public interest.* That'll be her get-out clause. I can't believe the editors of tabloid newspapers really do balance the rights of people like us against the public's right to know, especially when their driving force is to flog papers – and everyone knows salacious stories sell.

Pointing this out to Carter will only inflame the situation, however, so I bite my tongue and tell him lunch is almost ready.

Back in the kitchen, I bring peas to the boil and strain the potatoes. Fleming pulls himself out of his bed, lumbers over to the back door and starts whimpering.

'What is it, boy?' He gives a low bark. 'Need to pee?' I open the back door and he pushes past me, almost knocking me flying. I feel a flicker of unease. What if Tess Brown and her photographer have let themselves in through the gate at the bottom of the garden and are going through the wheelie bins right now, digging for dirt on us? I slip on my gardening shoes and let myself out of the door, preparing a speech in my head about my right to privacy as I walk towards the gate.

'Alex,' a voice says, and I jump a foot in the air as Freddie appears from nowhere.

'Jesus, Freddie,' I cry. 'Why didn't you come to the front door like a normal person?'

He is as white as a sheet. 'Someone just took my photo.' He glances over his shoulder, as if he's worried they've followed him into the garden and are snapping away behind his back.

'I know. They've been to the house. They're from the *Daily Post*. I would have called to warn you but I don't have your number. Carter's already made a formal complaint. You didn't say anything, did you?'

He shakes his head. His dark eyes are haunted. 'I shouldn't have come back.'

'What d'you mean?'

'You shouldn't have to put up with reporters knocking on the door because of me, Alex. It's not fair on you and the girls. Perhaps I should go.'

'No!' I fire the word like a bullet and Freddie's eyes widen. I take a breath, trying to calm myself. 'I mean, you can't leave before you've told me why you went in the first place.'

Freddie acknowledges this with a small nod.

'Anyway, I'm glad you're back,' I say quietly.

His face softens. 'I'm glad you're glad.'

For the first time since his return, I sense a chink in his armour and I press on. 'Freddie, you *have* to tell me what happened that night. And everything that's happened since. I deserve the truth.'

'I know you do.'

We lock eyes for a long moment, and my pulse quickens, because I'm finally about to find out why Freddie walked out of our lives. But then his gaze tracks from my face to the back of the house and he stiffens. I turn slowly, filled with a sudden dread, to see Carter standing in the kitchen doorway, whippet-still, his face expressionless. My heart hammers in my chest. How long has he been standing there? And, more importantly, how much has he heard?

25

FREDDIE

TEN YEARS AGO

I stand on the doorstep, my finger on the buzzer, when I pause, unsure of the reception I'll get. Thanks to the little scumbag who stole my watch, I have no idea of the time. If I was to hazard a guess, I'd say it was somewhere between two and three in the morning. Too late – too early? – to be ringing someone's doorbell, but I have nowhere else to go.

Sod it, I think, pressing the buzzer. The resulting chime is as loud as a foghorn in the quiet cul-de-sac. I bend down to peer through the letterbox. The hallway is empty. I gaze up the staircase, just making out two bare feet halfway up.

'Gemma, Gem, it's me. Freddie.'

The feet fly down the stairs and moments later the door swings open. Gemma stares at me, her mouth a perfect O.

I try a self-conscious smile. 'OK if I come in?'

She nods, mute, and stands aside to let me pass. I shrug off my coat and hang it on the end of the banister, where it drips onto the carpet. 'Oh, God, sorry. D'you have a towel?'

Gemma finally finds her voice. 'It's fine. What are you doing here, Freddie?'

'OK if we sit down?' I say, neatly sidestepping the question. 'I've been walking for hours.'

'Of course. Won't be a sec.' She dashes upstairs, returning a few seconds later with a vivid pink dressing gown which she hands to me. 'Give me your wet things and I'll stick them in the dryer.'

I do as I'm told, conscious of my flabby arms and belly fat as I strip down to my underpants and pull on the dressing gown. I hand Gemma the pile of sodden clothes and she disappears again. It isn't long before I hear the low rumble of the tumble dryer.

When she comes back she's holding a bottle of Elijah Craig bourbon in one hand and a couple of balloon glasses in the other. She sets them on the coffee table, pours two stiff measures and pushes one glass towards me before sitting cross-legged in the armchair opposite. Dressed in plaid pyjamas, her blonde hair tied in a plait over one shoulder and her face bare of make-up, she looks softer and less worldly than usual.

I reach for the glass and smile. 'I've known you for sixteen years, yet I never knew you drank bourbon.'

'I always used to keep a bottle in for Carter.' Gemma shrugs. 'And you looked like you could use a drink.'

The beginnings of a headache are tightening across my temples. I've sunk so much booze, what difference will another few units make? I take a sip. The rich, sweet, smoky drink transports me straight back to med school where Carter and I would drink Jim Beam with a splash of water because it was all our student grants ran to. I down the rest and pour myself another.

Gemma watches me over her glass. 'You still haven't told me why you're here.'

I sigh. She'll find out soon enough anyway. She and Alex

talk to each other at least once a day. In fact, I'm surprised she doesn't know already. 'Alex and I are over.'

Her eyes widen. 'Over? You mean you're getting a divorce?'

Though Alex hadn't spelt it out, I know that's what she meant. It's the inevitable next step. First separation, then divorce. There'll be solicitors and court orders. We'll have to decide how we divide our assets and who has custody of the girls. Inevitably, it'll be Alex, because she's a stay-at-home mum while I have a full-time job. At least I did. After yesterday I'm not so sure. Anyway, Alex will keep the house, in which case, where the hell am I supposed to go? One of the registrars at work moved back with his parents aged forty-five because his wife played hardball and took him for every penny. I love my parents but hell would have to freeze over before I moved back into my childhood bedroom.

'Over,' I confirm. 'It was news to me too.' I run a hand across my face, suddenly choked. 'I'm sorry,' I mumble. 'It's all been a bit of a shock.'

'Oh, Freddie, I'm so sorry. I knew things were rocky but I had no idea they were that bad.' Gemma sets her drink on the table and joins me on the sofa, wrapping her arms around me and pulling me into a hug. I rest my head on her shoulder and breathe in the scent of spearmint and Persil. Apart from cuddles with the girls, it's the most physical contact I've had for weeks. When I finally break away Gemma stays where she is, one hand resting lightly on my knee.

'I kept telling myself it was a touch of postnatal depression after Megan was born, but it's more than that,' I say. 'I'm not sure what I'm supposed to have done but she can't stand the sight of me.'

'People change, Freddie. I should know.' Gemma's face darkens for a second, then she smiles. 'Come on, drink up. I'm damned if I'm going to save it for Carter.'

'Are you and he—?'

'Also over,' she says. 'Apparently, he doesn't want to "muddy the waters" at work. That's his excuse anyway.'

'I'm sorry.'

'Don't be.'

'His loss,' I say, and I mean it. I love Carter like a brother but he has a ruthless side to him and never lets anything or anyone stand in the way of his career.

I reach for my bourbon and knock it back. Gemma's biting her lip, as if she has something to say but isn't sure she should.

'What is it?' I ask.

'Maybe some time apart would be a good thing for you guys. Alex might realise what she's missing.'

'You think?'

'You know what they say about absence making the heart grow fonder.' She gives a little laugh. 'Not that it ever worked with Carter.' She points an unsteady finger at me. 'You are a good man, Freddie Harris, don't let anyone tell you otherwise, and you deserve better, too, d'you hear me?'

'I do,' I say solemnly.

'You and me,' she continues. 'We've been through so much together. At work, you know? It's like a pressure cooker, that place, waiting to blow every single day. And what does Alex have to do? Wash a few nappies and put supper on the table. She needs to cut you some slack.'

'She does,' I agree, because hadn't the same thought occurred to me only the other day? 'She has no idea what it's like, the strain we're constantly under.'

The bourbon is blurring everything again and it feels good. I pour myself another measure, splashing some on the coffee table.

'Whoopsie,' I say, and Gemma giggles. I've always found her laugh infectious. Alex is more serious. She's certainly been short on laughs recently. I raise my glass. 'To us. The original members of the Lonely Hearts Club.'

'To us,' Gemma says, snuggling up to me. Without thinking, I drop a kiss on her hair. She lifts her face and smiles sleepily and I feel a surge of affection for her. Gemma appreciates me. She understands the stress I'm under. She doesn't bitch at me the minute I walk through the door or turn away from me when I touch her. My nerve endings tingle as she edges even closer, thigh against thigh. I close my eyes and when I open them again Gemma has shifted and is straddling my lap. She takes my glass, sets it on the floor, then starts massaging my shoulders.

'You're so tense, Freddie,' she whispers, kissing my neck. I groan. I can't help it. She pulls the pink dressing gown open and bends her head, her tongue tracing a line down my chest to my groin. The bourbon thrums in my veins, clouding my judgement. It's impossible to think straight. I close my eyes and go with it.

26

ALEX

NOW

After almost forty years on this earth, I have come to realise that, more often than not, the things you worry about most – from dentist appointments to parents' evenings – are never as bad as you think.

The one exception to this is childbirth, of course. But at least you're given drugs for that.

However, the story in the *Daily Post* is far, far worse than anything I could have ever anticipated. The headline alone, *Exclusive: Missing doctor returns to find wife married to his best friend!*, is enough to make my toes curl in horror.

And it gets worse.

A missing children's doctor who disappeared a decade ago has returned – only to find his wife married to his best friend.

Dr Freddie Harris hasn't been seen since he mysteriously vanished from the family home in August 2015.

But in a twist straight out of a soap opera, the father of two returned on Saturday night to find his wife Alex happily married to his best friend and former colleague, Dr Carter Petersen, the Daily Post *can exclusively reveal.*

Looking visibly distressed yesterday, Dr Harris refused to comment on the revelations, or disclose where he'd spent the last ten years.

His former best friend, Dr Petersen, the top paediatric consultant at Thornden Green Hospital – the same position Dr Harris held until his disappearance – was equally tight-lipped when he was approached yesterday.

And the woman at the centre of the love triangle, mother-of-three Alex Petersen, also refused to comment.

'Carter has really stepped into Freddie's shoes,' said a family friend who wishes to remain anonymous. 'He has taken Freddie's job, his wife and, effectively, his life.'

Dr Harris made headlines shortly after he disappeared when he was the subject of an investigation by the General Medical Council following a complaint by the mother of a young patient under his care.

Sapphire Kelly was admitted to Thornden Green's Dolphin Ward with suspected pneumonia but ended up in intensive care after Dr Harris failed to spot the youngster had sepsis.

Sapphire's mum, patients' rights campaigner Ingrid Kelly, has also been approached for comment.

I push the paper away, bury my head in my hands and groan softly. Across the table, Gemma smiles at me encouragingly. Between us lies a pile of thirty papers. She bought every single copy from the local newsagent on her way here so our neighbours wouldn't see our dirty linen being aired so publicly. They could easily look the story up online, of course, but it was sweet of her to try.

'It could be worse,' she says.

'Worse?' I look at her incredulously. 'I've been painted as a scarlet woman, Freddie like some flaky Doctor Death and Carter... Carter doesn't exactly come out of it well either, does he? The man who stole not just his best friend's wife, but his job too. You know how hung up he is about his reputation. It means everything to him. How exactly could it be worse?'

Gemma wrinkles her nose. 'I agree it's not ideal, but I think you're overreacting. You'll be yesterday's news by tomorrow. Quite literally.' She smiles at her own joke but I'm too angry to acknowledge it.

My anger has been simmering ever since I woke at five this morning and checked the *Daily Post*'s website to find Tessa Brown's exclusive about us was the fifth most-read story of the day. But if I was angry, Carter was apoplectic.

'How dare they print this garbage?' he hissed, as he buttoned his shirt and knotted his tie so savagely he was in danger of choking himself. 'Your newspapers are a total joke. This would never happen back home.'

Carter professes to love the UK and when everything is going well, he calls it his spiritual home and says he can't imagine living anywhere else. But when things go wrong, he's the first in the queue to slag off his adopted country. The UK's public transport system is 'archaic', the weather 'depressing', the food 'bland' and the customer service 'lousy'.

'Tessa Brown gave me her card yesterday. I could try calling and asking her to take the story down?' I offered.

He let out a bark of laughter as he slipped his jacket on. 'Why would she do that when it's the fifth most-read story of the day?' He checked his phone. 'No, wait, we're the third most-read now. Jesus.'

I straightened his tie and brushed a speck of lint off his collar. 'I'm sorry,' I said, because what else was there to say?

He softened. 'It's not your fault. Sorry I yelled. I'm just so goddamn furious. Who gave that rag the right to splash our private lives all over its pages? Look, I need to go. I'm meeting

the head of HR at nine to give her the good news that I'm
Public Enemy Number One. I'll see you later, OK? And if any
other reporters get in touch, tell them they can go fuck
themselves.'

Freddie was nowhere to be seen when I trooped downstairs
with Dylan on my hip to give the girls their breakfast before
school. Instead, I found a note propped against the kettle. *Gone
for a walk.* How typical, I thought bitterly. When the going gets
tough, Freddie gets going.

Erin and Megan were surprisingly unconcerned when I
told them about the story.

'Everyone knows journalists are liars, Mum,' Erin said, her
mouth full of toast.

'And I don't give a stuff what people think,' Megan declared
with enviable indifference.

I wish I could be as sanguine as them.

Now, I jab at the paper with my finger. 'And who is the
insider?' I ask Gemma. 'Which one of our supposed friends has
stitched us up?'

'I've been wondering about that.' She pulls the paper
towards her and scans the story again. Four pictures accompany
the article, which takes up the whole of page fifteen. There's a
photo of me staring anxiously through our open front door; a
shot of Freddie shielding his face with his forearm as he hurries
down our road, looking as guilty as any convicted felon; and one
of Carter pushing his bike up to the house, a scowl on his handsome face and the veins in his neck bulging. Finally, there is a
picture of Sapphire Kelly lying unconscious in her intensive
care cot, as waxen and lifeless as a porcelain doll.

'What if Ingrid Kelly tipped off the reporter?' Gemma says.
'She became a bit of a poster girl for patients' rights after the
thing with her daughter, didn't she? I bet she has loads of
contacts on the nationals.'

'You really think she would?' My eyebrows shoot up in

surprise. There's no doubt Ingrid placed Freddie firmly in her sights when Sapphire was taken ill, but that was ten long years ago. Surely by now she would have found closure? Besides, how would she know he's back?

Gemma chews her bottom lip. I can tell she wants to say something I'm not going to like, but whatever it is, I need to hear it.

'What is it, Gem?'

She lets out a long, drawn-out sigh. 'I wasn't going to tell you this, but she turned up on Dolphin Ward the other day.'

'Ingrid Kelly?' Gemma has my full attention. 'Why?'

'I wasn't on duty at the time, but a mate told me she was there to see Simi.'

The name rings a bell. I search my memory for a face. 'The ward sister?'

Gemma nods. 'Why Ingrid Kelly would be paying Simi a visit after all this time I have no idea. I just thought it was a bit of a coincidence.'

I consider it. Ingrid Kelly visits Dolphin Ward, then Freddie turns up out of the blue, and suddenly we're plastered all over one of the tabloid newspapers. There's something else. The anonymous letters warning that the truth will out. I don't know how all these things are connected, but Gemma's right, it's too much of a coincidence.

'You think she's been watching the house?'

Gemma tucks a strand of hair behind her ear. 'Seems unlikely, I know. But she doesn't live that far from here, does she?'

Ingrid's small, terraced home is a couple of streets away, between here and Megan's school. I saw her locking her front door one morning not long after Megan started in reception. Ingrid had a small brown dog on a lead and my heart had jumped into my throat when Fleming had woofed a greeting. I'd bowed my head and chivvied Fleming and the girls along before she saw me. After that, I changed my route, walking double the distance twice a day for years.

'Church Lane,' I agree. Perhaps Ingrid has been keeping tabs on us. I'm not someone who lives their life on social media, but I do occasionally post pictures of the children. I make a mental note to check my privacy settings. It's more likely Ingrid was out walking her dog the night Freddie shuffled up the path to our front door. Unless she's been watching us...

And if she has, what does she want?

27

FREDDIE

TEN YEARS AGO

Sunlight stabs my eyelids, the pain like red-hot pokers. I squeeze my eyes shut and drag the duvet over my head, inwardly cursing Alex for pulling the curtains when she must have seen I was still asleep. She's an early riser, the kind of person who's annoyingly cheerful in the mornings, whereas I've always been, always will be, a night owl. We're the polar opposite in so many respects. Alex likes cats. I prefer dogs. She's a Marie Kondo fanatic, I'm an inveterate hoarder. She loves travelling. I'm a home bird. Chalk and cheese. It's a wonder we're still—

'Morning, gorgeous. I brought you a cuppa,' a voice says, and my stomach flips as the memories rush in. Sapphire Kelly being whisked into intensive care, her life hanging by a thread. Alex throwing a pillow at me and telling me our marriage was over. Turning up on Gemma's doorstep, drunk as a skunk. And then...

Fuck. *Fuck*.

'I made it strong, just how you like it,' Gemma trills. I force my eyes open and gaze at her blearily.

She's wearing a silk negligee in a dusky apricot shade with a plunging lace-trimmed neckline. A spaghetti strap has fallen over one shoulder but my eyes are drawn to her nipples, which are clearly visible through the thin material. I feel myself harden, a physical reflex that fills me with self-loathing, because even if my marriage is over, I've committed the cardinal sin; sleeping with my wife's best friend is morally indefensible.

Gemma obviously feels no such guilt because she sets the mug on the bedside table, climbs astride me and unhooks the other strap so the gossamer-thin negligee slides over her breasts to her waist.

'No, Gemma,' I say, trying to wriggle away. 'Alex—'

Her eyes narrow. 'What about Alex? She threw you out last night, remember? You told me yourself. She doesn't want you any more.'

'I know, but it – *this*' – I flap a hand – 'seems wrong.' My voice has a pathetic note of pleading to it that I despise but seem unable to shake off. 'So soon, you know?'

Gemma wrenches the negligee back up, covering herself. 'It didn't seem "wrong" last night,' she retorts. 'You were practically gagging for it!'

Was I? The last thing I remember was Gemma making a move on me. A fresh wave of shame rolls over me. I could have stopped it at any point, but I hadn't. I was despicable. The lowest of the low. A single tear slides down my cheek.

'I'm sorry,' I say in a small voice. 'I behaved appallingly and if I could turn back the clock I would in a heartbeat—'

Rather than appease Gemma, my words seem to have the opposite effect, and her lips thin to the point of disappearing altogether. Shaking her head, she jumps off me and stalks across the room to the door.

'Gemma,' I call after her. 'I'm sorry.'

'Get lost, Freddie,' she hisses. 'You worthless piece of shit.'

Even though I know it's coming, I still jump out of my skin as the door slams shut behind her.

* * *

I hobble around Gemma's bedroom, trying to ignore the pounding in my head as I gather my clothes. My work shirt and trousers have been carelessly discarded on the back of a chair. My pants and socks are strewn over the wooden floor. My tie is crumpled under the bed like a sleeping viper. I comb every inch of the bedside tables and Gemma's cluttered dressing table looking for my watch. It's only when I've scoured the room from top to bottom that I remember it was stolen by the boy in the hoodie and I feel another pang of loss. Shallow, maybe, but my Omega represents everything I've always strived to be. Successful, assured, admired.

A bitter laugh escapes my lips. I'm not successful. I'm a failure: as a husband, a father, a doctor and a friend. A fraud who destroys everything I touch. This thing with Gemma is the final straw. I'm a grade-A piece of shit and everyone would be better off without me. Take Ingrid Kelly. She tried to tell me Sapphire was seriously ill and I hadn't listened. Thanks to my arrogance, Ingrid is probably mourning the loss of her daughter right now.

As for Gemma, I used her to bolster my own ego last night and turned down her advances this morning. Who was it who said hell hath no fury like a woman scorned? Shakespeare, probably. I shudder as I remember the contempt in her voice. She'll be glad to see the back of me.

And Alex? She's the only woman I've ever loved. The mother of my beautiful girls. I've been complacent, have assumed that even though we'd hit a rocky patch our relationship was strong enough to weather all storms. But, to continue the crap boat analogy, I've found myself up shit creek without a paddle.

I lick my cracked lips, a plan forming loosely in my mind. I turn it over, considering it from every angle. What if I just disappeared? Who would miss me?

No one, that's who.

28

ALEX

TEN YEARS AGO

When did I realise happy endings weren't a given? I can pinpoint the exact moment. It was the day Freddie walked out on us.

I'd woken to the sound of a baby's cries and groaned. Surely Megan couldn't be hungry already? I couldn't have been asleep for more than half an hour. The cries petered out, became whimpers. I turned onto my back and stared at the ceiling, willing Megan to go back to sleep.

The room fell blissfully silent and I heaved a sigh of relief. I hadn't had more than two hours of unbroken sleep since she was born and I was cross-eyed with exhaustion. I turned onto my side and was drifting off when Megan started mewling again. I clasped the duvet, ready to throw it off and haul myself out of bed, when I remembered I wasn't breastfeeding any more. Freddie could feed her.

'Freddie,' I muttered. 'Get up. It's your turn to feed the baby.'

Silence.

I was about to reach out a foot to prod his shin when I remembered throwing a pillow at him and telling him to sleep on the sofa. Huffing loudly, I dragged myself out of bed and peered into the Moses basket. Megan's face was working, her cries growing in volume. Any minute now and she'd wake her sister. 'Shush, shush,' I said automatically, scooping her into my arms and trudging downstairs.

In the kitchen, I flicked on a side light and warmed a bottle. I had a good mind to march into the living room and hand both the baby and bottle to my husband and crawl back into bed, but something stopped me. Freddie had looked knackered last night.

'We're all knackered,' I said to the empty room. Megan's eyes opened a little wider at the sound of my voice. I sat down, cradled her in the crook of my arm and gave her the bottle. Her gaze fixed on my face as she fed. Objectively, I could see she was a pretty baby, with her mop of brown hair, her tiny, pixie ears and perfect snub nose, but the whoosh of love I'd felt for Erin when she was born had failed to materialise when Megan came along.

I looked after her, of course I did. I fed and bathed her, I changed her nappy and soothed her when she was fractious, but I was going through the motions. When Freddie or his parents were around, I played the role of besotted mum, cooing at her, making funny faces, blowing raspberries on her tummy to make her giggle. With Erin it had all come naturally, this easy adoration, but with Megan it felt forced.

The guilt I felt was suffocating. It was the only word for it. It was as though I couldn't breathe. I knew there must be something badly broken inside me. So many women wanted babies they couldn't have, yet here was I, not wanting the thing they coveted above all else.

Look at Gemma. She was desperate to settle down and start a family. Only problem was, she seemed incapable of holding onto a man for more than a couple of months. She claimed it was because they were all commitment-phobic bastards, cut from the same cloth as Carter, but it wasn't that. She just had this uncanny knack of picking the players.

Sometimes, I think she saw through the image of the perfect mum I was trying so hard to project, because she'd look at me with those piercing blue eyes of hers and I'd feel stripped bare. But then she'd hug me and tell me I was doing brilliantly and I knew I was overreacting and that this madness, this desolation I felt, was temporary and one day I might start to feel normal again.

Megan finished her bottle and I carried her back upstairs, laid her in her Moses basket and crawled back into bed. When I finally fell asleep I dreamt I was drowning, waves crashing over my head, water filling my lungs and pulling me down into the depths of the ocean. I woke with a start. Rain was lashing against the window, a torrent of water running in rivulets down the glass. I stared groggily at the alarm clock. It was half past seven. I hadn't slept this late for months. Freddie must have crept in and taken Megan downstairs to feed her while I was asleep. I felt a rush of gratitude towards him, mixed with a big dollop of shame at the earful I gave him last night.

I stretched luxuriously and contemplated whether I might be able to grab another half hour's kip when I heard a snuffling by my feet. I pulled myself onto my elbows and squinted down at the Moses basket. A tiny fist punched the air, and the snuffle turned into a cry. I threw the duvet off with a sigh. Of course Freddie hadn't taken the baby downstairs to give me a lie-in. He was probably still on the sofa, snoring his head off, the selfish—

'Mummy!' Erin bowled into the room, her hair a bird's nest and sleep dust in the corners of her eyes. 'I'm hungwy.'

'Why don't you ask Daddy to get your breakfast while I change Megan's nappy? He's in the living room. Tell him there are some Cheerios in the cupboard.'

Erin nodded and trotted off and I pulled on my dressing gown and bent over the Moses basket. Megan cooed when she saw me, reaching up to grab a handful of my hair. I felt nothing.

Downstairs, Erin was sitting on the kitchen floor, the box of Cheerios in her lap, feeding a handful of the dry cereal to Fleming, then popping a couple in her own mouth.

'Eat it all up,' she said to the dog. His tail thumped the flagstones.

I felt a surge of irritation. 'Where's Daddy, Erin?'

She shrugged. 'Don't know.'

'Oh, for pity's sake.' I strapped Megan into her bouncy chair on the table, estimating I had about three minutes before she realised she was starving, and stalked into the living room.

The sleeping bag was still in its carry bag and the pillows were piled neatly on the armchair. Perhaps Freddie had got up early to buy my favourite cinnamon and raisin bagels from the bakery up the road. My mood softened. It's just the kind of thing he would do. A peace offering after turning up drunk last night. Then I spied his wallet, phone and car keys on the coffee table.

'Freddie?' I called, as I checked the dining room, snug and downstairs loo. No sign of him. I trudged back upstairs and looked in Erin's room, the spare room, the nursery and the family bathroom. 'Freddie!' I called again, my voice tight with irritation. I stomped into our bedroom and peered out of the window to the back garden. The rain was still coming down in stair rods. There was no sign of Freddie. Where the hell was he?

Fleming barked and I hurried into the kitchen to find Erin standing on a chair about to drop a handful of Cheerios into Megan's mouth.

'Erin, no!' I yelled, and she pulled her hand back in shock. 'You must never, *ever* feed your sister, do you hear me?'

Her eyes filled with tears. 'But she was hungwy,' she wailed.

'I don't care. She could have choked!'

I sank down at the kitchen table and buried my head in my hands. Erin's sobs were ramping up in volume and in her bouncy chair, Megan started to wail in sympathy. Outside, rain battered the kitchen window. Tears balled in my own throat. I couldn't cope. Not with the crying, the mess, the endless, grinding exhaustion.

I was drowning, and Freddie, the only person who could have thrown me a lifeline, had vanished.

29

ALEX

NOW

Once Gemma has left, I tidy up the breakfast things and put a wash on, hoping that by staying busy I can keep a lid on my anxiety. But it's no good. The house feels oppressive, the four walls pressing in on me. I need to get out.

'Dylan,' I call, dangling Fleming's lead in front of him. 'Want to take Fleming for a walk?'

His eyes light up and he drops the police car he was playing with. 'Me, me, me,' he says, reaching for the lead.

'OK, but you need to go in the buggy, all right?'

He nods, and I bundle him into his coat and strap him into his pushchair. Fleming, hearing the word 'walk', is already standing patiently by the front door, his tail pumping. I clip his lead on and hand the end to Dylan, whose little face beams with delight.

'Hold on tight, OK?' I tell him, even though I know for a fact that a squirrel could streak across the pavement in front of us and Fleming would still stick like glue to Dylan's side, the dear, sweet dog he is.

We set off for the park but when I reach the end of the road, I find myself turning right instead of left. Soon we are walking along Church Lane towards Ingrid Kelly's house, drawn to her cheery yellow front door like pilgrims to a holy relic. The red-brick house, with its wrought-iron gate and holly bush taking up most of the handkerchief-sized front garden, is exactly as I remember, apart from a grab rail next to the front door.

We reach the front gate. Fleming chooses that moment to take a dump, and I curse under my breath and ferret about in the bottom of the pushchair looking for a poop bag while glancing nervously at the house. My stomach swoops as a figure flits across an upstairs window. I turn my head, hoping Ingrid hasn't recognised me.

'Shit,' I mutter. In the pushchair, Dylan, growing bored, chants, 'Shit, shit, shit.'

I tie the bag and hook it over the handle of the pushchair while debating my next move. I want to confront Ingrid, to ask her how she thought she was justified in selling our story to a national newspaper, and I have one hand on the gate, about to open the latch, when I hesitate.

What actual proof do I have that Ingrid told the *Daily Post* Freddie was back? The truth is that I have none. Yes, I could point the finger at her to see her reaction, but the woman already hates our family for what happened to her daughter. Accusing her of something she didn't do will only fan the flames. I thought this morning's story was bad enough. Imagine the headlines if Ingrid called up Tessa Brown to say the woman in the centre of the missing doctor love triangle had turned up on her doorstep, threatening her. I can't take the risk.

Another movement in the upstairs window catches my eye and I glance back up. The windows are spotlessly clean, making it easy to see the woman staring down at me. Ten years have passed since I last saw Ingrid Kelly, but I'm in no doubt it's her. She has the same slim, athletic build I remember. My heart is racing, the palms of my hands damp. It was a mistake to come here. I need to stay out of Ingrid Kelly's way. Who knows what she's capable of? I release the brake on Dylan's buggy and march towards the park as quickly as my shaky legs will carry me.

* * *

By the time we reach the park my heart rate has returned to normal.

'Swings first, or ducks?'

Dylan kicks his buggy in excitement. 'Ducks!'

'Ducks it is.' We follow the path past the tennis courts towards the small duck pond on the far side of the park. I've been coming here for years, ever since Erin was a baby. In an age of smartphones and tablets, feeding the ducks offers fresh air and wholesome entertainment for the price of a packet of birdseed.

I unstrap Dylan from his buggy, hand him the food and he toddles towards the pond.

'Not too close,' I tell him, perching on the bench. A pair of mallards glide over. I've always thought the drake's shimmering green head, white collar and rich red-brown breast is a little in your face, preferring the muted beauty of the hen, with her chocolate-brown feathers, cat-flick eyeliner and flash of blue on her wing.

The ducks lose their grace the minute they jump out of the water, waddling over to Dylan, who shrieks with pleasure as they start gobbling up the bird food. They are soon joined by more ducks. From a distance, a pair of swans watch with haughty loftiness.

Swans mate for life. Megan did a project on it at school. So do lots of birds. Penguins and barn owls. Golden eagles. Not ducks, though. Ducks are monogamous for a season, then go their separate ways. No squabbles or petty jealousies at play in their world. They just get on with the business of procreating. No fuss, no drama. Nothing to see here.

If only my life were that simple.

I watch Dylan scatter birdseed on the grass with dogged concentration, my mind on the row Carter and I had last night.

It had started, like most spats, with a throwaway comment.

We were getting ready for bed when Carter asked if I needed him to pick up anything for tea on his way home from work.

'It's OK, thanks. Freddie's going to do spag bol.'

He balled his socks in his fist. 'He is, is he? How jolly decent of him,' he mocked.

'Don't be like that. He just wants to help.'

'That's not all he wants though, is it?'

'What d'you mean?'

'Come on, Alex. Don't be naive. He's trying to worm his way back into your life. Have you told him he's got to find somewhere else to stay?'

'Not yet, I—'

Carter exhaled loudly and climbed into bed.

'I get why you're angry, but there's no reason to be,' I said. 'Freddie came back for the girls, not me.'

'He told you that, did he?' Carter's jaw was tight, a muscle popping in his temple.

'Not in so many words,' I admitted. 'But he respects the fact that I'm married to you now.' I mentally crossed my fingers behind my back, because I wasn't sure this was true. Why would Freddie be warning me about Carter otherwise?

It seemed Carter was of the same opinion, because he shook his head. 'I don't think he does. I've seen the way he looks at you. He still loves you, Alex.'

I laughed, then. 'If he loved me, he would never have left.'

'Has it ever occurred to you that he left *because* he loved you?'

'What?' I frowned, because Carter wasn't making sense. Why would Freddie leave if he loved me?

Carter pummelled his pillow and slipped it under his head. 'Maybe he felt he wasn't good enough for you and the girls. Maybe he thought you'd be better off without him, especially after all that business with Sapphire Kelly.'

'You're wrong,' I said, a flush of shame creeping over me. 'There was more to it than that. I... I wasn't in a good place back then.'

Carter's expression softened. 'I know you weren't, babe. Look, I'm sorry for having a go. I'm just feeling a bit off balance, you know?' He looked sidelong at me. 'A bit insecure.'

Because Carter's an alpha male people automatically assume he's made of steel. They don't realise that inside that hard exterior is a loving, loyal man who would do anything for me and the kids.

My eyes glassed over. 'I don't want to fight you, Carter. I love you.'

'I love you too.'

He pulled the duvet open and I climbed in, shimmying across the bed and resting my head on his chest. I could feel his heart beating a steady tattoo.

'We'll be all right, won't we?' I said in a small voice. 'We'll get through this?'

He kissed my hair. 'Damn right we will. You, Dylan and the girls are my family now. I won't let Freddie take you away.'

I wrench my thoughts back to the present. Dylan has run out of birdseed. It's our cue to leave, and I strap him in his buggy, hand him Fleming's lead and set off for home.

We're rounding the corner into our street when I see the woman. She's standing on the opposite pavement a few doors down from our house. I don't know why she attracts my attention. Perhaps it's the way she's hugging her chest as if fighting the cold, even though it's a mild day. Perhaps there's something about her body language that stirs a distant memory.

As I approach our house, she sets off smartly down the street towards the park, her head tucked into her chest. Two lines of parked cars separate us, and I stand on tiptoes and crane my neck to get a better look at her. Fleming growls softly as she passes, which is strange, because Fleming never growls at anyone. My curiosity deepens to suspicion. And then it hits me with the force of a water cannon.

It's Ingrid Kelly.

But what the hell is she doing outside my house?

30

ALEX

TEN YEARS AGO

'Where *is* Daddy?'

I was giving Megan her bottle when Erin looked up from her bowl of Cheerios, a frown on her face, and asked me the one question I couldn't answer.

'I don't know, sweetheart.'

'Is he at work?'

'No, it's the weekend.' I mustered a smile. 'Maybe he's popped to the shops.' It was almost nine o'clock and Freddie still hadn't come home. Every time I heard a car outside I expected to hear his key in the lock, even though I knew he hadn't taken his keys with him.

'Is he with Uncle Carter?' Erin asked through a mouthful of cereal. I felt like planting a kiss on her forehead and telling her what a clever girl she was, because of course Freddie was at Carter's. It was obvious when I thought about it. Carter's achingly trendy bachelor pad overlooking the canal was only a thirty-minute walk from ours and Freddie often used to crash there after a heavy night's drinking in those long-ago carefree days before the girls were born.

'Let's see, shall we?' I picked up my phone and dialled Carter's number, wondering why it had taken a four-year-old's logic to locate my missing husband when it hadn't occurred to me. It was the lack of sleep. I wasn't thinking straight.

After an age, the line clicked and Carter's voicemail kicked in.

'Hey, I can't get to the phone right now, so leave a message after the beeps and I'll get right back to you.' Carter's Californian drawl always made me think of sunshine and sandy beaches. 'Beep, beep, beep,' he finished.

I cleared my throat. 'Hi, Carter. It's Alex. Can you ask Freddie to give me a ring when he's up? I'd have called him myself but the silly sod's left his phone here. Anyway, that's it. Just tell him to call me.'

I had put Megan down for her lunchtime nap, tidied the kitchen and folded two loads of clean laundry when Carter phoned back. I pushed the bedroom door shut and sat down heavily on our bed.

'Freddie's not here, Alex.'

The ground shifted beneath my feet. 'Are you sure?'

'Of course I'm sure. Why did you think he was?'

'He came home late last night, drunk, and I... I...' My skin prickled with shame. I didn't want to admit to Carter that I'd given Freddie a tongue-lashing and banished him from our bed.

'And you what?' Carter prompted.

'I... we... had words. When I woke up this morning he wasn't here. At first, I thought he must have popped to the shops, but it's been hours now and he's still not home and I'm getting worried.'

I waited for Carter to tell me not to fret, that Freddie was bound to turn up before long. He didn't.

'That's odd,' he said. 'I had a strange text from him last

night. He was in The Swan and wanted me to join him. Think he wanted to talk.'

My cheeks burned at the possibility that Freddie had told Carter I was a hormonal mess and struggling to cope.

'You didn't go?'

'I couldn't. I had someone over.'

'Ah.' I frowned. 'What did he want to talk to you about, anyway?'

'Sapphire Kelly.'

'Who's that, your new girlfriend?'

'What? No. One of the patients on Dolphin Ward. She's in PICU with sepsis. Unlikely to make it, to be honest. Freddie's blaming himself.'

'Why?'

'Because he didn't spot it sooner.'

'He didn't tell me.' The words were out before I could stop them. But when was the last time I'd asked Freddie about his day? I started complaining about my lot the moment he walked through the door. He didn't get the chance to offload.

'You know Freddie. He probably didn't want to worry you,' Carter said.

I was silent, the guilt like a gut-punch.

'Have you tried his mom and dad?'

'I didn't want to worry them.'

'I'll call them if you like.'

'Thank you.' I picked at a loose thread on the duvet. 'What should I do?'

'Sit tight. I'll come over once I've spoken to them. And Alex? Don't worry. He'll be home before you know it.'

Carter sounded so sure of himself that the tightness in my chest eased a little.

'You're right.'

'I'm always right, Al.' I could sense the smile in his voice. Thank God for Carter and his unshakeable optimism. Even so, as I pushed myself to my feet and made my way slowly downstairs to the snug, where I'd left Erin glued to the Disney Channel, I couldn't stop my thoughts galloping. What if Freddie, staggering along the canal towpath on his way to Carter's flat, my recriminations ringing in his ears, had stumbled on the uneven ground and toppled into the oily water? What if he'd tottered into the path of a speeding car, his body tossed into the air by the force of the collision? What if he'd had a heart attack, a stroke? He was only thirty-three, but it happened. He could be hooked up to a life support machine in his own hospital for all I knew.

I cradled my head in my hands and groaned, so caught up imagining the worst that I jumped out of my skin when a hand touched my knee.

'Mummy?' Erin asked, her wide eyes mirroring my own fear. 'What s'matter?'

I swiped at my tears and wrapped my arms around her, burying my face in her curls. 'Nothing's the matter, darling. Mummy's just a bit tired, that's all.'

I knew she didn't believe me. How could she, when I didn't believe myself?

31

FREDDIE

TEN YEARS AGO

I nurse my pint and let my mind drift. The pub, more of a sports bar really, with three huge screens and cheap beer, is busy, but I welcome the babble of voices and laughter. It's like white noise, a soundtrack to my thoughts.

I came here after finding a twenty-pound note in the pocket of my trousers. Truth is, I've nowhere else to go. The two pints I've drunk already dulled my hangover. The third, I hope, will dull the ache inside me.

It's not like I'll be missed. It's Saturday, my day off, and Alex apparently couldn't care less where I am. Even so, I've spent the last half an hour debating whether or not to ask the man sitting at the table next to mine if I can borrow his phone, which is lying in tantalising reach beside a copy of the *Racing Post* and an empty pint glass. The man is glued to a horse race on the nearest screen, his tapping foot the only giveaway that he might have more at stake on the outcome than a couple of quid.

By my calculations, it must be almost six o'clock. Alex will be running Erin's bath by now while Megan has a kickabout on her play gym. Once Erin emerges from the bath, all rosy-skinned and smelling of baby shampoo, Alex will help her into her pyjamas and, once she's settled Megan in her cot, they'll reconvene in Erin's bedroom where Alex will read *Mr Men* stories – Erin's current favourite is *Mr Silly* – until her eyelids droop.

A stab of longing shoots through me, sharp as a knife. I've never missed the girls' bedtime. Never. Even when I'm away at a conference or working late I always take five minutes out to FaceTime Alex so I can say goodnight to them.

I eye the phone on the next table again, the question forming on my lips, *I don't suppose I could...* when a dark-brown horse and its jockey in butter-yellow silks romp home by a length. The man slams a fist on the table, causing his pint glass to wobble precariously, and mutters, 'Feckin' donkey,' before grabbing his phone and paper and stalking out of the pub.

It's probably just as well, I think, as I drag myself to the bar and order another pint. Alex would have hung up on me anyway. I remember the coldness in her voice as she dropped the pillow by my feet. *You can sleep on the sofa tonight. I'm done.* Tears pool in my eyes, and the barman, a burly guy with a nose ring and sleeve tattoos, regards me with concern.

'You all right, mate?' he says, setting the pint glass on the bar.

I nod and hand over the last of my change.

The barman counts it out. 'You're fifty pence short, but don't worry. I won't tell the boss if you don't,' he says, tapping his nose and winking at me.

'Thanks,' I manage, before retreating to my table, away from the barman's sympathetic gaze, because I know it'll be the undoing of me.

By the time I've reached the bottom of my fourth pint I've

drunk myself sober. I stand, feeling at peace for the first time in months.

'You off then?' the barman says as I set my glass on the bar.

'In a manner of speaking,' I say, then pause. 'Thank you.'

The barman frowns. 'What for?'

'For caring.' I give him the ghost of a smile. 'Not everyone does, you see.'

* * *

It's about half a mile from the pub to the motorway as the crow flies. I walk with purpose, my mind set, eager to get on with it now. Should I have left a note? Probably. But what would I have said?

I love you. I'm sorry.

The words feel hollow, a pathetic attempt at explaining the mess inside my head. In time, Alex will realise she's better off without me.

The hum of traffic grows louder as I near the motorway. After another ten minutes, I reach the top of the slip road. The chill wind is biting, but I barely notice. My gaze is fixed on the road ahead. The rush-hour traffic has thinned, which suits me. This isn't meant to be some grand gesture. It's just a fork in the road of my miserable life.

Left or right.

Leave or die.

A car pulls onto the slip road, its headlights on full beam. Slow to react, I catch the full glare square in the face and am momentarily blinded. I stumble backwards, almost toppling over the crash barrier. I right myself, and carry on walking, one foot in front of the other. Left foot, right foot. Rinse, repeat. Before long I've reached the hard shoulder. Cars and vans race past, a blur of steel and rubber.

An articulated lorry crests the brow of the hill, its cab lit up like a Christmas tree. Erin loves Christmas – what kid doesn't? I think of Sapphire Kelly, who will never see another Christmas because of me.

I take a breath, my mind made up.

And I step into the lorry's path.

32

ALEX

NOW

By the time I've wheeled the buggy round, Ingrid has disappeared. I scan the street, my heart pounding. For the briefest of moments, I consider leaving Dylan with Fleming on the path outside our front door and sprinting after her, but then I catch myself. It would be madness. What if someone took him? Instead, I find my keys, lift Dylan out of the buggy and head into the house.

I let out a hollow laugh when I spy the envelope on the doormat. I set Dylan down and snatch it up, not bothering about fingerprints this time because I don't need to. I can guess exactly who posted it through our letterbox. I rip it open and scan the scrawled words on the sheet of paper inside.

LIARS SHOULD GET EVERYTHING THEY DESERVE.

I feel a flash of anger. How dare Ingrid Kelly try to intimidate me like this? I'm certain the notes are from her. She was vocal enough in her condemnation of Freddie at the time, but now she's crossed a line. I ought to be able to feel safe in my own home. She has no damn right to taunt me with threats over something I had no part in. What happened to Sapphire was every parent's worst nightmare, I get that. But Freddie never meant for it to happen. He was a good doctor who made one mistake.

''Nana,' cries Dylan, grabbing hold of my hand and pulling me along the hallway. ''Nana, 'nana, 'nana.'

I scrunch the note into a ball and let him lead me into the kitchen where he climbs onto a chair and points at the bunch of bananas in the fruit bowl. ''Nana.'

'Hands first.' I lift him up to the sink to wash his hands, then settle him in his highchair. My own hands are trembling as I slice the banana and when the letterbox snaps, I jump a foot in the air. The knife slips, slicing through my finger.

Yelping, I rush to the tap, holding my hand under the cold water until the bleeding stops.

''Nana, Mummy,' Dylan says again, his little face screwed up.

'Won't be a minute, sweetheart.' I pull off a square of kitchen roll and wrap it around my finger before rinsing the knife and finishing the banana. I give it to him, then scoot into the hallway and grab the post from the mat. I flick through the letters, my pulse racing. There are a couple of bank statements, a water bill and a reminder from the optician to book an eye test. My shoulders slump with relief.

I carry the post back into the kitchen. A dark red stain is seeping through the kitchen roll wrapped around my finger. If I were prone to fanciful thoughts, I'd draw some hidden meaning from this. Something about the insidious power Ingrid has to penetrate our lives.

* * *

Megan is in high spirits when Dylan and I pick her up from school that afternoon. She's been pleading with me to let her walk home on her own since she started in Year Five in September. So far, I've managed to deflect her entreaties even though it won't be long before she's catching the bus to secondary school with Erin. At least I'll have Dylan at home for a few more years.

I never pictured myself as a stay-at-home mum. I'd assumed I would go back to work full-time after my maternity leave ran out. I found a nursery I liked and Erin enjoyed the taster sessions. But as the date of my return to work drew nearer, the more I dreaded leaving her. I loved hanging out with her.

Freddie had been behind me one hundred per cent. As a registrar, he was on a decent salary at the time, whereas I'd barely be taking home five hundred pounds a month after paying the exorbitant nursery fees. I handed in my notice with glee.

'Can we go to the swings, Mum?' Megan asks, as she skips alongside me. Strands of her fine blonde hair are escaping their plait and her white socks are wrinkled at the ankles.

I'm about to say no, but the sun is shining and Erin won't be back from school for another half an hour, and I'd rather be in the park than at home waiting for another threatening note.

'Ten minutes,' I say. Megan whoops with pleasure and my chest tightens with love for my sunny-natured middle child.

A decade on, I find it impossible to believe that it took so long for me to bond with Megan. I know the crippling postnatal depression I suffered after she was born was to blame. I'd felt hormonal for a couple of weeks after Erin's birth and had naively assumed that was as bad as the baby blues got. I wasn't stupid, I knew life with two young children would be hard, but the depression I experienced after Megan was born was so debilitating that if someone had offered me a pill to end it all, I would have gladly taken it.

Alongside spiralling anxiety, I was wracked with insomnia, my nights plagued by intrusive thoughts. What if Erin dies in her sleep? What if I drop Megan? What if social services find out how I'm feeling and take my babies away?

Freddie was endlessly patient when I was in the depths of my depression, which only exacerbated my feelings of uselessness. I refused all offers of help. I was a bitch to him. I correct myself. I wasn't the bitch; the illness was the bitch. But the outcome was the same. He was my verbal punchbag and he took every barbed comment, every criticism, on the chin because he's that kind of guy.

It's only now, with the benefit of hindsight, that I can look back at the stranger I had become during those dark, muddled months, and wonder if I was the one who drove Freddie away. Was this all my fault?

33

ALEX

TEN YEARS AGO

When, at six o'clock, Freddie still hadn't come home, I phoned the police to report him missing.

Carter had arrived just after two, and between us we'd phoned every friend and colleague of Freddie's we could think of and every hospital within a fifty-mile radius, but no one had heard from him and there were no reports of a man matching his description being admitted.

The call handler sounded almost bored as she took Freddie's details.

'Has he ever stayed out without letting you know before?'

'No, never. It's completely out of character.'

'What was his state of mind when you last saw him?'

I hesitated. I'd shut myself in the living room to make the call while Megan was napping and Erin was on my iPad in the kitchen. I could see Carter pacing the back garden, his phone pressed to his ear. I'd been loose with the truth when he asked me what I meant when I'd said Freddie and I had had words, downplaying it to little more than a petty quarrel. To my shame, he'd believed me.

'He was fine,' I told the call handler. 'A bit stressed about work – he's a paediatric consultant at Thornden Green – but otherwise OK. That's why I'm so worried.'

'Understood. Has he left a note at all? Sent you a text?'

'I told you already. He's left his phone here. And, no, I haven't found a note.' My voice was rising and I took a deep breath and tried to calm myself down. 'Sorry. I shouldn't take it out on you.'

'No need to apologise, Mrs Harris,' the call handler said, her voice gentle. 'And try not to worry. Most missing people are either found or come home in a few days. I'll start a missing person's report and an officer will be in touch shortly to take some more details. If you hear from your husband in the meantime, be sure to let us know.'

As I ended the call my phone pinged with a text from Gemma.

Hey, honey. I saw you've been trying to get hold of me. I snagged an agency shift so couldn't call you back. Everything OK?

As I dialled her number, the tears I'd been bottling up all day came pouring out.

'Something's happened to Freddie,' I sobbed, the moment she picked up. 'He's gone missing, Gem. We had an argument last night and I told him to sleep on the sofa. When I woke up this morning, he'd disappeared.'

On the other end of the line, Gemma was silent as she digested my news.

'He didn't leave a note and he didn't take his phone with him so I can't even call him. I'm so worried.'

'I'm sure he'll come home when he's had a chance to cool off. You know how much he adores you and the girls.'

'But what if he's had an accident?' I wailed.

'What makes you think he has?'

'Why else wouldn't he have come home?'

'Have you called the police?'

'Yes, they're sending someone over.'

'OK. Want me to come too? Help with the girls?'

'Would you?'

'Course. I'll get changed and come straight round.'

My shoulders sagged with relief. Gemma was the kind of person you needed in a crisis. Calm, capable, level-headed. It's why she was such a good nurse. 'Thank you,' I said, tears springing into my eyes again. 'Thank you.'

* * *

Was it my imagination, or did Carter's eyes narrow when I told him Gemma was on her way? I couldn't figure out why, since according to Gemma, they hadn't hooked up in ages.

'Auntie Gemma's here,' Erin yelled. She'd been keeping watch from the landing from the moment I told her Gemma was coming. I used to joke that if Gem and I ever went head-to-head in a custody battle and the judge asked Erin who she'd rather live with, it would be Gemma every time.

I opened the door and, as she gathered me in a hug, I felt myself sagging against her. 'Thank you so much for coming.'

'Don't be silly. What can I do?'

'We've phoned round everyone we can think of. There's a list in the kitchen. I'll show you, in case there's anyone we've missed.'

'We?' she queried.

'Carter came over earlier.'

'He's still here?'

I nodded. 'He's set up a mini command centre in the living room.' I gave her a weak smile. 'You know Carter.'

Erin thundered down the stairs and flung herself at Gemma.

'My daddy's wun away,' she said, her bottom lip wobbling.

Gemma tucked a strand of Erin's hair behind her ear. 'Oh, sweetheart, Daddy hasn't run away. He's just taken some time out. I'm sure he'll be back before you know it.'

'He's wun away,' Erin repeated stubbornly. 'He told me.'

My eyes met Gemma's, and I asked Erin sharply, 'When did he tell you that?'

'When I was asleep.'

'Last night?'

Erin didn't answer, her attention caught by the gold locket around Gemma's neck. She reached for it, but Gemma was quicker, tucking it into her top before she could grab it.

'Erin,' I said, trying to keep my voice steady. 'Listen to me. This is important. When did Daddy tell you he was running away? Last night?'

She shrugged. 'Fink so.'

I wanted to press her further but at that moment, the doorbell rang. I looked through the spyhole. Two uniformed officers stood on the doorstep, their faces distorted by the fisheye lens. My hand fluttered to my chest. I only reported Freddie missing an hour ago. Considering how stretched the police were, their arrival seemed too fast. Were they here to take details of his disappearance, or had they come bearing bad news?

I opened the door, my heart in my mouth.

34

FREDDIE

TEN YEARS AGO

I stand frozen in the carriageway, trapped in the beam of the lorry's headlights, as though caught in suspended animation. The lorry is two hundred metres away and bearing down on me fast. One hundred and fifty. One hundred and twenty. A car in the outside lane hurtles past, horn blaring, its driver gesticulating wildly as he tears by.

The piercing blast of the horn snaps me out of my trance. Do I really want to die like this, splattered over the front bumper of a forty-tonne HGV? What about the driver? They'd be haunted by the sight of my broken body for the rest of their life. I've caused enough pain already. I can't be responsible for more.

Just as I make the decision to step back onto the hard shoulder, the lorry's brakes screech. The smell of burning rubber fills the air as the artic shudders to a stop, barely ten metres away. I notice the Lithuanian number plate as the driver winds down the window and unleashes a volley of expletives. I don't need to know a single word of Lithuanian to understand how furious he is.

I hold my arms wide. 'I'm sorry.'

'You should be!' the driver cries, shaking his head. 'No one should walk here. Not safe!'

'I know. I was just—' My voice cracks. 'I'm sorry,' I say again.

The driver leans out of the window. He's about my age, with a thick beard and heavy black eyebrows that are drawn together in concern. 'You need lift?' he asks.

I pause. Do I need a lift? 'Where are you going?'

'Ullapool,' the man says.

I wrack my brains. Ullapool. It sounds as if it should be in the Lake District. I went there on holiday with Mum and Dad when I was about nine. My memories are hazy, but I remember with a sudden pang how much I enjoyed scrambling up the craggy fells to be rewarded with three-hundred-and-sixty-degree views of green valleys and sparkling lakes. Wainwright's country. The image dances in front of me like a mirage. It would be so easy to take up this kind man's offer, jump into his cab and leave my life behind. After all, what is there left for me here? My marriage is in tatters, my career's on the rocks and I've just slept with my wife's best friend. There's nothing left. I've destroyed it all.

'I can't pay you,' I tell him, my voice low. 'I don't have any money.'

'I do not want your money,' the man says. 'You want lift or not?'

I make up my mind. I don't know much at the moment, but one thing I do know is that Alex, the girls and my patients are better off without me.

'I do,' I say decisively. 'Thank you.'

* * *

I climb into the cab and look around as I fix the seat belt. It's a small space, but ordered. A soft tartan blanket is neatly folded on the seat beside me, and in the footwell sits a battered duffel bag and a Thermos flask. A small Lithuanian flag, its yellow, green and red stripes faded by the sun, hangs from the rear-view mirror. Tucked into the sun visor is a photo of a pretty, dark-haired woman and a young boy, who can't be much older than Erin.

'Your family?' I ask, gesturing to the photo.

The man nods. 'Daina and Lukas. They still live in Kaunas, my home town.' He pulls out into the traffic and glances at me. 'I'm Tomas.'

'Freddie.' I smile. 'Thank you for stopping.'

'Pleasure. The road can be lonely place. It is many, many miles to Ullapool. It is nice to have company.' He grins at me, displaying a row of crooked teeth. 'And chance to practise my English. Eez not so good.'

'It's a bloody sight better than my Lithuanian,' I say, and Tomas roars with laughter, as if I've just cracked the funniest joke at the Edinburgh Fringe Festival.

We fall silent for a while, and I gaze out of the window, watching the world whizz by. After a while, Tomas says, 'You look like man with many troubles. Sad man.'

Once again, my eyes well with tears at the kindness of strangers. Tomas is a big guy, well over six foot, with meaty hands and muscular forearms, but I feel safe in his company. Safer than I've felt for weeks.

I sigh. 'My life is a complete shitshow.'

'Shitshow?' Tomas repeats. 'I do not know this word.'

'It's on the skids. It's... it's a disaster.' I play with a tassel on the tartan blanket. 'I have two girls. Erin, who's four, and Megan, who is three months old.'

'Tiny baby,' Tomas exclaims. 'Hard work!'

'It is, but she's perfect, you know? So is her sister.' My voice thickens. 'But their mother, she doesn't want me any more. That's why I'm coming with you, to Ullapool. To give her some space.'

Tomas nods.

'What about your family?' I ask. 'You must miss them when you're away.'

'It is hard, but this job pays well so I can send money home. Sometimes, leaving is good, yes? We do it for our families. Our sacrifice. Like Jesus.' Tomas glances at the small crucifix hanging from a hook on the dashboard. He grins again. 'My wife always very happy to see me when I get back.'

I can't imagine a time when Alex will ever be pleased to see me, but I agree with Tomas and congratulate him again on his excellent English.

After a couple of hours, we pull into a service station so Tomas can take a break. We pass Birmingham and Manchester and stop to refuel. We chat. I doze. Tomas turns on the radio and hums along to Absolute 80s. When we see the first brown tourist sign for the Lakes the sun is peeping over the horizon.

Ullapool must be at the northernmost tip of Cumbria, I think, as we pass the signs for Kendal and Penrith. I turn to Tomas, confused, when we reach Carlisle.

'Have you missed the turning?'

Tomas guffaws. 'We have another three hundred miles to go.'

'Three hundred?' I cock my head at my new friend, wondering if he's winding me up.

'Five and a half hours,' Tomas confirms. 'We go almost to the top of Scotland.'

I've never been much good at geography and revise my mental picture of the Lake District, replacing it with rugged Scottish mountains and vast sea lochs, golden eagles and herds of red deer.

'It is pretty, Ullapool. Friendly. Nice place to live,' Tomas says, looking sidelong at me. 'From there you catch ferry to Lewis. Very remote. No one would find you there. If that's what you want,' he adds.

Is that what I want? I picture myself living in a tiny croft on the edge of a sweeping bay, the sand ground to fine grains by the waves rolling in from the Atlantic. I could get work as a labourer or on the local fishing boats. I wouldn't need much; just enough to buy food and pay rent. I wouldn't have to worry about inspections by the CQC or Alex's disdain. Fleetingly, I think of the children: Erin, even at four, a serious, thoughtful little girl. Megan, still so small, her personality yet to form. Alex may have struggled after Megan was born, but she's a good mother. They would thrive whether or not I was there. In fact, they would be better off without me.

'I think it is what I want,' I tell Tomas. 'For now, at least.'

Tomas drops me off outside Ullapool's small ferry port on his way to pick up a load of aggregate from a quarry just outside the town. We embrace like brothers, and I catch myself thinking how strange it is that the Lithuanian understands me better than Carter, who has been my best friend since I was eighteen.

'Thank you,' I say, my voice thick with emotion.

'I am glad to help.' Tomas fumbles in his back pocket, pulls out a shabby leather wallet and peels off a roll of notes. 'Take this, please.'

I shake my head. 'No, Tomas. It's so kind of you but I couldn't possibly. This is for Daina and Lukas.'

Tomas waves my protestations away. 'Is fine. I get more overtime, how you say it, easy-peasy. You need money more than me, I think.'

'I don't know how to—' I begin, as Tomas thrusts the notes into my hand.

'Is my pleasure. You are good man, Freddie. Kind man.' He holds my shoulders and looks me in the eye. 'I understand you want to give space to your wife. But not forever, OK? This would be big mistake. Trust Tomas. He is always right.'

I nod, suddenly unable to speak, and start walking towards the harbour, knowing it isn't the sea spray wetting my face, but tears for everything I've lost and everyone I'm leaving behind. Because despite what Tomas says, I know it's too late for me.

I can never go back.

35

ALEX

NOW

Carter arrives home from work just after six, grey with exhaustion. Megan looks up from my iPad and smiles.

'Hey, Carter,' she says.

'Hey, honey. How was your day?'

'I scored a goal in netball.'

'Atta girl.' He ruffles her hair then, with a frown, glances at Freddie, who is stirring a pan of bolognese sauce on the hob.

'Want a beer?' I ask Carter.

'I'll grab a shower first.' He checks Freddie's back is still turned, then bends towards me. I'm expecting a peck on the cheek, but instead he whispers, 'You and I need to talk about—' He points a thumb in Freddie's direction.

'I know,' I mouth.

He nods, his lips a thin line, and disappears upstairs.

Freddie tips a packet of spaghetti into a saucepan and I put bowls in the oven to warm and cut chunks from a sourdough loaf. The doorbell sounds as I'm laying the table. I startle, dropping the fork I'm holding, and it clatters onto the floor. Freddie looks round in concern.

'Everything all right? You seem a bit jumpy.'

'Just tired.' I go into the hallway and peer through the spyhole. Gemma is standing on the doorstep, her back to me. My shoulders sag with relief and I turn the catch and let her in.

'Mmm, something smells good,' she says, breezing past me into the kitchen. Her eyes widen. 'Look at you, looking like you never left,' she says to Freddie. I wince inwardly. Gemma doesn't mean to be rude, she just has no filter. Freddie doesn't turn round.

'Auntie Gemma!' Megan cries, jumping off her chair, my iPad in her hands. 'Taylor's uploaded a new video. Wanna watch it with me?'

Gemma and I share a smile.

'I'd love nothing more.'

'Freddie's catered for a small army,' I say. 'There's plenty if you want to stay and eat with us?'

She heels off her trainers and folds her coat over the back of the sofa. 'That would be great, thanks. It's been a complete bitch of a day, but I expect Carter's told you all about it.'

'He hasn't actually.' I lay another table setting. 'He went straight up to shower. What happened?'

Gemma glances at Megan, who's glued to the Taylor Swift video, then looks around. 'Where are Dylan and Erin?'

'Dylan's in bed and Erin's upstairs doing her homework.' My curiosity is piqued now. Over by the hob, Freddie still shows no sign that he's registered Gemma's arrival, let alone that he's listening to her.

'We had a boy in who'd...' Gemma motions tying a noose around her head and pulling.

My eyes widen. 'Oh my God, that's awful. Is he all right?'

'Luckily his mum found him in time and she was a trained first aider. She kept him alive until the paramedics arrived. He's having CT and MRI scans in the morning to see if he's suffered any brain damage. He was lucky he didn't break his neck.'

'Poor kid.' I shudder. 'How old is he?'

'Thirteen. He was being bullied at school.' Gemma's voice thickens and I reach across and squeeze her hand.

'Want a glass of wine?'

'Please.' She pulls a tissue out of her pocket and blows her nose. 'Sorry.'

'No need to apologise. I can't begin to imagine how awful it must be.'

'You don't have to, do you?' she says, her voice suddenly tight.

I bristle. I know Gemma thinks my life is one long party and that I spend my days meeting mummy friends for coffee and lounging around. She doesn't understand how exhausting it is, the relentless grind of looking after a young family. The endless shopping, cooking, washing and cleaning. Gemma sees what she wants to see: the Friday night takeaways and the Sunday roasts, the summer barbecues and winter walks. The edited highlights. She doesn't see the bits that end up on the cutting room floor: the tummy bugs and the tears, the mountains of laundry and the sleepless nights. She thinks I'm living the dream. She doesn't know, for instance, that sometimes I'd give anything to swap places with her. To step off the merry-go-round, just for a day. To go to a wine bar or a spin class. To lie in until eleven or eat cereal for tea. To remember who I am.

One day, I might tell her.

'You're right, I don't.' I pat her hand and go to the cupboard in search of wine glasses. It's clear we could all do with a drink tonight.

* * *

Anyone watching us through the window would see two couples and two kids enjoying a relaxed midweek dinner.

The atmosphere is anything but relaxed.

Carter is in a cranky mood, telling Erin off for resting her elbows on the table and nagging Megan for talking with her mouth full. I can tell he's miffed with me, too, because he's flirting outrageously with Gemma, which is something he always does when he wants to point-score. He knows nothing is guaranteed to wind me up more.

Gemma, of course, is lapping it up, her earlier moodiness forgotten as she basks in the warm glow of his attention.

Even though it's been years since he and Gemma were an item and their relationship was dead in the water long before Carter and I started dating, even though he's assured me count- less times he never loved her, it still needles.

And where's Gemma's loyalty? She was the one who talked me into going on that first date with Carter. She was adamant she'd moved on. So why do I sometimes get the feeling she'd give anything to have him back?

An image of them in bed together pushes its way into my mind; limbs writhing, eyes glazed with lust, slick skin glistening. I close it down with a snap. It's pointless torturing myself. Carter loves me now. He loves *me*.

At either end of the table, the girls shovel food into their mouths with grim determination, keen to escape this charade as soon as possible. Beside me, Freddie picks at his bowl of pasta. He hasn't said a word since we sat down to eat, though I can hear his foot tapping against the leg of his chair, something he always did when he was nervous.

Gemma listens avidly while Carter brags about a recent success on the squash court. She is playing with a strand of her hair, curling it round and round her index finger. Irritation builds like a stabbing headache behind my eyes. She's so transparent. Can't she see he's using her to get at me? Maybe she doesn't care.

I roll my eyes and turn to Freddie.

'Not hungry?'

He shakes his head.

'You should eat. You've got too thin.'

I haven't seen Freddie this skinny since his student days. He always used to joke that he was a distant cousin of the praying mantis, all arms and legs. When he hit his thirties he put a bit of weight on and it suited him. Now, his cheeks are like razor blades and I have the urge to feed him up, as if he were an abandoned puppy.

'I'm good,' he says, pushing the bowl away. He's barely touched his wine either. I, on the other hand, am halfway down my second glass, though any hopes I had of it helping me to relax were in vain. I can't shift the feeling that we're teetering on the brink of a catastrophe. Is this how people feel in the moments before a tsunami, or when they're trapped in the eye of a storm? Paralysed with dread, yet powerless to do anything about it?

I'm scrabbling about for something to say when Gemma jumps to the rescue.

'You guys haven't had any more journalists turning up asking awkward questions?' she asks.

I turn to her with relief. 'No, thank goodness.'

'Apart from that lady at school,' Megan says through a mouthful of spaghetti, blissfully unaware of the bombshell she's just dropped.

36

ALEX

TEN YEARS AGO

'Mrs Harris?' the older of the two police officers enquired. I nodded. He extended his hand. His handshake was firm and assured. 'PC Dev Desai, and my colleague PC Tom Evans. We understand you've reported your husband, Freddie Harris, missing?'

'That's right.' I swallowed. 'Have you found him?'

'Not yet,' he said. 'But you can rest assured we're working on it. That's why we're here. To get a few more details so we can try to establish where Freddie might have gone. Is it all right if we come in for a chat?'

'Oh God, of course,' I said, shaking my head. 'I'm so sorry. I'm not thinking straight.'

'That's totally understandable, Mrs Harris.'

'Please, call me Alex. This way.'

As I led them into the living room, Gemma touched my arm and murmured, 'I'll take Erin upstairs. Get out of your hair.'

'Thanks. There's a bottle made up in the fridge if Megan wakes up.'

Carter slammed his laptop closed and jumped to his feet as the two officers followed me into the room. 'Doctor Carter Petersen,' he said, pumping PC Desai's hand. 'Family friend.'

'Carter's been helping me phone round everyone we know in case Freddie's been in touch,' I explained, and PC Desai nodded. He was a trim man, with neat, coal-black hair and a cropped beard. In contrast, PC Evans's shirt strained across his stomach and his face bore the bulbous nose and veined skin of a heavy drinker. They sat either end of the sofa like mismatched bookends, one ramrod straight, the other slouched like a sack of potatoes.

PC Desai took a small black notebook from his pocket and flipped it open. 'I know you may have given some of these details to the call handler already, but it's important we don't miss anything.'

'Sure,' Carter said, leaning back in his armchair. 'Shoot.'

PC Desai ran through a series of questions: When did I last see Freddie? What was he wearing? Had he ever gone missing before? Finally, what frame of mind was he in?

It was the question I'd been dreading and I faltered, grateful when Carter interjected.

'I might be best placed to answer that.'

PC Desai's ears pricked.

'We've had a situation at work in which a six-year-old girl was misdiagnosed. Freddie was treating her for pneumonia, not realising she'd developed sepsis,' Carter explained. 'Her mother has been very vocal, threatening to go to the press and to report Freddie to the General Medical Council.'

I looked at him, shocked. He hadn't mentioned *that*.

PC Desai's pen hovered over his notebook. 'Do you have the child's name?'

Carter laced his hands together. 'I do, but I can't give it to you. Patient confidentiality.'

'I appreciate that in normal circumstances you would need

the patient's consent to share personal information, but this is a live police investigation, sir. I would say it's in the public interest to provide her name, wouldn't you? Especially if it might prevent a serious threat to Doctor Harris.'

My mouth fell open. 'You think this woman might have caused Freddie *harm*?'

'Let's not jump to conclusions,' PC Desai said smoothly. 'But it's certainly a line of enquiry.'

Carter exhaled slowly. 'As you wish. But I want it on record that you consider the information to be in the public interest.' He dipped his head towards PC Desai's notebook.

'Noted,' the PC said. 'And the name of the girl you're referring to...?'

'Sapphire Kelly. Her mother's name is Ingrid.'

PC Desai nodded at PC Evans, who eased his bulky frame off the sofa and started talking into his radio as he left the room. 'Control, this is PC Evans, requesting a PNC check on one Ingrid Kelly, over.'

'How is Sapphire doing?' PC Desai asked, once his colleague had closed the door behind him.

'I spoke to the paediatric intensive care unit about an hour ago,' Carter told him. 'Officially, she's in a critical but stable condition. Between you and me, she's gone into septic shock. Her body is shutting down.'

'She's not going to make it?' the officer asked.

Carter looked away, a muscle twitching in his jaw. When he finally spoke, his voice was grave. 'I'm sorry to say, I don't think she will.'

37

FREDDIE

TEN YEARS AGO

I step off the ferry at Stornoway into driving rain that soaks me in seconds. The sky is gunmetal grey, the clouds so low and oppressive that I find myself stooping as I walk through the tiny harbour. I would turn on my heels and catch the ferry straight back to the mainland if I didn't feel so bloody seasick from the choppy two-and-three-quarter-hour crossing here. Boats and I have never mixed well.

I pull my collar up and follow the smattering of people heading into town. The briny air reminds me of childhood holidays to Brixham and Looe, where Dad and I would spend hours perched on harbour arms crabbing while Mum sat in a deckchair and snoozed.

I wonder what my parents will make of my disappearance. Dad is a stolid, pragmatic man who, until he retired earlier this year, was the union rep at the engineering firm he'd worked at since he left school. I've never seen him ruffled; have never seen him show emotion at all, come to that. No, that's not true. He dotes on Erin, playing with her for hours when we go over for Sunday lunch, building complicated tracks with my old Brio trains that he's fetched from the loft specially. When Dad peered into Megan's cot in the hospital I thought I saw a tear in his eye, but it was so out of character I put it down to my own exhaustion after Alex's fourteen-hour labour.

With me it was different. Dad has never so much as clapped me on the back, let alone told me he loved me or was proud of me, even when I graduated from medical school.

Dad will be his circumspect self when he discovers I'm missing. He'll raise a bushy eyebrow, mutter something about flaky Gen X-ers and go back to his paper.

Mum, on the other hand, will wring her hands with worry as she imagines the worst. She'll cope, but I know I'll carry the weight of my guilt for leaving her for the rest of my life. She's the diametric opposite of my father. Emotional and impulsive, she has the tendency to engage mouth before brain, which sometimes leads to friction between her and Alex, especially where the girls are concerned.

'Your mother,' Alex would snipe – Mum was always 'your mother' when she'd pissed her off – 'Your mother says she doesn't know why I bother with real nappies when disposable ones are so much more convenient. Spoken like a true Baby Boomer. No wonder the planet's fucked.' Or, 'Your mother says she's surprised we haven't taken the stabilisers off Erin's bike yet because you could ride a bike when you were three. Well, bully for you, Freddie, and thanks for nothing.'

Mum phoned me at work a couple of weeks ago to ask if I thought Alex was coping, and although I wanted to admit that no, she wasn't, and everything was turning to shit, out of loyalty to my wife I assured her that everything was fine.

Fine. Such a small word that hides so much... so much *subtext*. Because nothing is fine. Nothing has been fine for a long time, if ever. It's as if the distance between us has given me the courage to admit that I have never truly believed Alex loved me as much as I loved her.

She was on the rebound when we met at that student party all those years ago. She'd found out, minutes before she kissed me, that her long-term boyfriend had been cheating on her. She was drunk and she was heartbroken, and I'd been there, willing and able to confirm that, yes, she was not only desirable, she was *hot*. I could have been anyone. Our geeky housemate, Rob. The earnest guy with the glasses who Rob knew through the uni's anime and manga society. The asshole rugger bugger who was hitting on anyone in a skirt. Even Carter. I give a bitter laugh. *Especially* Carter. I've seen the way her eyes follow him when she thinks I'm not looking. No one is immune to Carter, the charming bastard.

I have to face it. I've been nothing more than a Band-Aid for her broken heart.

And now I'm nothing at all.

I find myself re-examining our marriage as I troop past towering piles of lobster baskets and brightly painted houses. Although we are worlds apart in some respects, we are compatible in so many others. We both prefer an evening in with a takeaway and a bottle of wine to a night at the pub. We like the same films, share the same sense of humour. We were thrilled when we discovered our birthdays were two days apart, like it was a sign from the universe that we were meant to be together, when really it was a simple coincidence, because everyone was born sometime, right?

Carter joked that I was punching above my weight when I fell in love with Alex, and I knew deep down he was right. I'd been blindsided by the strength of my feelings for her. I worshipped her, and she'd basked in the warmth of my love. It had been enough to sustain us through university and when we moved into our first rented studio flat. It had kept us going through the early days of our marriage and as we'd forged our careers. Years passed. Our jobs became more stressful, our responsibilities mushroomed. We had the girls. Our family should have been complete, but somewhere along the line, the Band-Aid had come unstuck, exposing the raw wound underneath.

I shiver. The wind is biting, the rain dripping down the back of my neck and seeping into my socks. I reach the end of the harbour and, on impulse, turn right, past the imposing Martin's Memorial Church with its impressive spire, into a residential street that climbs steadily uphill.

Stornoway shares the same closed-off feel as every other out-of-season seaside town, but as I explore the quiet streets, I feel strangely at peace, as if I've come home.

I buy a toasted sandwich and a mug of tea in a café with steamed-up windows and a cheerful waitress who asks if I've come far.

'About six hundred miles,' I tell her, handing over a tenner from the roll of notes Tomas gave me. I'd counted the money in the gents on the ferry. It was just over four hundred pounds. I felt both profoundly grateful and humbled by the Lithuanian's generosity. It's enough for six, maybe seven nights in a cheap bed and breakfast while I figure out what I'm going to do.

'Where are you staying?' the waitress asks. She's called Aileen, according to her name badge, and is about my mother's age, with kind eyes and an easy smile.

'Nowhere at the moment,' I admit. 'I just arrived on the ferry this afternoon.'

'A blow-in, then!' Aileen smiles again. 'You'll be needing somewhere to rest your head. I might be able to help you there. My sister, Ruth, runs a B&B across the way. I'll see if she has any vacancies.' She bustles over to the counter and disappears into the kitchen, returning a few moments later, beaming.

'You're in luck. She has one single room, forty pounds a night, mate's rates. I've written down her phone number and address.' She tears a page from her order pad and hands it to me with my change.

'You're very kind.' Fortified by the tea and toastie, I stand and shrug on my sodden coat. Outside, the rain has finally stopped, and a watery sun peeks through the clouds. It's another sign, I think, as I wave goodbye to Aileen and set off with purpose towards her sister's bed and breakfast on the opposite side of the street.

I still feel crushed by the weight of all my mistakes, but I know I'm doing the right thing: by Alex, the girls, my patients. They will thrive without me, and maybe I can start again, here, on this remote, windswept island where no one knows my name.

38

ALEX

NOW

We stare at Megan, open-mouthed.

'What lady, Megs?' I say.

She twirls spaghetti on her fork. 'The one who asked about Freddie.' Her gaze slides to him and she flushes. 'I mean, Dad.'

'One of the teachers?' Carter asks. I know what he's thinking because I'm thinking the same. How dare a member of staff quiz a ten-year-old to satisfy their own morbid curiosity about our affairs?

'Not a teacher. A lady.'

We have all stopped eating, our attention fixed on Megan. She finishes chewing, takes a sip of water and says, 'She called me over to the fence by the footpath. Bella said I shouldn't talk to her because she was probably a weirdo, but she wasn't. She was just a lady.'

'What did she look like?'

'What did she ask you?'

Carter and I fire the questions in unison, and Megan's forehead crinkles. I'm quick to reassure her. 'It's all right, darling. You're not in any trouble. We just want to know what she said.'

'She asked if it was true my dad was back.'

'And what did you say?'

'I said it was.' Her eyes cloud with tears. 'I didn't want to lie.'

'Of course you didn't. When was this, sweetheart?' I ask.

'Lunchtime. Bella and I were playground buddies, which is why we were standing down by the fence.'

'Can you describe her?'

Megan scrunches her eyes shut. 'She didn't really look like anything. I mean, she was just ordinary.'

'Old? Young?' Gemma asks.

'Pretty old.'

As Megan considers anyone over the age of thirty – with the exception of Taylor Swift – as past it the woman could be anywhere from middle-aged to in her eighties.

'Did she say anything else?'

'Only that I must be glad to have my dad home. Then she said, "Take care because you never know what's round the corner." That's when Bella came over.'

'Bella spoke to her too?' I ask.

She shakes her head. 'She saw Bella coming and she went. Can I get down now?' Megan, clearly having had enough of the interrogation, is already sliding out of her seat with the air of a prisoner of war trying to escape his captors. At the other end of the table, Erin is also pushing her chair back.

'Go on then, but put your bowls in the dishwasher first, please, and don't wake your brother.'

'What d'you make of that?' Gemma says, once the girls are safely out of earshot.

Carter refills our glasses. 'It'll be some freelance reporter trying her luck.' He sees my doubtful expression and frowns. 'Who else is it going to be?'

'I'm sure you're right,' Gemma says, but that means nothing, because Carter could argue the earth was flat and Gemma would agree with him. Freddie, it appears, doesn't have an opinion. He has left the table and is stacking saucepans in the dishwasher.

'I'll pop into school in the morning to let them know in case she turns up again.' I drain the last of my wine. 'It's all right, Freddie. You cooked. I'll clear up.'

'In that case, we'll get out of your way.' Carter picks up his and Gemma's wine glasses and beckons her to follow him to the living room. 'Tell me what you think about the new staff rosters,' he asks her as they disappear into the hallway.

I carry my bowl over to the dishwasher. 'Honestly, Freddie, you really don't need to help. I've got this.'

'I want to.' He hands me a tea towel and smiles. 'I've got to earn my keep somehow.'

Now is probably the time to tell Freddie that he's going to have to start looking for somewhere else to stay because he can't sofa-surf at ours forever. I'm deciding how best to approach it when he asks, 'D'you still have kitchen discos?'

When Freddie and I first moved in together, kitchen discos were a weekly occurrence. We'd crank up the CD player and dance our hearts out to Blur and Pulp. When Erin was old enough, Freddie would sit her on his hip and spin her around the room until she was dizzy.

After Freddie left, I was too grief-stricken to feel like dancing, and Carter is way too cool to be seen goofing around. I shake my head, suddenly bereft, which is ridiculous, because even if Freddie had stayed, we wouldn't still be dancing round the kitchen. We're too old, too jaded, too knackered.

'Not any more.'

'I'm sorry.'

I sigh. 'Me too.'

* * *

At eight, I check on Dylan and say goodnight to the girls. I bend my head over Dylan's cot. His breathing is clear. He must have finally shaken his cold. With any luck he'll sleep through. I hope so. My bones droop with weariness.

'Night night, Dyls,' I whisper. I kiss his cheek and he lets out small sigh.

Erin is in bed, the latest copy of *BBC Wildlife* magazine propped against her knees. She has her heart set on studying wildlife conservation at university despite Carter's best efforts to convince her to go to med school.

'Humans are the reason the planet's on the brink of oblivion, Carter,' she points out whenever he attempts to change her mind. 'I need to save the animals we've failed, not the people who messed everything up.'

She has a point.

I cross the room and ruffle her hair. She ducks if I try to kiss her these days. She's growing up so fast.

'Not too late tonight,' I tell her.

'No, Mum,' she says, too engrossed in her magazine to even look up. I leave her to it and cross the landing to Megan's room. Her nose is buried in *The Lion, the Witch and the Wardrobe*, which is not a good sign. I sit on the end of her bed.

'You OK?'

She closes the book, clamps it to her chest and regards me with round eyes.

'You're not cross with me for talking to that lady, are you?'

'Of course not. But if you see her again you need to tell someone straight away, OK? Me or Carter, or one of your teachers.'

'Why?' Megan fidgets in her bed, her face knotted with worry. 'She's not going to hurt me, is she?'

I force a little tinkle of laughter. 'She is definitely not going to hurt you. I'm sure Carter's right and she was a reporter from another paper. Either that or she'd read the story about Dad coming home and was just being nosy. I don't want you to worry about her, all right?'

'All right.'

I drop a kiss onto her forehead. 'Night night, Megs.'

'Night, Mum.'

She grabs my wrist as I lean across to turn off her bedside light.

'Can you leave it on tonight?'

Anger that a stranger has the power to make Megan feel anxious in her own bedroom erupts inside me. I do my best to push it back down, and smile.

'Of course you can, sweetheart.'

I've reached the door when she calls me again. 'Mum? I've remembered something about the lady.'

'What's that, Megs?'

'She was tall. Like, *really* tall.'

'Tall?' A knot tightens in my chest and my mind races, trying to pin a memory down. But it lingers at the edge of my consciousness, stubbornly out of reach.

39

ALEX

TEN YEARS AGO

During those first few days after Freddie disappeared, I became obsessed with the statistics on the Missing People website. I took comfort from the fact that of the nearly 97,000 adults reported missing each year, 77% were found within twenty-four hours, and 87% within two days. Only 3% – just under three thousand people – remained missing for longer than a week, and fewer than a thousand for more than a month.

The odds seemed in our favour.

But with each day that passed with no news, the odds lengthened and my hopes of Freddie returning started to fade. Every time the police called, I held my breath, bracing for the news that a dog walker had found Freddie's lifeless body dangling from a tree, or bloodied and broken at the bottom of a cliff.

On the third day, PC Dev Desai called to ask if I would consent to a missing person appeal.

'What would it involve?'

'Our media team would release a recent photo of Doctor

Harris with a description and details of where and when he was last seen, asking anyone who has seen him to get in touch. Appeals can be powerful tools in a missing person enquiry.'

The thought of Freddie's face splashed across the newspapers filled me with dread. I could already picture the headlines: *Have you seen Dr Freddie?* Or worse, *Doctor at centre of hospital blunder goes missing.* Sapphire Kelly was still in intensive care, clinging onto life by the thinnest of threads, and Carter had warned me she was unlikely to pull through. People would assume Freddie had fled because he was to blame. Whether he was guilty or not was irrelevant: he would be made the scapegoat in his absence.

But if a media appeal helped bring him back to us, wasn't it worth the risk?

'Let me think about it,' I told PC Desai.

I shouldn't have been surprised when Carter and Gemma both declared it to be a terrible idea.

'You'd be opening Pandora's box,' Carter said, pacing the kitchen. 'Think of the damage it would do to his reputation. When he comes home – and he will, Alex, I know he will – it'll be out there. He'll be the doctor who ran away because he couldn't cope with the pressure. It'll follow him for the rest of his life.'

Gemma was even more emphatic. She gripped my hand. 'Sorry to be blunt, but it's not your call to make. The last thing Freddie would want is a media circus. Can you imagine how he'd feel if he saw his face plastered everywhere? Let the police do their job, and you concentrate on holding the fort till he comes home with his tail between his legs.'

It was an odd thing for her to say, but we were all a little crazy by then – the lack of sleep, the feelings of helplessness and frustration, were taking their toll.

I phoned PC Desai back. Even as I told him I wouldn't be

authorising a media appeal, I wondered if I was making a dreadful mistake.

On day seven, Desai phoned with an update.

'We've carried out financial enquiries with Doctor Harris's bank and his credit card company. The last transaction was at The Swan public house at eight thirty on the night he disappeared. It was for a pint of bitter. I've spoken to the landlord and he's checked the CCTV. Doctor Harris spent a couple of hours in there alone, leaving just before nine o'clock.'

'Which is when he came home,' I told him wearily. 'We know he texted his friend Carter from the pub. And, as you know, he left his wallet and phone here, which is why you won't find any more transactions after that. Wherever he is, he doesn't have any money.'

On day fifteen, PC Desai called round to the house to ask if Freddie owned an Omega watch.

The contents of my stomach plummeted. My worst nightmare had come true. They'd found Freddie's body and needed me to identify it.

Too late, Desai realised his mistake. 'It's all right, Mrs Harris. It's just his watch we think we've located, not Doctor Harris.'

'Right. You'd better come in.'

Desai pulled an evidence bag from his pocket and showed me the watch inside. 'Is this your husband's?'

I knew it was Freddie's the second I saw the gold and silver wristband and the black face, but I took the bag from Desai and turned it over, studying the letters engraved on the back. FJH. Frederick John Harris.

'It's his. Where did you find it?'

Desai ran a finger round his collar. 'One of our aspiring career criminals, a particularly odious seventeen-year-old called Kieran Doyle, tried to sell it at a pawnshop in town yesterday. Luckily, the owner did his due diligence and called us. We have

Doyle on the shop's CCTV.' He passed me a printout of a skinny boy in a grey tracksuit standing at a shop counter, his hands in his pockets. 'I take it you don't know him?'

I shook my head.

'His MO is to target men walking home from the pub. He asks them if he can use their phone. If they hand it over, he scarpers. If they refuse, he threatens them with a knife, which is usually enough to change their minds.'

'Jesus.' I looked up at Desai. 'But Freddie didn't have his phone with him.'

'Which is why we think Doyle stole his watch. There's a warrant out for his arrest but, unfortunately, he's also gone AWOL.'

Seeing my expression, he quickly added, 'I wouldn't read too much into it. Knowing Doyle, he's lying low. The last time he was in court the magistrate told him he was a whisker away from being sent to a Young Offender Institution. Don't worry, we'll find him.'

'What about my husband?' I was picturing Freddie curled on the ground with a knife protruding from his stomach, bleeding out in some dank alleyway. 'What if this Doyle character has hurt him?'

'Doyle's pond life, but he's all talk. He's never laid a finger on anyone in all the years he's been offending. Please try not to worry.'

After Desai left, I leaned against the door, my forehead pressed against the cool wood. I didn't know whether to feel relief that Freddie's watch had been located without his body attached to it, or despair that we were no closer to finding him.

It was all well and good PC Desai reassuring me that Kieran Doyle would never attack Freddie, but he didn't know this for sure. What if he'd flipped when he realised Freddie didn't have his phone? One plunge of the knife was all it would take.

A tear trickled down my cheek as I stumbled back into the kitchen, wondering if this nightmare would ever be over.

40

ALEX

TEN YEARS AGO

In the end, it was immaterial that I told the police I didn't want a media appeal, because the press found out Freddie had disappeared anyway.

Someone leaked the story to the local paper, and by the following day it had been picked up by the tabloids, who ran with it. Who could blame them? It made for juicy reading. A six-year-old girl was fighting for her life in hospital while her doctor – the man responsible for putting her there – couldn't answer the allegations brought against him because he'd vanished off the face of the earth.

I was hounded relentlessly, reporters camped outside the house, shoving microphones in my face and shouting questions every time I stepped out of the front door.

Carter blamed Ingrid Kelly for contacting the press, and it made sense. She was proving to be a thorn in the side of the hospital trust. She had already reported Freddie to the General Medical Council and the hospital to the Care Quality Commission.

'She's hired one of the top clinical negligence solicitors in the country,' Carter said. 'She means business.'

It was a month after Freddie had gone missing. Carter and Gemma had taken to coming round every Saturday evening with a couple of bottles of wine and a takeaway, ostensibly to talk about our efforts to find Freddie, but in reality I knew it was to keep me company. They were worried I wasn't coping.

I was, but only just. I managed to look after the girls and Fleming, but I didn't have the bandwidth to look after myself. I survived the days on autopilot, numb with grief. I couldn't eat. I couldn't sleep. The baby fat had fallen off me; my face was gaunt, my hair unwashed. I was a mess. In many respects I was lucky: Freddie's parents were a tower of strength. Alan provided practical help, like plastering the missing posters I'd had printed all over town, and arriving on the doorstep with his toolbox whenever anything needed fixing. Mary stepped in when I needed someone to pick Erin up from pre-school, or if I'd run out of groceries. She was as lost as I was without Freddie, but spending time with her granddaughters gave her a purpose, a positive way to channel her grief, and I was glad, for her sake.

We did what we could to find Freddie ourselves. Alan and Mary visited all Freddie's childhood haunts, showing his photo to everyone they met. I joined forums for the friends and families of missing people and, with Carter and Gemma's help, reached out to everyone who knew him, from kids at his primary school to every single person he'd worked with at Thornden Green.

'That Kelly woman's a money-grabbing cow,' Gemma said, with venom. 'She should be with her daughter, not getting lawyered up.'

Sapphire was still critically ill. Ingrid had released a photo of her wired up to a life support machine in the intensive care unit, her waxen face as blank as a mannequin's, which had whipped up a storm of hatred for Freddie, the negligent doctor who'd done a runner.

Although I would never have admitted it, privately I agreed with Gemma. Surely Ingrid's energies were better spent by her daughter's bedside than ruining the reputation of a good man who'd made one mistake because he was under too much pressure? Sapphire wasn't the victim of one doctor's incompetence, she was the casualty of a system in crisis after years of underfunding.

Carter set his plate on the coffee table and reached for his laptop. The strain was telling on him too. Deep grooves had appeared across his forehead and some of his natural optimism had worn off. Freddie had always joked about Carter being a control freak. His compulsive need to micromanage stemmed from his childhood when he was powerless to stop his brother dying. Freddie reckoned it explained why Carter's flat looked like a show home, why his car appeared as if it had just been driven out of the showroom and why he was always so immaculately dressed. It also explained the high standards he expected from everyone around him. By disappearing, Freddie had broken all the rules and Carter was struggling to deal with it.

'Did you get anywhere with PC Desai?' he asked me.

There had been a flurry of calls to the police after the story had broken. A guy working in a sports bar on the other side of town remembered serving Freddie the day after he left home. He'd arrived in the bar at around four in the afternoon, had drunk four pints of beer, paying in cash, and had left just after seven. He'd seemed upset, the guy said. But when he'd asked Freddie if he was all right, Freddie had brushed off his concern and disappeared into the night.

Another sighting came in a few days later. A man who'd been driving along the motorway later the same evening reported seeing a man matching Freddie's description standing on the London-bound carriageway. He'd sounded his horn as a warning, and Freddie had stepped back onto the hard shoulder.

When a search of the area yielded nothing, the police concluded Freddie must have hitchhiked out of town.

'They've downgraded Freddie to low-risk,' I said, and held my breath as I waited for Carter to explode. He found it hard to stomach the fact that the police were also out of his control.

I didn't have to wait long. His expression darkened. 'They've *what*?'

'PC Desai says an inspector's reviewed Freddie's case and feels he isn't in any immediate danger. There's no history of self-harm or mental health issues and no signs of foul play. Basically, they think he's left voluntarily and will come back when he's good and ready. It's not a crime to walk out on your life, apparently.'

'Well, it freaking well should be!' Carter cried, banging his fist on his knee.

'Even if they do find him, it's up to Freddie whether he comes home or not. The police won't force him to, nor would they tell me where he was if he asked them not to. It's his choice. His life.' My voice was flat.

'You sound like you've given up on him.'

'I haven't. It's just that...' The baby monitor emitted a wail and I jumped to my feet, glad to escape Carter's reproachful look. 'Time for Megan's bottle. Won't be long.'

I warmed the milk and headed upstairs to the nursery. Megan's arms and legs pumped with excitement when she saw me. She was four months old and her personality was beginning to form. Erin had been a placid baby, just like her father, but Megan's moods changed like the wind.

'She's her mother's daughter, all right.'

Freddie's voice was so clear, it was as if he was standing right next to me, but when I spun round there was no one there. It was just my mind playing tricks on me. Shaking my head, I bent down and stroked Megan's cheek before lifting her from her cot and settling her on my lap.

As she started to drink, her eyes locked onto mine. This time, instead of looking away, I held her gaze, studying her soot-black eyelashes, her peachy cheeks, the soft fuzz of hair and those dark-blue eyes that seemed to stare right into my soul.

And then, something inside me shifted. A warmth rushed through me, catching me unawares. It was the same whoosh of love I'd felt for Erin the day she was born, a rush I never thought I'd feel again.

A tear plopped onto Megan's cheek and her eyes widened in surprise. 'Sorry, sweetheart,' I whispered, thumbing it away. But more tears came; I couldn't stop them.

For four long months, I had lived a lie. Only Megan and I knew the shameful truth. Finally, I could stop the pretence.

But as I cradled Megan in my arms, my relief was tinged with sadness. How could I truly be happy when Freddie was gone?

41

ALEX

NOW

Dylan doesn't get up in the night, but I still sleep badly, dipping in and out of dreams about faceless women trying to steal my children. I wake at five, my hair damp with sweat and my legs tangled in the duvet. Beside me, Carter snores softly, the frown lines on his forehead ironed out by sleep and the hint of a smile on his face.

I stare at the ceiling, thinking about the woman who quizzed Megan yesterday and wondering how she knew where Megan went to school. Not just that. How she picked her out from almost four hundred other kids in the playground.

I roll onto my side, squeeze my eyes shut and try to drift back off, but it's no good. My thoughts are racing. Who is this woman? Who *is* she?

Giving up on all hope of sleep, I snatch up my phone and find Tess Brown's article in the *Daily Post*. It mentions we have kids but doesn't name them. So how the hell did she know who Megan was?

Maybe Carter is right and this woman is another journalist

who's done some digging and is looking for a new angle. But surely any self-respecting reporter would come to me for a comment before they approached my ten-year-old daughter? I tap away at my phone some more, frowning when I see the answer Google throws up.

In the UK journalists aren't allowed to interview children under the age of sixteen without the consent of a parent or guardian.

So she's either morally bankrupt or she isn't a journalist at all. And if she isn't, who the hell is she?

There is someone she could be, of course. Someone who would know where Megan's school is because she only lives a few streets away. Someone who has a vested interest in Freddie's return because she holds him responsible for misdiagnosing her daughter's sepsis. Someone who holds a grudge against our family because we ruined hers.

Ingrid Kelly.

I'm certain she's the one who's been sending the notes. Perhaps she felt they weren't having the impact she intended so she thought she'd threaten a ten-year-old instead. What exactly did Megan say this woman told her? *Take care because you never know what's round the corner.*

It sounds uncannily like a threat.

The memory that was hovering at the edge of my mind last night suddenly takes shape. Ingrid is tall. I remember noticing it when I saw her outside her house all those years ago. At least five ten, maybe even taller. It must be her.

Another thought hits me. What if Gemma's right and it was Ingrid who tipped off the *Daily Post*? Ingrid would love seeing our secrets splashed across a tabloid newspaper. It would have been so easy for her to orchestrate. Just one anonymous phone call to the news desk and let the paper do its job. A spiteful act of revenge.

The question is, what's her next move? And how far is she willing to go to make Freddie pay for his terrible mistake?

* * *

I don't have time to brood for long because at ten to six Carter's alarm goes off, heralding the start of the morning merry-go-round. He pulls on his running gear, pecks me on the cheek and disappears. I shower, dress and head downstairs to make a coffee, which I sip while I put a wash on and make Erin and Megan's packed lunches.

At seven, I give the girls their first wake-up call. I am their human snooze button. Megan usually appears, her hair mussed and her face creased with sleep, after the second call. Erin, who will be fifteen in July, takes three, sometimes four increasingly irritable reminders before she drags herself out of bed.

Dylan babbles away as I change his nappy and coax him into some clothes. Downstairs, I make three breakfasts: porridge for Dylan, granola for Erin and toast and jam for Megan. I find Megan's plimsolls and Erin's history textbook. I chop up a banana for Dylan. Carter arrives back from his run and I pour him a black coffee – he recently started intermittent fasting and won't eat a thing until noon – and iron him a shirt. Megan has a meltdown when she remembers she has a spelling test after lunch, so I test her while plaiting Erin's hair into a French braid. I take some chicken out of the freezer for our dinner, and feed Fleming. Carter, showered and shaved, reminds me I need to book my car in for its MOT, then, in a low voice, asks me to make sure I speak to Freddie about finding somewhere else to stay. He shrugs on his jacket, pecks me on the cheek and heads to work. Erin reminds me I promised to make flapjacks for her form's cake sale tomorrow. Megan reminds me it's book week and she needs a Hermione Granger fancy dress outfit for Friday. I make sure all three kids have cleaned their teeth, then kiss Erin goodbye before she leaves for her bus. I clean my own teeth and yank a brush through my hair, strap Dylan into his pushchair, clip Fleming's lead on and check Megan has picked up her rucksack.

'Why are we going the long way round?' Megan moans when I march past the top of Church Lane. 'I'm going to be late *again*.'

I can't tell her that there's no way I'm risking bumping into Ingrid Kelly, so I lie.

'I need to get my steps in. And we won't be late, not if you get a wiggle on.'

She huffs loudly but lengthens her stride, and we reach the playground moments before the bell. She gives Fleming a hug and the old dog wags his tail. Dylan makes star shapes with his hands.

'Bye-bye, Meg-Meg,' he says.

I unhook her packed lunch bag from the handle of the buggy. 'Remember, if anyone tries to talk to you again today you must tell a teacher, OK?'

She looks up from Fleming, the worried expression back. 'OK.'

'I'm sure they won't,' I reassure her. She nods, though I'm not sure she believes me. 'And good luck with the spellings!'

She trails into school, her slight shoulders drooping, and I make my way to the office. The school secretary, a thin, po-faced woman called Mrs Smedley, is on the phone but motions that she won't be long and I'm to wait. Snippets of a conversation about the poster for the summer fair filter through the hatch. Five minutes later, she finally puts down the phone and meanders over.

'I want to report an incident at school yesterday involving my daughter, Megan Harris,' I begin.

Behind her, the phone rings again. She holds up a hand, her palm facing me, and bustles off to answer it. I tap the counter impatiently. Dylan, growing bored in his buggy, kicks his legs against the footrest and arches his back in an attempt to slide out of the straps. My patience snaps.

'Tell you what,' I say to Mrs Smedley's scrawny back. 'I'll phone, shall I?' It's obviously the only way I'll get the damn woman's attention.

She either doesn't hear or chooses to ignore me. Huffing, I haul open the door and head back into the playground.

* * *

'Ducks?' Dylan asks hopefully as we set off for home.

'Not this morning, sweetheart. Maybe this afternoon?' I feel bad for fobbing him off but the house is a tip and I have flap-jacks to bake and a flipping Hermione Granger costume to source. 'Tell you what, you can watch some cartoons as a treat, OK?'

''Toons!' Dylan says, instantly mollified.

I don't feel even a flicker of guilt. To Carter, using the TV as childcare is even worse on the Petersen scale of bad parenting than relying on a pacifier, but Carter is at work. What he doesn't know won't hurt him.

We reach the house and I unclip Fleming's lead and let Dylan out of his buggy. I shoulder open the door while collapsing the buggy with the other hand, and Dylan runs into the kitchen chanting, ''Toons, 'toons, 'toons.'

I'm surprised to see the door to the living room still closed. Freddie must be sleeping in. Out of nowhere, a familiar feeling of resentment blooms in my chest and I think, *all right for some*. It's as automatic as muscle memory, this grievance that Freddie's life is a breeze compared to mine. The perpetual 'my life is worse than yours' thought loop that used to play constantly when the girls were babies, when in fact there was no competition: we were both as knackered as each other. The difference was, Freddie had to function in a job where a wrong decision was the difference between life and death, while I just had to make sure the girls and Fleming were fed and watered. It's something I lost sight of in those blurry days after Megan was born, when I was an angry, anxious, vicious mess.

It was only after Freddie disappeared and I learnt what had happened to Sapphire Kelly that I understood how wrapped up in myself and my own misery I'd become. I had no idea Freddie wasn't coping. I'd been too self-absorbed to spare him a thought. He was a brilliant doctor with an impeccable record who, through sheer exhaustion, had missed something he shouldn't have missed. If I'd cut him some slack it might never have happened. What Sapphire endured was as much my fault as it was Freddie's.

I've wondered more than once over the years if Ingrid knew we had a young family at the time. Surely she remembered the debilitating tiredness that came with the territory? Did it never occur to her that, while it wasn't an excuse, it might have been a reason for what happened?

I settle Dylan in front of the TV in the kitchen with a beaker of water and some strawberries, then put the kettle on. On impulse, I pull two mugs from the cupboard and stick a couple of slices of bread in the toaster for Freddie. Tea and toast. It was what I had in hospital after all three kids were born. Nothing has ever tasted as good before or since.

Humming to myself, I pop the tea and toast on a tray with butter and a knife. I open the cupboard and reach for the Marmite, which is what Freddie always used to slather on his toast. I have no idea if his tastes have changed in the last ten years, so I grab a jar of raspberry jam and the honey too, just in case.

I tap gently on the living room door. 'Room service,' I call, pushing the door open.

The curtains are closed and the air is stuffy. The sleeping bag is rolled and neatly stacked on the pillows. Freddie is sitting in the armchair by the window, his elbows on his knees and his head bowed.

'Freddie?'

He lifts his head but doesn't reply. A dart of fear pulses through me. I set the tray on the coffee table.

'Freddie,' I say again. 'Are you all right?'

Even though the room is dark, I am close enough to see his face. His eyes are puffy, his cheeks wet and blotchy. Scenarios race through my head. Erin has been hit by a car on her way to school. Megan's been snatched by Ingrid Kelly. Carter's had a heart attack.

My hand flies to my chest. 'Freddie, you're frightening me. What is it? What's wrong?'

42

ALEX

TEN YEARS AGO

The months turned into years with a crushing inevitability, each blurring into the next. Birthdays, Christmases, Easters, summer holidays all came and went without Freddie. He missed so many milestones it's hard to remember them all. Erin's first day at school, Megan's first tooth. The day Erin was voted head girl. Megan's Taylor Swift obsession. His mum Mary's cancer diagnosis and her all-clear five years later.

I stopped expecting him to walk through the door and found a certain contentment as a single mum. The girls and I were a tight-knit unit of three. Freddie leaving had made us stronger. I learnt how to change a plug and turn off the stopcock. I could hang a shelf and build flat-pack furniture. Money was tight but – with help from both sets of grandparents and some freelance book-keeping – we managed.

Some days stretched endlessly, every hour a lifetime, yet years slipped by in the blink of an eye.

Eighteen months after Freddie disappeared, Carter announced he was moving back to the States. My shock must have been visible, because he reached across the kitchen table to take my hand.

'I'm sorry, Al,' he said, his voice thickening. 'But I'm really struggling. I miss the old bastard so much.' He shook his head. 'I need a change.'

'I understand.' A lump formed at the back of my throat, because Carter had been my rock this past year and a half. How would I cope without him? 'Where will you go?'

'I've been offered a job at Boston Children's Hospital. It's one of the top paediatric hospitals in the country. I'd be a fool not to take it.'

'That's amazing.' I squeezed his hand. 'I'm so pleased for you.'

And I really was. Carter had seemed somehow diminished after Freddie left. Some of the swagger, the endless optimism, had worn off. He hadn't dated in months. Instead, his focus was on his career and doing what he could to help me and the girls.

When it was time for him to leave, we clung to each other like the survivors of a storm. It had been a tumultuous year and a half; a roller-coaster ride of dashed hopes and heartbreak. The hole Freddie had left in our lives gaped like an open wound, raw and bloody. I wasn't sure we'd ever get over it.

'I love you,' Carter whispered in my hair.

'I love you too.' I pulled away and forced myself to smile. 'Now, you go and show your fellow Yanks how it's done, OK?'

Six months after Carter moved back to the US, he called to tell me he'd met someone at a charity fundraiser. Elizabeth was a six-foot Amazonian beauty with a Harvard law degree and a summer home in Nantucket.

'I really think she could be the one,' he said, sounding self-conscious. 'You remember? For the kids and the dog and the picket fence I always wanted?'

'I'm glad,' I said and, again, I meant it. He'd been through the mill and I wanted him to be happy.

Carter and Elizabeth married in a lavish ceremony in the garden of her beautiful, white, weatherboarded Nantucket house. I didn't go; I didn't want to take Erin out of school. Gemma refused to attend on principle. 'If he thinks I'm flying across the Atlantic to watch him drool over some trust fund princess, he can think again,' she said, her mouth a thin line.

The marriage lasted four years. Elizabeth, it turned out, was too in love with her glittering career to give it all up to have babies. Carter was devastated and fled again, this time back to the UK and Freddie's old job in the paediatrics department at Thornden Green Hospital.

We slipped back into our easy friendship. The girls loved having him around, and he doted on them. Gemma wasn't on the scene much at the time. She'd fallen head over heels in love with a semi-professional footballer she'd met online. Privately, I thought Ryan Shaw was a jerk, but Gemma was smitten.

When, out of the blue, Carter asked me out on a date, I'd been so gobsmacked I'd phoned Gemma in a panic.

'What should I do, Gem? He's bought tickets to see *La Traviata* at the Royal Opera House!'

'Go, you twit. Anyone can see he has the hots for you,' she said, laughing.

'Seriously?'

'Seriously.'

'You don't mind?'

'Of course I don't mind. I'm so over Carter. Did I tell you Ryan's booked us on the Eurostar to Paris next weekend?'

With Gemma's blessing, I said yes to the date. Mary, who'd always had a soft spot for Carter, babysat.

'You two have fun. You deserve it,' my mother-in-law said with feeling as we left the house. Carter looked handsome as hell in his black dinner jacket. I wore a crushed velvet dress the colour of mulberries that brought out the green of my eyes.

If I'd had concerns that the date might feel weird, I needn't have worried. We'd always got on well; falling in love felt like the most natural thing in the world. I ignored the nagging voice in my head that said Carter was still on the rebound after his divorce. Mary was right: after everything we'd been through, we deserved to be happy. Six months later, when Carter proposed, I said yes again. How could I refuse? Carter was handsome, funny, charismatic.

I think I'd always been a little in love with him.

43

ALEX

NOW

Freddie looks at me with bloodshot eyes.

'It's Aileen.'

I swallow. Here it is, the betrayal I've subconsciously been waiting for from the moment Freddie turned up on the doorstep. The admission that the reason he stayed away for so long was because he'd fallen in love – maybe even started another family – with someone else. I lick my lips. Force the words out.

'Who is Aileen?'

He looks at me quizzically, then his face clears. 'You think she... you think I would have...? No, Alex, I would never...' He shakes his head.

'Then who is she?'

'She's a friend. *Was* a friend,' he corrects himself.

'You mean she's dead?'

He nods, his eyes filling with tears. I should pass on my condolences, I suppose, but how can I when I have no idea who the hell Aileen is, let alone the role she's had in Freddie's life for the last ten years? Instead, I give him a tissue and say, 'I think it's about time you told me where you went, don't you?'

Meekly, he nods, blows his nose and balls the tissue into his fist. He looks me in the eye. 'Lewis. It's an island off the west coast of Scotland.'

'I know where Lewis is,' I say, although I don't, not really. The only time I've been north of the border was to attend a friend's wedding in Edinburgh not long after I graduated. 'Why there?'

He shrugs. 'I hitched a lift and that's where my ride was heading.'

'There was no planning, no forethought? You just hitched a ride and saw where it took you?'

'Pretty much.' He glances at me. 'What did I have to lose? You'd said we were over.'

'What?'

'That night. You said, "I'm done." That's why I left. I thought you wanted me gone.'

I think back to the night Freddie walked out. I've replayed our final conversation so many times over the years that I can recite it word for word. 'I said you could sleep in the spare room because I was done *in*, not "done". I was shattered, and the last thing I needed was you snoring your head off next to me all night. You were drunk, if you remember.'

'Of course I remember.' He shakes his head. 'You meant you wanted me to sleep in the spare room? That was it?'

It hits me, then. All that pain, all that heartache, over one simple misunderstanding. The girls lost their dad – I lost my *husband* – because he hadn't heard me properly that awful night. I push my shock aside, because it's too late for us now. There's too much water under the bridge. Anyway, if he was prepared to throw our marriage away over one careless comment, he doesn't deserve me. I change the subject.

'Did you work there? On Lewis?'

Freddie's shoulders have sagged like a collapsed soufflé and his head is buried in his hands. 'What?' he mumbles through his fingers.

'Did you work on Lewis?' I repeat, louder this time.

'Work?' He looks up blearily, then runs a hand through his hair. 'Um, yes. Labouring, mainly, though I did a bit of beating for a couple of the local estates during the shooting season. Cash-in-hand jobs. It was all a bit hand-to-mouth, but I didn't need much.'

When we were married, Freddie's idea of getting close to nature was a visit to our local petting zoo. Walks in the country were reserved for dry, sunny summer days when there was no danger of Erin finding a puddle to stamp in. He didn't even own a pair of wellies, for God's sake. I find it hard to reconcile the Freddie I knew with a man of the land, someone who eked out a living as a gamekeeper and labourer.

'I love it up there, Al. The beaches, the moors, the wildness of it. It gets under your skin.'

'Scabies gets under your skin,' I say tartly. Freddie guffaws, and it's the infectious, easy laugh I remember from old and I can't stop a smile creeping across my face.

'God, I've missed you,' he blurts, then shakes his head. 'I shouldn't have said that. I'm sorry.'

I want to tell him it's fine, but the words catch in my throat, because it's not. He can't breeze back into my life after ten years and tell me how much he missed me.

He just can't.

Freddie gazes at his hands, perhaps regretting his outburst. I used to joke that he should have been a surgeon with hands like his. Now, they are calloused and rough and his long, elegant fingers are ingrained with dirt. With a jolt, I notice the tip of his right index finger is missing.

'What happened to your finger?'

'Caught it in a trap.'

'A trap? What kind of trap?'

'For stoats.'

'You killed stoats?'

'If we're being pedantic, I didn't kill them, the traps did. Their numbers have to be controlled because they're a bit too fond of grouse eggs and chicks for dinner.'

Again, it's impossible to equate the Freddie who talks so matter-of-factly about trapping small mammals with the man who would rescue spiders from the bath and carefully carry them downstairs to release them in the garden.

As if reading my thoughts, he says, 'I didn't enjoy it, but I could see it was necessary. Stoats might look harmless, but they're highly adaptable and efficient predators. If the stoat population was allowed to get out of control there would be no ground-nesting birds left in Scotland.'

'You're a consultant paediatrician, Freddie, not a game-keeper or an odd-job man.'

He shakes his head and burrows his hands deep into his pockets. 'I left all that behind. Up there, I was just a guy who was good with his hands.'

'No one knew you were a doctor?'

'Only Aileen.'

I raise an eyebrow but Freddie shakes his head.

'It wasn't like that. She helped me out when I first arrived on Lewis. She was the same age as Mum. Her son, Roddy, lives in London. She brought him up on her own after her husband died at sea. He was a fisherman. Aileen used her husband's life insurance to buy a café down by the harbour. It's the first place I went after I arrived on the ferry. She found me a room in her sister Ruth's B&B and got me work on one of the big estates that came with accommodation. Just a tiny croft with one bedroom and a peat fire, but it was all I needed.'

I think about our house, with its mod cons and gas-fired central heating. 'That must have been a shock to the system.'

'Aileen said that if I survived my first winter on the island I'd be fine, and she was right. The Lewis winters are brutal, but you get used to them. And the pay-off is the scenery. It's stunning, Al. The beaches on the west coast are as beautiful as any in the Caribbean.'

The longing in Freddie's voice irks me and I frown.

'If you love it so much, why bother coming home?'

Freddie's head jerks back like I've slapped him, but I'm unrepentant. 'It's a simple enough question, isn't it? Why come back now?'

He rubs a hand across his face. 'Aileen was diagnosed with pancreatic cancer just before Christmas. She was in the hospice in Stornoway when I left. She made me promise to come.'

'She knew about me and the girls?'

'She knew everything.' He hangs his head. 'She guessed I wasn't just running from my job.'

'Good for Aileen,' I mutter. I can't help it. Perhaps I should be grateful she was the reason Freddie came back, but all I feel is a childish resentment. It took a dying woman's wish to bring Freddie home. Erin, Megan and I didn't figure in his decision.

'Don't be like that,' he pleads.

'Like what?'

'Bitter. It doesn't suit you.'

I fix him with a look. 'Can you blame me?'

He sighs. 'Probably not.'

We are both quiet for a moment, each lost in our thoughts, then I ask, 'You just found out she died?'

He glances at his battered Nokia and nods. 'Her sister Ruth rang to say she passed away this morning.'

'I'm sorry.' I reach out to touch his hand.

'I thought she had at least a couple of weeks left. I never had the chance to thank her.' His voice is ragged.

'For finding you a job and somewhere to stay?'

He shakes his head. 'For convincing me to come home. If it wasn't for Aileen I'm not sure I would have.' He finally looks at me. 'It's easier to keep running.'

'Well, I'm glad you did. For the girls' sake. And your parents. Have you managed to speak to them yet?'

He nods. 'I talked to Mum this morning. They've just arrived in Barbados.'

'How was she?'

'She said she couldn't decide if she wanted to hug me or have my guts for garters.'

I smile. 'That sounds like Mary.'

'I've promised to meet them at Heathrow when they land.'

'Good.' My thoughts drift to Carter and my promise to him. 'How long are you planning on staying with us?'

He leans forward, his elbows on his knees and his chin in his hands. 'Why? Do you want me to go?'

I fidget in his gaze. 'I have no opinion either way.'

'But?' he prompts.

'But Carter would like to know. Three's company and all that. You've got to admit it's a bit weird, us all being under the same roof.'

'To be honest with you, Alex, I didn't come here with a plan. I just wanted to see you, Erin and Megan. I know you'll find it hard to believe, but there hasn't been a single day when I haven't missed you and the girls. I should never have walked out like I did. I kidded myself that you were better off without me, but I was a coward.' He glances at the ceiling, then lets out a long breath. 'I'll go, if that's what you want. You only have to say and I'll be out of your hair.'

Is it what I want? I picture Freddie saying goodbye to Erin and Megan, slinging that tatty rucksack over his shoulder and walking back out of their lives. Even though I promised Carter

I'd fix it, I can't throw Freddie out yet. The girls are just beginning to get to know their father. I can't do it to them. I massage my temples.

'No, stay. I'll talk to Carter. We'll work something out.'

44

ALEX

NOW

I push the tray towards Freddie. 'I brought you breakfast. I wasn't sure if you still liked Marmite.'

'I'll always like Marmite.' He cradles his mug of tea and gives me a watery smile. 'Aileen made the best breakfasts in the whole of Scotland. So she reckoned, anyway.'

'Tell me about her.'

Freddie sips his tea but leaves his toast untouched. 'She was larger than life, you know? The heart of the community. She used to open her café on Christmas Day for anyone who was on their own. She looked out for all the waifs and strays. Including me.' His voice breaks. 'She was so kind to me, Al. She never once judged me for what I did...' His shoulders shake as the tears take hold. The only other time I've ever seen him cry was when Erin was born, but those were tears of relief, of joy. My chest aches with compassion. The urge to comfort him is so ingrained it's instinctive, and I wrap my arms around him.

'It's all right,' I whisper. 'I'm here.'

I don't know how it happens. Perhaps it's muscle memory,

our bodies remembering how we used to slot together just so, but Freddie turns his head towards me and before I can stop to think, my lips are on his.

The kiss is tender, his hand gentle as it cups the back of my head. He groans, and I feel an answering tug of desire deep inside me.

'Alex,' he murmurs. 'I—'

The front door clicks open, followed by the tap of heels on the wooden hallway floor. We pull away like scalded cats.

'Hello!' Gemma calls. 'Anyone home?' She peers round the door jamb, her smile fading as her gaze slides from me to Freddie. Her eyes widen as she takes in my flushed face and Freddie's proximity. I cough and shuffle away, hoping I've imagined the fleeting look of triumph on her face.

'Don't you two look cosy,' she says, one eyebrow raised. 'Just like old times, eh?'

'Freddie's just heard that a friend of his has passed away.' My voice sounds strained, defensive. I push myself to my feet. 'The kettle's just boiled. Want a cuppa?'

She follows me into the kitchen, pulls a protesting Dylan into a bear hug and smothers him in kisses until he wriggles out of her arms. She watches as I spoon coffee into the cafetière.

'I feel like I've interrupted something.'

'Don't be silly. I told you, Freddie's just heard one of his friends has died. It's hit him hard. I was just... talking to him about it.'

'If you say so.' Her lips twitch.

'He finally told me where he's been. The Isle of Lewis. He's been working as a labourer.'

'A labourer? Freddie?' Her mouth falls open. 'Blimey.'

'I know.' I ram the plunger down, spraying coffee onto the worktop, hoping that Freddie's revelation is enough to distract Gemma from what she thinks she's seen. 'I thought you were working today?'

'I'm on lates. Oh, I nearly forgot.' She reaches into her bag. 'I found this sticking out of your letterbox.'

My heart sinks as she hands me the white envelope.

'Great. Another one.' My voice is flat.

'Another what?'

'Someone's been sending me anonymous letters. I think it's Ingrid Kelly.'

'Ingrid Kelly's been sending you letters?'

'Look.' I rip the envelope open, scan the message and hand it to Gemma.

'"Secrets never stay buried forever"?' she reads, then looks at me. 'What's that supposed to mean?'

'I wish I knew. I've had at least ten, all with variations on the same theme: you can't hide the truth. What "truth" she's referring to, I have literally no idea.'

Gemma studies the heavy black scrawl and frowns. 'Wait. How d'you know they're from Ingrid Kelly if they're anonymous?'

'Who else would they be from? Besides, I saw her skulking about outside the house yesterday.'

Her eyebrows shoot up. 'She was here?'

I nod. 'And I found another letter on the doormat when I got in.'

'Show me,' Gemma says suddenly. 'I want to see them all. I assume you've kept them?'

'They're upstairs. Won't be a sec.' I pass Freddie in the hallway. Without meeting my eye, he mumbles something about getting some fresh air and lets himself out of the front door. I'm glad I finally know where he's been for the last ten years, but I could kick myself for not asking him what he meant about not trusting Carter. I also know we should talk about what just happened, but even if we did, what would I say? That his return has thrown me off-kilter and I have no idea how I feel about anything any more? It's not a conversation I'm sure I want to have, least of all in Gemma's earshot.

I carry on up the stairs, returning with all of Ingrid's letters. Gemma opens them carefully, as if the envelopes have teeth and they'll nip her fingers, like the book of monsters in *Harry Potter*. This reminds me that I still need to find Megan a Hermione Granger outfit before Friday, which in turn reminds me I need to bake Erin's flapjacks. I wonder if Gemma is planning to stay for lunch. I'm about to ask her when I clock her expression. A deep frown scores her brow and she pushes the letters away.

'What's she trying to say?' she asks with bitterness.

'I don't know. She probably doesn't even know herself.' I pick up the nearest letter and scrutinise it. It's the one that was posted through the door the night Freddie came back. *The truth will out.* 'She's just trying to put the wind up me.'

'Who else has seen these? Have you shown them to Carter?'

'Of course. He says they'll be from some nutter and I should ignore them.'

'You haven't told him you know who they're from?'

'I haven't actually had a chance. It's been a bit full on round here recently, if you hadn't noticed.'

Our eyes meet and she nods. 'Of course. So you haven't reported them to the police, or the hospital?'

'No. Carter said there's no point. They're not exactly threatening, are they?' But I'm starting to doubt myself. What if Carter's wrong? I chew my bottom lip. 'I don't know, Gem. Perhaps I should go to the police.' I look at her worriedly. 'What do *you* think I should do?'

'For once, I agree with Carter.'

'So, what, I do nothing?'

She nods decisively. 'Absolutely. Ingrid Kelly's a headcase. If you react, it'll only encourage her, and who knows what she might try next.' Her gaze flickers to Dylan, who is curled up on the sofa, sucking his thumb and gawking at an ancient episode of *Tom and Jerry*.

My stomach turns liquid with fear. What is she trying to say? That Ingrid would harm Dylan to avenge Sapphire? Gemma must sense my worry, because she flashes me a quick smile.

'Don't worry. I'm sure she wouldn't actually do anything.' She draws in a long breath and releases it slowly. 'Though it's probably best to stay on your guard.'

45

ALEX

I'm relieved when Gemma says she can't stay for lunch. She left an hour ago, and I've spent the time since baking Erin's flap-jacks and sourcing a fancy dress costume for Megan. Luckily, the big out-of-town supermarket has one in stock, so I reserve it online.

'We'll pick it up after lunch,' I tell Dylan. He's in his high-chair, ramming pieces of fishfinger in his mouth. The kitchen smells of sweet, buttery flapjacks but my appetite has deserted me, the only silver lining in this whole messy business.

Freddie's still not back when we leave for the supermarket and my relief is replaced by a low-level anxiety. Every time he leaves the house, I can't shake the fear that we'll never see him again. It's the legacy of the night he walked out. At least his absence spares us an awkward conversation about the kiss. I've got too much on my mind to deal with that right now.

I prop a note next to the kettle telling Freddie where we've gone, grab a couple of shopping bags and find Dylan's shoes and coat. As I'm strapping him into his car seat, I remember I haven't booked the car in for its MOT. I decide to call into the garage on the way home from the supermarket.

I slide into the driver's seat and take a deep breath. I'm not a confident driver. In fact, I only learnt to drive when I was thirty. Mum and Dad offered to pay for driving lessons for my seventeenth birthday. Gemma had already passed her test by then – her dad's a mechanic and taught her to drive himself – and if we went out, she drove. I told my parents I wanted to wait until after I'd finished university. When I graduated, I was living and working in the same town and there didn't seem any need to start. I only learnt to drive out of necessity after Freddie left. It took thirty lessons, three attempts and a gallon of Rescue Remedy to pass my driving test. Nine years later, I would still rather catch the bus or walk. I tell Carter it's because I'm worried about climate change and I am, but we both know it's not the real reason.

I still have Freddie's old Volvo. Carter has offered to replace it on numerous occasions, but I use it so infrequently there's no point. I'm only taking it today because we'd have to catch two different buses to reach the supermarket and we don't have the time.

I fix my seat belt and catch Dylan's eye in the rear-view mirror.

'We'll pick Megan up from school on the way home, shall we?'

He nods, his big blue eyes so like his dad's that my heart quickens. If Carter knew I had kissed Freddie...

No, I can't think about that now. I need to concentrate. I turn on the ignition, check the mirrors and ease the car into the street. The narrow residential roads near our house are lined with parked cars and navigating them requires all my focus. I am hyperaware, watching out for pedestrians and giving cyclists a wide berth. Carter hates the town's new 20 mph speed limit but I was glad when it was introduced; it gives me an excuse to drive slowly.

I pull onto the main road out of town. It's a quarter past two and traffic is light. There are roadworks ahead, and the brake lights of the car in front flash on. The Volvo's brakes feel strange, much softer than normal, though it might be my imagination. I haven't driven for well over a fortnight. Still, it won't do any harm to ask the garage to check them when we pop in on our way home. Once through the lights, I accelerate, and before long I'm pulling onto the bypass. Carter is always telling me that driving too slowly on a dual carriageway is just as dangerous as driving too fast because it disrupts the flow of traffic and causes drivers to swerve to overtake, so I grip the steering wheel tightly and put my foot down.

I glance at Dylan in the rear-view mirror again. He's sucking his thumb, looking adorable.

'Nearly there,' I tell him.

A black BMW in the outside lane cuts in front of me so sharply I have to stamp on the brakes to avoid hitting him. The Volvo slows, but the brake pedal still feels spongy. The BMW screeches up the slip road, missing us by inches.

By the time we reach the supermarket, my nerves are shot to pieces and it takes three attempts to park. I rest my head on the steering wheel until my breathing is back under control before gathering the shopping bags, lifting Dylan out of his car seat and heading to the customer service desk to collect Megan's costume. My legs are weak, and my heart is racing. How people drive for pleasure is beyond me. Don't they realise that cars are potential killing machines? All it takes is one wrong decision, one lapse in concentration, and it's someone's funeral.

I pay for Megan's costume and pick up a few bits of shopping before we head back to the Volvo. The three o'clock news is just beginning on the radio as I drive out of the car park. Megan's school finishes in fifteen minutes. It's going to be tight.

Back on the bypass, I change up through the gears until the speedometer reads sixty miles an hour. In the back of the car, Dylan munches on the soft white roll I bought him from the in-store bakery.

I see the line of brake lights snaking in front of me in plenty of time. The stopping distance at 60 mph is eighteen car lengths – the thing about nervous drivers is that they know the *Highway Code* off by heart – and I've left plenty of space between me and the driver in front. But when I step on the brakes nothing happens. Nothing. I press my foot down again, but the pedal sinks straight to the floor and the car shows no signs of slowing.

I have a split second to make a decision. Swerve left onto the hard shoulder, or plough into the line of cars in front of me. I yank the steering wheel to the left and the Volvo hits the hard shoulder, but before I can correct the steering it lurches onto the verge, slamming into a fence with a sickening crunch and pitching down a small embankment where it finally comes to a stop. With a whoosh, the airbags inflate and I am enveloped in a white, pillow-like sack. For a moment, I drift in and out of consciousness, the impact of the crash rippling through my body, but Dylan's screams pull me back. Wildly, I look around. His face is scrunched up, tears spilling onto his cheeks, but he seems OK. *Thank God he's OK.* I unclip my seat belt and swivel in my seat, reaching out to him. As I do, pain radiates through my chest and I almost pass out.

'Mummy,' Dylan sobs, and I steel myself to ignore the pain.

'It's all right, baby. It's all right.' I turn off the ignition and stumble out of the car, scooting round to Dylan's door and pulling him into my arms. He clings to me like a monkey, burying his head in my neck as I cradle him.

'You're all right,' I soothe. 'We're safe now.'

But, as a siren wails in the distance, I think about those spongy brakes and wonder if we are...

46

ALEX

NOW

The paramedics are efficient and kind. They check Dylan over first and although they are pretty sure he's fine they tell me they're going to take him to hospital as a precaution.

They're turning their attention to me when a solitary police patrol car arrives.

Two officers, a man and a woman, step out, exchanging words with one of the paramedics before they approach me.

'Mrs Harris?' the female officer asks.

Confusion clouds my already foggy brain, then I realise I must have given the paramedics the wrong name.

'It's Mrs Petersen, actually. Alex Petersen. Sorry, I think I bumped my head when we crashed.' I touch my forehead and wince. The skin feels tight and tender.

'That's all right, Mrs Petersen. Can you tell me what happened?'

'We were on our way back from the supermarket when I saw a line of traffic. I braked but nothing happened.'

The male officer joins us. 'Are you sure you didn't press the accelerator instead? The right pedal instead of the left?' he adds helpfully.

'I... no... I—' Suddenly I'm not sure. Driving has never felt instinctive to me. I have to think about every manoeuvre. I could have easily panicked and hit the wrong pedal. But no, the brakes had felt spongy before we crashed and I tell the two police officers this.

They share a sceptical look, and the male officer turns and walks back to the patrol car, returning a few moments later with something in his hands. My stomach lurches when I realise it's a breathalyser.

'Are you going to breath-test me?'

'It's force procedure to breath-test all drivers involved in road traffic collisions.' He holds the machine to my lips. 'I want you to take a deep breath, seal your lips and blow nice and slowly till I tell you to stop.'

I do as he asks, feeling a sharp stab of pain in my ribs as I blow. He peers at the reading. 'That's fine. Thank you.' He turns to his colleague. 'If you finish taking Mrs Petersen's details, I'll arrange recovery.'

I glance at the Volvo. Apart from the two front airbags, which have deflated like a pair of limp party balloons, the car looks surprisingly unscathed.

'I can phone our garage and ask them to pick it up,' I offer. 'It's due to have an MOT next week anyway.'

He nods, clearly glad to have one less thing to do, and proceeds to wrap a length of police tape round the car. I find the garage's number on my phone and explain what's happened. The receptionist says they'll send someone to pick it up this afternoon.

Dylan toddles over, holding the hand of one of the paramedics.

'I've just been showing Dylan here the inside of our ambulance,' she says. She releases his hand and he throws his arms round me. I yelp, and the paramedic frowns.

'Everything all right?'

'It's just my ribs. They're a bit sore.'

'You may have fractured them. Let's get you both to hospital.'

The female officer turns to me. 'Can I get you anything from the car?'

'My bag, please. And there's a shopping bag in the passenger footwell. Oh, God.' The blood drains from my face.

'What is it?'

'What time is it?'

She consults her watch. 'Twenty to four.'

'My little girl, she finishes school at quarter past three. I was on my way to pick her up.'

'Which school?'

'Beechwood Primary.'

'I'll phone the school now and let them know what's happened. Please don't worry. I'll make sure they ask one of your emergency contacts to collect your daughter.'

Gemma and Freddie's mum, Mary, are Megan's emergency contacts. I didn't put Carter down as it's often impossible for him to get away from work, especially if there's a crisis. Mary and Alan are still on their cruise, but I know that Gemma will drop everything to pick Megan up, even if it means leaving work early. Everything is going to be fine.

* * *

When I tell the A&E doctor checking Dylan over that my husband is Doctor Carter Petersen, she promises to call Dolphin Ward to let him know we're here. He sweeps into the waiting area fifteen minutes later, his commanding presence turning heads. Dylan spots him first and scrambles out of his chair to meet him.

'Hey, little man.' Carter lifts him into his arms and kisses his cheek. 'Are you OK?'

Dylan nods solemnly. Carter looks at me, one eyebrow raised.

'They gave him the all-clear,' I confirm.

'Thank God.' Carter takes the seat next to mine and asks in a low voice. 'What happened, Alex?'

I've been thinking about nothing else since we've been here. Replaying every mile of the journey to and from the supermarket. Did the brakes really feel spongy or was it all in my head? When the Volvo's clutch was replaced last year the clutch pedal felt weird. I was so worried I made the garage recheck it, feeling a little silly when the mechanic said it was perfectly normal for the bite point to change when a new clutch was fitted.

Was it possible I stamped down on the accelerator, not the brake? I flex my feet surreptitiously and for a moment can't remember where any of the pedals are. I close my eyes and put myself in the driver's seat. Right foot on the middle pedal, left foot on the clutch. Turn on the ignition. Depress left foot and put the car into gear. Switch right foot to the accelerator on the right. Lift the clutch until the engine bites.

I can remember it now, but had I remembered when I saw the brake lights ahead, or had I been too busy recalling the stopping distances in the *Highway Code*?

I look up at Carter. 'It was my fault. I think I accelerated instead of braked.'

'Jesus, Alex.' Carter shakes his head. 'You could have both been killed.'

I shiver. 'Don't say that.'

Dylan takes a pen from Carter's shirt pocket and clicks the lid with his thumb. Delighted, he clicks it again, and again, and again. The sound pulls at my frayed nerves, but Carter is too focused on me to notice.

'I've spoken to the A&E consultant. She says the para- medics think you might have fractured some ribs. She's trying to get you in for a chest X-ray. There's not much she can do for you if you have, but at least we'll know you haven't damaged anything else. Does it hurt to breathe?'

'A bit,' I admit. I shift in my seat. 'How long will it take?'

Carter shrugs. 'Your guess is as good as mine. Why?'

'I need to get back for Gemma.'

'Gemma?'

'She's Megan's emergency contact. School would have asked her to collect Megan when I didn't show.'

Carter's brow furrows. 'You've spoken to the school?'

'No. One of the police officers promised to ring them for me. Why?'

'Gemma's on Dolphin Ward, Alex. She was taking some- one's bloods when I left.'

The ground shifts beneath my feet. If Gemma is still at work, who the hell picked Megan up from school?

47

ALEX

NOW

I stare at Carter, dread solidifying like ice in my stomach.

'We need to phone the school,' I cry, reaching for my bag.

'Use mine.' Carter pulls his iPhone from the back pocket of his trousers, unlocks it and asks for the number. I've phoned the school so many times over the years I know it off by heart and I rattle it off. He dials and presses the phone to his ear, then whispers out of the corner of his mouth, 'No one's picking up.'

Of course. They wouldn't. The school office closes at half four and it's now just gone five. Almost two hours since Megan would have trotted out of her classroom, unaware that I wasn't there to pick her up.

Dylan presses the top of Carter's pen again and again, chortling quietly to himself every time it clicks. My gaze darts to Carter who has started talking.

'Good afternoon, this is Doctor Carter Petersen, Megan Harris's stepfather. Please could you call me urgently regarding Megan's whereabouts.' He leaves his number and ends the call. 'Now what?'

I think hard. 'There's a mobile number for the caretaker on the school website. Give me your phone.' I tap quickly, calling up Beechwood's website and scrolling through to the contacts page. The caretaker's number is a link. *Please answer*, I think, as I press it.

The phone rings once, twice, three times, then there is a click.

'Jeff Townsend speaking,' a gruff voice says.

'Oh, hello, Jeff. It's Alex Petersen, Megan Harris's mum. I need to speak to Mrs Pendlebury. Could you please give me her number?'

'I'm afraid I can't—'

'I'm in hospital after a car crash, so I couldn't pick Megan up from school. We think she might have gone home with someone, but I need to know if she's still at school before I call the police.'

There is a pause and a long exhalation of breath. 'Mrs Pendlebury is in a governors' meeting. I'll ask her to call you as soon as it's convenient.'

I want to scream at him to walk straight into the governors' meeting and hand the head teacher his phone, but I don't, because we are already attracting curious glances from other people in the waiting room. 'I'll call the police if I haven't heard from Mrs Pendlebury by a quarter past five,' I say, hanging up.

'I need to go.' I reach for my bag and push myself to my feet.

'What about your X-ray?'

'Sod the bloody X-ray. I can't wait here for hours while Megan is God knows where. I need to see if she's home, and if she isn't, I need to phone the police.'

'How will you get home?'

'I'll call an Uber.'

Carter runs a hand down his stubble. 'No, I'll take you. Give me ten minutes.' He hands Dylan to me and is gone from the waiting room before I can argue.

The minutes crawl by. Dylan still has Carter's pen clasped in his chubby fist and I can tell the constant clicking is getting on the nerves of the elderly woman in a mobility scooter to my left. Five minutes pass. Ten. When my phone rings, I leap to my feet, instantly regretting it as I'm gripped by a wave of pain. I hobble over to the back of the waiting room, Dylan on my hip.

'Mrs Petersen? It's Sarah Pendlebury. I understand you have some concerns about Megan.'

I explain what's happened as quickly as I can. 'The police said they were going to contact you to let you know about the accident.'

'What time did it happen?'

'Just after twenty to four.'

'I'm afraid I wasn't made aware of a call. Perhaps it was an oversight on their part.'

I swallow my frustration. 'I'd assumed you must have contacted my friend Gemma Lawrence, one of Megan's emergency contacts, as Megan's grandmother is currently on holiday, but I've just found out Gemma is at work.'

'We didn't call either of your emergency contacts,' Mrs Pendlebury says.

My heart lifts. 'So Megan's still at school?'

'I'm afraid she's not.' The head teacher's voice is grave. 'Miss Abbott is off sick today and Willow Class had a supply teacher. I've checked with her, and she says Megan told her she had permission to walk home from school. I'm afraid the supply teacher took her at her word.'

Once again, the ground spins. 'Are you telling me Megan walked home on her own?'

'I'm afraid she did. Have you tried calling her?'

'She doesn't have a mobile.'

'Is there no one at home?'

I think. Erin has drama club after school today and won't be home until a quarter to six. I suppose Freddie might be there, but what if he isn't? Megan can't use the spare key because we've given it to Freddie. I spot Carter in the corridor heading our way. He raises his eyebrows but I shake my head.

'Mrs Petersen?' the head teacher says in my ear. 'Did you hear me?'

'What? No, sorry.'

'If Megan isn't at home you might want to try phoning round a few of her friends to see if she's gone home with them. If not, it's probably best to call the police. I'll be in school until at least six tonight. Please let me know when you find her.'

* * *

I hit the phone on the way home from the hospital. No one picks up the landline and Erin's mobile goes straight to voicemail. I leave a message asking her to call me back urgently, then try the mums of Megan's three closest friends. Sophie and Jess were both at after-school club and didn't see Megan leave. Bella heard Megan telling their supply teacher her mum let her walk home.

'Sorry,' Bella's mum says. 'She didn't think to question it.'

'It's fine. Plenty of Year Five kids do walk home. It's understandable.'

I thank her, end the call and glance at Carter. 'I'm going to call the police.'

'We'll be home in five minutes. Let's check she's not there first.'

'OK.' My voice is thick and Carter squeezes my knee.

'I'm sure she's OK.'

I turn away, scouring the streets for a glimpse of Megan's flyaway blonde hair. I wish I could believe him.

48

ALEX

NOW

Megan isn't at home.

Deep down, I think I already knew.

Freddie's out too. The note I left him is still propped against the kettle, untouched since breakfast. Erin isn't due home for another fifteen minutes. I leave her another message, then text her for good measure. She doesn't reply.

Once we've searched the house, Carter disappears through the back door to check the garden, Fleming trailing behind him. He's back before I've taken Dylan's shoes off, his expression grim.

'She isn't there.'

I nod numbly and walk into the living room to make the call. As the operator asks which emergency service I require I get a flashback so vivid it's like I've been transported back in time.

I was standing in this exact spot when I reported Freddie missing.

I was scared then, but this fear is like nothing I have ever experienced. It is brutal. Blood rushes in my ears, and my chest is tight with panic. I have to force myself to slow my breathing so I don't start hyperventilating.

'Police,' I manage.

The line clicks and in the silence I replay the call I made ten years ago. The call handler told me most missing people were either found or came home in a few days. She was wrong about that.

'What is your emergency?' a voice says in my ear and I startle. *Get a grip, Alex.*

'It's my daughter. She's missing.'

'How old is your daughter?'

'Ten.'

'And how long has she been missing?'

'She left school at three fifteen and hasn't come home.' I stifle a sob and force myself to concentrate as the call handler asks my name and address and whether we've checked the house.

'Twice.'

'What's your daughter's name, Mrs Petersen?'

'Megan. Megan Harris. I remarried.' I feel the inexplicable need to explain.

'I'm dispatching a crew to your house now. In the meantime, please can you give me a description of Megan and what she's wearing?'

'She's just under five foot with shoulder-length blonde hair and brown eyes. She's in her school uniform. Royal-blue sweatshirt, grey pleated skirt and socks. Black lace-up shoes.'

'Thank you. I'll get that description out to all patrols in the area. Just to confirm, you've searched your house and garden?'

'We have,' I say, my voice rising. 'She's not here.'

'Is there any reason why she might have decided not to come straight home? An argument, anything like that?'

'No.'

'And this is out of character for Megan?'

'Yes!'

'Please stay calm, Mrs Petersen. Eight in ten children are found within twenty-four—'

'I don't want you to give me bloody statistics. I just want you to find her.' I break off, tears spilling onto my cheeks.

'I understand. Please don't worry. We'll do everything we can.'

Erin arrives home, her heart-shaped face paling when she discovers her sister is missing.

'Didn't you see my text?'

'Sorry, Mum. My phone died.'

'D'you know where she might have gone? You won't be in any trouble. I just need to know.'

She shakes her head. 'I'd tell you if I did, I promise.'

The girls are close. I'm sure Erin would have known if Megan was planning to run away. It's a tiny crumb of comfort, but I hold onto it, trying not to think about the alternative – that Megan was taken against her will.

Every atom of my being wants to run out of the house and scour the streets for my little girl, but the call handler insisted I stay inside until the patrol arrives. I'm putting Dylan to bed when the front doorbell rings. I rush downstairs to find Carter leading two police officers into the kitchen. They decline his offer of tea and take seats at the kitchen table, pens poised over their black pocket notebooks.

The endless questions begin again. Where and when was Megan last seen? What was she wearing? Was she worried about anything? Is this out of character? Where might she have gone?

'If we knew where she'd gone she wouldn't be missing,' I snap, even though it's the same question I asked Erin earlier. Carter shoots me a warning look but I ignore him. Megan's been missing for over three hours, and every minute we waste talking is a minute we're not out there looking for her.

'What about family or friends?' the older officer asks. 'Is there anyone she might have gone home with? Anyone at all?'

My blood runs cold. Suddenly it's obvious. There is someone who has a reason for taking Megan. Perhaps I knew subconsciously all along. I drag my hands down my face.

'What is it, Alex?' Carter says.

'She's with Ingrid Kelly,' I mutter.

'Who's Ingrid Kelly?' the older officer asks at the same time Carter cries, '*What*?'

'Ingrid Kelly,' I repeat, my voice growing stronger, more certain. 'She lives a couple of streets away. She's been sending me threatening notes and—'

'You think those notes are from *Ingrid Kelly*?' Carter interjects.

'I saw her hanging around outside the house yesterday.' I turn back to the officers. 'And she tried to talk to Megan at school.'

The younger officer reaches for his radio. 'Do you have her address?'

'Thirty-two Church Lane.'

Carter is staring at me like I've lost my mind, but I know I'm right. Who knows how long Ingrid's been hanging about outside school waiting for a chance to approach Megan. Today, the one day Megan decides to walk home on her own, was the perfect opportunity.

'Why would Ingrid Kelly take Megan?' the officer asks.

I pick distractedly at a loose flap of skin on my thumb. 'Because we have something she doesn't.'

49

ALEX

NOW

Carter stands in the doorway watching as I follow the two officers down the street. He told me to leave it to them, but I can't. I have to be there when they find her.

'It's left at the top, then second left.' My voice is breathless, as if I've just walked up a dozen flights of stairs. We turn into Church Lane. I lick my lips. 'It's the one on the right with the holly bush in the front garden.'

'Stand back, please, Mrs Petersen,' the older officer says, as his colleague strides up to the front door and raps sharply.

It swings open, and Ingrid appears. She looks at the officer in confusion, her face jaundiced by the glow of a nearby street lamp.

'Ingrid Kelly?' the officer asks, showing her his warrant card. 'We're carrying out enquiries into the report of a missing ten-year-old. Can I come in?'

Ingrid's hand flies to her chest and she says something I can't catch, then steps aside to let the officer through the front door.

'Wait here,' the older officer instructs me. I nod and he follows his colleague into the house.

I edge closer to the front gate, every instinct screaming at me to tailgate him so I can find Megan myself. I have one hand on the wrought-iron gate when Ingrid sees me. She stiffens, her eyes narrowing.

'What are you doing here?'

I swallow. 'It's my daughter Megan who's missing.'

She frowns. 'What's that got to do with me?' The frown deepens. 'You think I have something to do with it?'

'You were at her school yesterday, Ingrid. Don't try to pretend you weren't.' She looks away and I know I was right.

Her gaze flits to the house at the sound of heavy boots stomping up the stairs. 'I heard Doctor Harris was back. I wanted to check it was true.'

'Why?'

'Because there's something he needs to know. Look, I might have spoken to your daughter yesterday, but I promise I haven't seen her since. So you can call your Rottweilers off. She isn't here.'

As if on cue, the older officer appears. He is talking into his radio. '…No sign of the misper.' He glances at me apologetically then turns away. 'Copy that. All units, misper Megan Harris is still unaccounted for. She is just under five feet tall with shoulder-length blonde hair, last seen at three fifteen this afternoon leaving Beechwood Primary School, wearing a royal-blue sweatshirt, grey pleated skirt and black shoes. Over.'

As we walk down the front path to the street, Ingrid calls out, 'I hope you find her.' I stop, turn. She is silhouetted against the light of the open front door, her face in darkness, so I can't read her expression. Her arms are wrapped around her thin body despite the warmth of the evening, her earlier defensiveness gone.

'Do you?' I call back. 'Really?'

'I do,' she says, rubbing the tops of her arms. 'No one deserves to lose a child.'

* * *

My tread is heavy as I follow the police officers back to the house. I'm trying not to think about the time we've wasted on my wild goose chase. I was convinced Megan was with Ingrid but I was wrong. She's now been missing for three and a half hours. She should be watching a bit of TV after her dinner. Taylor Swift on YouTube, probably. 'YouToob,' I whisper, tears pricking my eyes. But she isn't at home watching YouToob. She is out there somewhere, alone and afraid.

Unbidden, my thoughts stray to all the other girls snatched from the streets. Girls made infamous by their fate, their names imprinted on the human psyche like soldiers' names engraved on a war memorial. Girls whose faces are aged by AI on the fifth, tenth, twentieth anniversaries of their disappearance. Please don't let Megan be one of those girls.

The younger officer stops so suddenly I almost cannon into him.

'What is it, mate?' his colleague asks.

He is pointing down our street. 'Is that her?'

Hope surges through me and I push past him. That's when I see them: Freddie and Megan walking casually down the road. She is holding a box of popcorn and is laughing at something he's said. He sees me and waves, as if nothing is wrong.

'Megan!' I cry. My legs are weak with relief.

'Hey, Mum,' Megan says. She is glowing, her face smooth and untroubled until she notices the two police officers flanking me and worry lines fan out across her forehead. 'Is everything all right?'

'Where have you been?' I cry hoarsely. They are both looking at me strangely, as though I've lost my mind.

Freddie speaks first. 'I bumped into Megan walking home from school. I thought I'd treat her to pizza and a film. I left you a voicemail.'

Voicemail? I pull my phone from my back pocket. In all the panic I hadn't thought to check my voicemail. My cheeks are suffused with heat as I see the missed call.

The older of the two police officers steps forward. 'And you are...?'

'Freddie Harris,' Freddie says. 'Megan's dad.'

'Mrs Petersen?' the officer asks. 'I need to let control know Megan's been found.'

'OK.' I nod. 'I'm so sorry to have wasted your time.'

Freddie gapes. 'You reported Megan missing? Is that why they're here?' He shakes his head, horrified. 'But I left you a message.'

'I didn't see it. I thought Megan had... I thought—'

'I'm sorry, Al. I didn't mean to worry you.' He touches my arm and I give an involuntary shiver, remembering the feel of his lips on mine. Was that only this morning? I've aged a decade since then.

'It's not your fault. I should have checked my phone, but I crashed the car—'

'What?' Freddie's brown eyes search mine. 'Are you all right?'

As soon as he says it, the ache across my ribcage, dulled by adrenaline, is back with a vengeance.

'I'm fine.' I fumble with my phone. 'I should let Carter know Megan's safe.'

'Of course.' He slips his hands into his pockets and hangs back.

Carter picks up before I've caught a breath.

'Any news?'

'We've found her.'

'Thank God. Where was she?'

'With Freddie.'

'*Freddie*?'

'He took her to the cinema.'

'He *what*? Who said he could—?'

'He found her walking home from school on her own,' I interject. 'He left a voicemail. I didn't see it.'

'You hadn't checked your voicemails?' Carter says with disbelief. 'Jesus, Alex.'

'I know. I'm sorry. But the main thing is she's OK, right? Look, I've got to go. The police are just leaving. We'll be home in a minute.'

I apologise to the officers again and they troop back to the patrol car and their next job. They were pretty understanding, all things considered. Ingrid, not so much. I should never have accused her of taking Megan. She already hated me. She must really loathe me now.

'We saw the Minecraft movie,' Megan says, offering me the box of popcorn. I shake my head. 'It was so terrible it was genius.' She grins at Freddie. 'Dad hadn't a clue what was going on.'

'It's true,' Freddie says, grinning back at her. 'It was a surreal experience.'

'And I had a Sloppy Giuseppe and a Coke at Pizza Express.'

'That's nice,' I say automatically. I walk beside them as Megan chatters about the film, nodding and answering in the right places, while feeling as though I'm standing on shifting sand with nothing to anchor me to stable ground. I tell myself it's the shock, that anyone would feel bewildered after the day I've had, but it's more than that.

I can't shake the feeling that my life is unravelling and there's nothing I can do to save it.

50

ALEX

NOW

As we troop into the house, I force myself to push my misgivings to one side for tonight. Megan is safe and that's all that matters. If anyone's at fault it's me. I should have checked my voicemail before launching into full-on panic mode. But I wasn't thinking straight after the accident.

Carter makes a beeline for his study and Freddie offers to give Dylan his tea. My ribs are aching and I swallow a couple of painkillers, then peer into the fridge, looking for something I can knock up for Carter, Erin and me. But it's dismally empty.

'Why don't I phone for a takeaway?' I say.

'Can we have Thai?' Erin asks.

'Sure.'

'Can Auntie Gemma come?' Megan says.

'I don't think—'

'But it's her favourite!'

'She's at work today. I doubt she'll be finished in time.'

'*Please*, Mum,' Megan wheedles.

Two hours ago, I was prepared to sell my kidney for my

youngest daughter's safe return. It seems churlish to refuse her this small wish, even though I'd been looking forward to a Gemma-free night tonight. I sigh. 'All right.' I hand her my phone. 'You text her while I fetch the menu.'

Megan announces that Gemma knocks off at seven and would love to join us for a takeaway. I pretend to be pleased and phone the restaurant with our order, then stick plates in the oven and pour myself a large glass of wine.

Gemma arrives at the same time as the delivery guy. I try to hide my wince of pain as she draws me into a hug.

'Carter told me about the accident. You poor thing. It must have been terrifying.'

I pull away. 'Not as terrifying as thinking Megan was missing.'

'What?'

Her jaw drops as I relay what happened.

'It was my fault. I should have checked my phone.' I take the plates from the oven and set them on the table. I can't keep still; a nervous energy is ripping through me like an electrical current. 'I just wish I hadn't accused Ingrid of snatching her.' I grimace. 'You should have seen her face when the police knocked on her door. As if she didn't hate me enough already.'

'It must have been awful for her.' Gemma peels open the takeaway cartons. 'I wouldn't wish what happened to Sapphire on anyone. But...' She trails off.

'But what?'

'She's a bit... intense, isn't she? And not in a good way.'

'What do you mean?'

'Look at the way she gunned for Freddie after what happened. She wouldn't let it go. It makes you wonder what else she's capable of, doesn't it? Do you have a bowl for the prawn crackers?'

I find her one and call everyone to the table. The food looks delicious but once again my appetite has deserted me. All I can think about is Ingrid, and what she might do now she knows Freddie's home. I can't get Gemma's words out of my head. *She's intense, but not in a good way. It makes you wonder what else she's capable of.* Is Gemma blowing things out of proportion, or is she right?

'Alex,' Gemma says sharply. 'Did you hear what I said?'

'Sorry. Miles away.'

'My mate Estelle and her new man have a table booked at The Oak and Ivy tomorrow night, only she's got a tummy bug and they can't make it.' She points her knife at me. 'I've told her you and Carter will take it.'

'Oh, I don't think—'

'Nonsense,' Carter interjects. He turns to Gemma. 'We'd love to. Thanks for thinking of us.'

'I know how much you were looking forward to going on Saturday.' Gemma spears a prawn with her fork. 'I'm working, otherwise I'd offer to look after the kids.'

Freddie clears his throat. 'I'll babysit. Least I can do.'

'Good,' Gemma says with a satisfied smile. 'The table's booked for eight.'

* * *

The following night, I slip on the clingy red dress again, pin my hair up and step in front of the mirror. My heart sinks. Everything looks wrong. My smoky eye make-up is too heavy, the lipstick too bright, the dress too showy. Despite the painkillers I'm popping like sweets, my ribs still hurt like hell. On Carter's advice, I took myself to our local minor injuries unit this morning where an X-ray revealed hairline fractures in three ribs.

'Not much you can do about them other than rest, ice and painkillers, I'm afraid,' the cheerful nurse practitioner told me as he pointed out the thread-like cracks on the X-ray. 'But look on the bright side. At least you haven't damaged your internal organs, eh?'

'Lucky me,' I said wryly, and he laughed and sent me on my way.

I'm on my knees with exhaustion and a night out at a fancy gastropub is the last thing I need, but Carter has wanted to go for so long I don't want to disappoint him, so I paste on a smile and head downstairs.

He's standing in the hallway, car keys in his hand, one foot tapping the floor impatiently.

'We're going to be late.'

'I just need to check Freddie knows where everything is. Won't be a sec.' The sound of his sigh follows me down the hallway to the snug, where Freddie is sandwiched between Erin and Megan in front of the TV watching *Pitch Perfect*, bowls of popcorn balanced on their knees.

What I'd give to ditch the heels, throw on something comfy and join them.

'We're off,' I say.

Freddie looks up, his eyes flicking over my dress, and I pat my hair self-consciously.

'You look nice,' he says. 'Red always did suit you.'

I hesitate, caught off guard. If he hadn't left, would this be our normal, all snuggled up on the sofa together? It's immaterial, because he did leave, and I am now married to Carter, who is waiting for me by the front door.

Heat colours my cheeks and I change the subject. 'You've got our numbers if you need anything,' I say briskly. 'We won't be late.'

'We'll be fine, Mum,' Erin says, her eyes not leaving the screen.

'Shush, Mum,' Megan adds, holding a finger to her lips. 'They're about to have a riff-off.'

'All right, all right, I know when I'm not wanted. I'll see you later.' I back out of the room, trying to ignore the small sting of rejection.

* * *

The Oak and Ivy is every bit as gorgeous as its Instagram profile, with oak beams, an open fire and candles on every table. Carter raves over the eight-course tasting menu, which is advertised as 'playful and theatrical' but to me seems plain pretentious. The mushroom consommé has truffle foam; the deconstructed fish and chips comes with malt vinegar jam and the lamb loin is served on a bed of hay.

I'm about to joke that I'm glad my dinner's come with its own bedding, when I stop myself. Carter is taking it all way too seriously.

'Don't you love how the chef has elevated what is tradition-ally comfort food to new heights, while paying absolute homage to its roots?' he says.

'Oh, absolutely,' I agree, taking another slug of my deli-cious, but no doubt hideously expensive, Barolo. Maybe it's the alcohol, maybe it's the painkillers, but the evening is starting to blur and I'm finding it hard to focus. My thoughts dart here and there, as slippery as the truffle foam on my over-sized plate.

Freddie would see through the pomposity of this place, I think, as the waiter places two soft-boiled eggs on the table, gives a small bow and leaves. He'd poke fun at the edible sand and the liquid nitrogen-frozen Bloody Mary palate cleanser. He'd gently mock the snooty sommelier and the tiny portions, some barely a mouthful.

The soft-boiled eggs turn out to be the first of our two desserts. The tempered white chocolate shells are filled with a passion fruit 'yolk' and yet more foam – coconut this time. A dribble of the stuff oozes onto my dress and as I dab at it with my starched white napkin a flicker of irritation crosses Carter's face.

'Careful, it's dry-clean only.'

'I'm sure it'll be fine,' I say, although the more I rub away, the worse the stain seems to spread. I lay the napkin over it and smile at him. 'It's funny. I'd forgotten I was wearing a red dress the first time we met. D'you remember?'

There is a moment's hesitation before he nods, and I know he doesn't. I'm not sure I even registered on his radar that night. He only had eyes for Gemma. Not that I cared.

I only had eyes for Freddie.

51

FREDDIE

NOW

The Isle of Lewis will always hold a piece of my heart, but as I sit on the sofa hemmed in by my daughters, I feel a different kind of contentment. This is my happy place. Sandwiched between Erin and Megan, watching the Barden Bellas do their thing, Fleming snoring softly at my feet. Why did I ever leave?

Beside me, Megan yawns and stretches.

'I think it's probably time for bed,' I say. 'You've both got school tomorrow and I don't want to get into trouble with your mum.'

Both girls grumble softly but oblige, scrambling to their feet and kissing first Fleming, then me goodnight.

'Don't forget to clean your teeth,' I call after them as I head to the kitchen to make a cup of tea. Back in the snug, I flick through the channels, eventually settling on a rerun of *The Office*. I'm drifting off when the sound of the front door jolts me awake. I glance at my watch, a cheap digital Casio I bought for a tenner, and frown. It's only half past nine. Alex and Carter aren't due back for another hour at least.

'Only me,' trills a voice from the hall. My heart plummets. Gemma.

I heave myself up, meeting her in the hallway.

'I thought you were working tonight?'

'I got off early. Thought I'd see if you needed a hand with the kids.'

'They're fine. Not a peep from Dylan all evening, and the girls went to bed half an hour ago.'

Gemma either doesn't notice or doesn't care about the sullen tone to my voice. She pulls a bottle of Prosecco from her slouchy suede handbag and waves it in my face.

'I was going to get an early night.'

'Don't be boring, Freddie. Alex and Carter are out having fun. Why shouldn't we? You open this and I'll find a couple of glasses.' She thrusts the bottle into my hands and breezes into the kitchen.

I hover in the hallway for a moment, my fingers sticking to the neck of the ice-cold bottle, then, with a sigh, I follow.

Gemma flits around the kitchen opening cupboards and drawers with an easy familiarity. She always treated our house like her own. I used to tolerate it, because I knew how close she and Alex were, but now I find myself unaccountably irritated at the way she saunters in and takes over.

When I first met Gemma and Alex at that party in our grotty student digs all those years ago, I'd assumed Gemma was the bright light, the one people gravitated towards. Alex had seemed happy in her shadow. But the longer I knew them, the more I realised how wrong I'd been. Under the surface, Alex had a quiet strength that drew others to her like moths to a naked flame, while Gemma was needy and insecure.

I often wondered how the friendship had lasted, especially when Alex and I married and started a family. It felt precarious, like a fault line in the earth's crust, waiting for the right pressure to set it off. I'd half expected it to have imploded by now, but here they were, still as close as ever.

Gemma takes a tub of olives from the fridge and shakes a bag of Kettle chips into a pretty earthenware bowl Alex bought on our honeymoon in the South of France.

She glances at the bottle. 'Haven't you opened that yet?'

I blink, then begin to untwist the wire cage with fumbling fingers. Six clockwise half-turns. Grip the cork and twist the bottle. I hold my breath. There's a soft hiss and a pop and I exhale slowly, then pull out a chair.

'Not here,' Gemma says. 'The snug's so much cosier.'

I hesitate. I'd rather stay in the kitchen under the unforgiving gaze of the ceiling lights, surrounded by appliances and the detritus of family life, than retire to the squashy corner sofa in the softly lit snug, but Gemma has already disappeared. Reluctantly, I follow.

She pours us each a large glass of Prosecco and sinks into the sofa, tucking her legs under her. I perch on the edge and take a cautious sip of my drink. She watches me with amusement.

'Relax.' She pats the cushion beside her. 'I don't bite.'

I focus on the bubbles in her glass as they glide effortlessly to the surface.

'I still can't believe you're back.' Gemma twirls the stem of her glass. 'How's the whole "spare prick at a wedding" thing going?' Her mouth twitches. 'I bet Carter's pissed off. He hates playing second fiddle to anyone.'

'He seems OK.'

'And Alex?'

'Alex?' I repeat. Alex is an enigma. I used to think I knew her inside out, but since I've been back she's kept me at arm's length. Perfectly polite, but distant. Until the kiss. But that should never have happened. 'Um, yeah. I'm sure she's fine with it all.'

Gemma takes a long sip from her glass. 'If you say so. *I'm* glad you're back.' She edges closer to me. 'I've missed you.' The scent of her perfume hits me, something spicy and intense that makes my head swim. 'Have you missed me?'

She smiles coquettishly and leans forward to brush a speck of lint off my jumper. Carter's jumper, to be accurate. My own clothes have mysteriously vanished. I have a sneaking suspicion Alex has chucked the lot of them.

'I've never forgotten that night you turned up on my doorstep,' Gemma says softly.

I haven't forgotten either. How could I? It was easily the worst night of my entire life.

Her hand drops to my chest. She is so close now that I can see the blobs of mascara clinging to her eyelashes like spiders caught in a web.

'Gemma—' I begin, but she cuts me off.

'Come on, Freddie, what's the problem?' Her eyes narrow. 'Unless I'm not good enough for you. Is that it?'

'Gemma, please.'

She pulls back, her expression darkening. 'Oh, I get it,' she says slowly. 'You're still in love with Alex, aren't you?' She shakes her head. Smirks. 'You're deluding yourself if you think she'll have you back. Not when she finds out what we did.'

An icy dread seeps into my bones.

'You're not going to tell her?'

She tilts her head, considering me. 'Well, that's the sixty-four-thousand-dollar question, isn't it?'

I lick my lips. 'What d'you mean?'

'I might, and I might not.' She smiles. 'It all depends on you.'

52

ALEX

NOW

The receptionist at the Volvo dealership gives me a concerned look when Carter drops me off to pick up my car the following morning.

'Mrs Petersen,' she says, suddenly flustered. 'Do you have a moment to speak to Jim, our lead technician?'

'Of course,' I say, wondering what this is about. I shift Dylan into a more comfortable position on my hip. My ribs are still killing me and I'm dosed up to the eyeballs on paracetamol and ibuprofen. 'It won't take long, will it?'

'Not at all. Please, take a seat and I'll let him know you're here.' She gestures to the empty waiting area, then disappears into the workshop, returning moments later with a man in blue coveralls with oil-stained hands, a waxed quiff and salt-and-pepper sideburns.

Jim says hello and takes the seat opposite us. He has a clipboard and a length of cable in his hands. Dylan immediately leans forward and tries to grab it.

'No, Dylan. It's not a toy,' I say, and he howls in protest.

'We have some Matchbox cars and a playmat if your little boy would like to play with them?' The receptionist pulls a plastic box from a bookcase next to the water cooler and tips it onto the carpet. Toy cars topple out. Dylan wriggles out of my arms and races over to investigate. I turn my attention back to Jim.

'Sorry about that.'

'No need to apologise.' He smiles. 'Reckon you've got the makings of a fine mechanic there.' He fingers the cable, his smile fading. 'One of the lads spotted something strange when he carried out your MOT. This is your brake cable.' He flexes it, exposing a small slit in the rubber. 'This isn't normal wear and tear.'

'What do you mean?'

'It's been cut. Look.' He runs the tip of his index finger along the tear. 'Sliced clean through, using wire cutters, by the look of it, and the brake fluid has leaked out. No fluid means no pressure on the brakes. When you braked, the pedal would've gone straight to the floor.'

'That's why the car didn't stop.' I stare at him. 'I thought it was my fault. I thought I'd hit the accelerator instead of the brake.'

He shakes his head. 'It definitely wasn't your fault.' He holds out the cable. 'I didn't know if you wanted to keep it. As evidence,' he adds.

I blink as I take it from him. 'You don't think it was an accident?'

'I've only ever seen a brake cable tampered with once before, and that was the car of a woman whose husband had just taken out a very large life insurance policy, if you get my drift.'

The hairs on the back of my neck stiffen. 'I... I do. Thank you.'

He nods, apparently glad his message has hit home. He

consults his clipboard. 'We've replaced your windscreen washers and changed your oil, and there's an advisory on your two front tyres, which'll need replacing in the next couple of months. I also had my lad check over for any damage from the accident, but it was fine. He says you ended up on the embankment?'

I nod. 'I swerved to avoid the cars in front.'

'I think you were probably very lucky, Mrs Petersen.' He glances at Dylan, who is making 'vroom vroom' noises as he pushes a car along the grey ribbon of road that stretches across the middle of the playmat. 'It could have been a lot worse. You did the right thing.' He hands me the invoice. There's an oily smudge in the top right-hand corner. It looks like a police thumbprint. 'In fact, if it wasn't for your quick reactions, I'm not sure we'd be having this conversation at all.'

'Thank you.'

'No problem.' He pauses. 'I'll happily confirm what I found to the police if you need me to. All you have to do is say the word.'

I pay the bill on autopilot.

'Your keys, Mrs Petersen,' the receptionist says, pressing them into my hand. She bends down and gives Dylan one of the Matchbox cars, then straightens and frowns. 'Are you all right to drive home? I can call someone for you if like?'

'No, I'll be fine, thank you.' I grab Dylan's hand and hurry past the dazzlingly shiny new SUVs and saloons towards the doors, keen to get out of the fishbowl-like showroom.

The Volvo has been valeted, a 'perk' of the expensive dealership service charge, and the grey metallic paintwork gleams. It's no good for fingerprints now, I think, as I strap Dylan into his car seat. Not that I'm going to report the tampered brake cable to the police. Not after falsely accusing Ingrid Kelly of kidnapping Megan. I can just imagine the reaction I'd get. They'd label me neurotic and file my report in the bin. I'm not sure I'm even going to tell Carter, because what would be the point? Unbidden, the mechanic's story about the husband who cut his wife's brake cable pops into my head. I bury it as quickly as it appears.

Carter would never do that to me. I know our marriage has weathered its fair share of storms, but he loves me.

Does he? a vindictive voice whispers in my head as Freddie's words come back to me. *You'd be a fool to trust him.*

And just like that, all my insecurities rise to the surface, like scum on a stagnant pond. The nagging fear that Carter was on the rebound when he asked me out; that I can never compete with the leggy blondes he used to date.

That he only married me because he felt sorry for me.

53

ALEX

NOW

I did everything I could not to slip back into postnatal depression after Dylan was born. I'd looked up the stats. Women who've experienced PND with one child have a thirty to fifty per cent chance of suffering from it again.

I was determined not to be one of them.

I swallowed my pride and told my midwife how ill I'd been after my last pregnancy, and I signed up for a course on cognitive behavioural therapy, hoping to learn strategies to manage the negative thoughts if they struck. I ate well and I went to bed early. I swam three times a week and walked everywhere, hoping that if I was physically strong I could beat the depression into submission.

When Dylan was born, after a frenetic four-hour labour, I was euphoric. Carter was over the moon to have a son, and Dylan was such an easy baby I fell instantly in love with him. Carter was adamant he wanted me to breastfeed Dylan and, with perseverance and the help of an amazing midwife on the labour ward, I cracked it. Finally, I felt as though I knew what I was doing.

My euphoria lasted until the day Carter went back to work after his paternity leave. Dylan was two weeks old, the girls were at school and once again I was stuck in the house with a tiny baby.

I tried to keep busy, to keep well, but the depression was always there, like an old lover impatient to welcome me back into his arms.

I tried so hard not to give in, but I was powerless to stop it.

The days seemed to solidify and swell like expanding foam as the depression took hold. Simple tasks, those I could be bothered to tackle, like making packed lunches or preparing dinner, took me hours. I couldn't see the point of washing my hair, or wiping down the work surfaces, or anything much at all, really.

I pinned a smile on my face when I picked the girls up from school and when Carter came home from work, but they weren't stupid. They knew.

Dark thoughts filled my mind. I was a useless mother who couldn't do anything right. Erin had more maternal instinct in the tip of her little finger than I did.

Every time Carter tried to talk to me about how I was feeling, I shut him down. I began to dread seven o'clock, the time he usually arrived home from work, in case he didn't come home at all. I was terrified history would repeat itself and another husband would walk out on me.

Things came to a head when Dylan was nine weeks old. It was a Wednesday, I think. I'd been awake since four, staring, gritty-eyed, at the ceiling, wondering how I would ever find the energy to drag myself through another day. Carter left the house at seven, barely saying goodbye. Erin and Megan would not stop bickering. Dylan was fractious. I reached the end of my tether.

It was still no excuse.

I let myself into the house after walking the girls to school, settled Dylan in his cot, fed Fleming and walked right back out again, locking the door behind me.

I didn't go far, just down the road to the park, where I sat on the bench by the playground and watched the other mothers push their kids on the swings. Mothers who knew what they were doing, who enjoyed having children. Mothers who weren't broken like me.

I felt as though I was at a crossroads. Turn left, and walk right back into my mundane, familiar life. A life of packed lunches and school concerts, nappies and feeds. A life which, at the time, felt suffocating; my children vampires, sucking the blood out of me.

Or I could turn right and keep walking into a new life where the only responsibility I had was myself. Where I could rediscover who I really was, where I could be *me*.

Is this how Freddie felt, the day he disappeared? Had he felt suffocated by marriage and parenthood? Had he wanted to shrug us off like a coat on a warm spring afternoon? I pictured him that last night, as I had so many times in the months and years after he left. He hadn't seemed like a man keen to start a new life. He'd seemed like a man on the brink, a man who was struggling to hold it together. A man who didn't think he was good enough; for his patients, for his children, for me.

Had he walked away because he thought we'd be better off without him?

If he had, he was so wrong.

I sat on the bench for what felt like ages but was in reality only about ten minutes, paralysed with indecision, as children played and mums gossiped. It wasn't until a small girl – she couldn't have been much older than three – ran past me to her mother and said in a faux whisper, 'Why's that lady crying?' that I realised tears were streaming down my face.

The woman, looking impossibly wholesome in a stripy

Breton top, denim dungarees and shiny red Dr. Martens, approached me cautiously and asked if I was OK.

'I'm fine,' I said thickly, though I clearly wasn't.

'I've seen you here before,' she said. 'You have two girls, yes? And a new baby?' Her expression froze, and her hand flew to her mouth. 'They are all right, aren't they? You're not upset because...' She trailed off, and I tried to smile, wanting to reassure her.

'No, they're all fine. The girls are at school, and Dylan, he's—'

I pictured my baby growing fretful in his cot, with no one there to comfort him. It was the wake-up call I needed and I hauled myself to my feet.

'He's at home,' I said. 'Which is where I should be.' I met her gaze. 'Thank you.'

She smiled uncertainly. 'What for?'

'For giving a damn.' I touched her arm and started running, and where the path split in two, I turned left towards home.

* * *

Gemma's car had been parked outside our house. Stomach churning, I let myself in and stood, listening, at the foot of the stairs. I could hear Gemma talking over the sound of Dylan's muffled sobs. She was using the quiet, calm voice she used when Megan fell and grazed her knee, or when Erin had a bust-up with a friend at school. The soothing voice she no doubt employed when she was looking after the sick and injured children on Dolphin Ward.

For a split second I considered turning round and leaving, because Gemma was so much more suited to motherhood than I was. Sometimes I hated the way she made it look so easy. She was patient and capable. She adored my kids and they adored her. I couldn't compete.

To this day, I don't know what made me stay. Maybe it was because the girls had already lost their dad and I couldn't let them lose me, too. Maybe I was worried Gemma would slip a little too easily into my shoes. I like to think it was love for my children, pure and simple. Whatever the reason, I heeled off my shoes and took the stairs two at a time.

The door to the nursery was closed, and I turned the handle gingerly, as if I wasn't sure what I'd find, which was crazy when you think about it. But I was a little crazy at the time.

Gemma's head was bent over Dylan as she rocked him in her arms.

'There, there,' she soothed. 'You're all right now.'

I hovered in the doorway, watching. Gemma had everything under control, as always. I was the hopeless one, the one who couldn't cope. I dithered, unsure whether to go in or stay back. Eventually, I cleared my throat.

'Hello, Gemma.'

She whipped round. 'You left him,' she said, her voice tight with tension. 'You left him on his own.'

'I just popped out for a—'

'You're his mum. You don't get to "pop out" without him.'

Something inside me hardened. I held out my arms.

'I'll take him now.'

She pressed her lips together and for a moment I thought she might refuse, but she gave a little shake of her head and handed him to me.

I felt her eyes on me as I dropped a kiss on Dylan's forehead and inhaled his milky, baby smell. When I turned, she was at the door, her hand on the frame.

'This can't happen again, Alex,' she said in a low voice. Then, without waiting for an answer, she stalked out, leaving me with my baby in my arms and a sick feeling in the pit of my stomach.

54

ALEX

NOW

I booked myself an appointment with our GP the day after I left Dylan at home on his own. She prescribed me antidepressants that were safe to take while breastfeeding and, gradually, I began to feel myself again. Normal service was resumed. Our blended family of five felt complete. If Carter was occasionally a bit strict with the girls, it was only because he expected everyone to meet his own high standards. Megan didn't mind. Carter could do no wrong in her eyes. Sometimes, Erin pushed back, but she'd hit her teens, a time when all kids flexed their muscles. It wasn't a problem. And Dylan worshipped his father.

The more I think about it on the drive home from the garage, the more ridiculous the notion that Carter tampered with my brakes seems. Of course he wouldn't. He loves me and I love him. We are rock solid.

I pull up outside the house and lift Dylan out of his car seat. He toddles up to the door, but before he has a chance to bang it with his chubby fist, Freddie appears from behind us.

'Fweddie!' Dylan cries, and Freddie's gaunt face lights up, like he's just won the lottery.

'Clever boy, Dyls,' he says, perching him on his hip.

Dylan waves the red car in his face. 'Vroom vroom,' he babbles. 'Beep beep.'

'Where've you been?' I ask.

'For a walk.' He peers up at the sky. 'It's supposed to rain later.'

I unlock the door, kick off my shoes and Freddie follows me into the kitchen. Fleming lifts his head and woofs softly when he sees us.

'Tea?' I ask, filling the kettle.

'Please.' Freddie sets Dylan down, then looks at me. 'Are you all right? You look like you've seen a ghost.'

The longing to offload is so tempting I almost give in and tell Freddie what I've just learnt, that the accident wasn't my fault and only happened because someone sliced through my brake cable. Someone who wanted to hurt me, perhaps even wanted me dead. I'm gripped by a raw horror, because I could so easily have ploughed into the car in front on the bypass and killed us both. But I banish the dark thoughts, because there's no point dwelling on something that didn't happen. I need to concentrate my energies on working out who did it.

'I'm fine.' We sip our tea in silence. It should feel awkward, but it doesn't. Since his return, there's a stillness about Freddie. He used to be such a busy person, always on the go. I marvelled at how he thrived on the insane workloads at university and during his foundation and specialty training. The hours were even more gruelling when he took up the consultant's post on Dolphin Ward, but he still had the energy to help me with the girls when he came home from work. He was a force of nature, always so driven and focused. One of those people who got things done.

Now, his quiet presence is a balm. He seems at peace, and

this new serenity suits him. I suppose it's rubbed off from his time on the Isle of Lewis, a benefit of living in the middle of all that stunning scenery. I could use some myself.

A cool draught lifts the hairs on my arms. I frown.

'Is the back door open?'

'I locked it when I left.'

'Are you sure?' I push my chair back and investigate. The door is ajar. Freddie joins me as I peer into the back garden.

He looks stricken. 'I'm so sorry, Alex. I let Fleming out for a wee just before I went out, but I could have sworn I locked it.'

'No harm done.' As I pull the door closed, I spy the pile of dirty washing sitting in the basket on top of the tumble drier. I'd meant to put a wash on before I picked up the car. I lean across to pick it up, inhaling sharply at the resulting twinge of pain.

'Are you OK?'

I straighten and balance the basket on my hip. 'I'm fine. It's just my ribs. They're still a bit sore.'

'You need to be careful.' Freddie takes the basket from me. 'You sit yourself down. I'll do it. Which cycle?'

'The forty degrees daily one. Thanks.' I finish my tea but it's no good. There are jobs everywhere I look. The dishwasher needs emptying and the surfaces need a wipe. I haven't cleared up our breakfast things, let alone thought about dinner. At the other end of the long room, the coffee table is hidden under a pile of books and newspapers, and the roses Carter bought me for our anniversary have wilted and are dropping petals all over the hearth. Dylan sits in the middle of the rug surrounded by toys, humming quietly to himself as he tries to balance a plastic triceratops on top of his new car.

I carry the breakfast things over to the sink and, without asking, Freddie starts to unload the dishwasher. Before I know it, we've slipped into our old roles. He empties the bin and refills Fleming's water bowl while I wipe the worktops and sweep the floor.

Once the kitchen is shipshape, we move to the other end of the room. Freddie squats down to Dylan's level.

'Want to play a game with me?'

Dylan nods.

'I hoped you'd say that. This is how it works. The first one to pick up all the toys gets a chocolate biscuit.'

Dylan scrambles to his feet. While they toss toys into the toybox, I plump cushions and clear the coffee table.

I'm carrying a couple of the photo albums across to the bookshelf when one of them slips out of my grasp and falls on my foot. Yelping, I bend down to pick it up, instantly regretting it as I'm gripped by another wave of intense pain.

'Jeez,' I gasp, clutching my sides. Freddie guides me to the sofa. 'Take a minute. Dylan and I have got this, haven't we, mate?'

Dylan nods and waves a Brio train at me.

Absently, I check the spine of the album. *Our family* 2010 in Erin's neat handwriting. She took charge of the albums the moment she was old enough to, painstakingly filling them with photos, one for every year of the last decade. Once she'd finished, she went back further in time. This is the earliest, the year Freddie and I were married.

It's been years since I've looked at it, and I'm opening the album before I can stop myself. I pause at the first page, staring at a photo of me and Freddie standing outside the church as our friends and family throw handfuls of confetti. But something's wrong.

Thick, jagged lines slash through both our faces, scratching out our features, the pen biting so deeply it scores the glossy paper. I turn the page with trembling fingers to find more of the same. Every photo Erin has lovingly stuck into the album – our vows, signing the register, cutting the cake, our first dance – has been defaced in the same brutal fashion. Each memory destroyed.

I sway, suddenly light-headed, and the album slips from my lap, landing on the floor with a thud. Across the room, Freddie looks up in concern.

'Alex?' he says. 'Are you all right?'

Wordlessly, I nudge the album towards him with my foot. He picks it up, his eyes bulging as he flips through the pages, taking in the angrily scored lines obliterating our faces.

'Christ,' he mutters. His gaze slides to Dylan, who is dropping crayons into an old ice-cream tub.

'It wasn't Dylan,' I say, my voice low. 'This isn't doodling, it's a warning.'

Everything is falling into place. The threatening letters. The reporter. My slashed brake cable.

I know exactly who is behind this campaign of terror...

55

ALEX

NOW

'A *warning*?' Freddie gapes at me. 'What do you mean?'

My thoughts are racing. 'The back door was ajar when we came home. She must have found the key under the flowerpot and let herself in. It makes sense.' The thought of Ingrid Kelly inside my house sends a chill down my spine. 'The letters weren't working and the story fizzled out. Then the brakes, well, that didn't work either, so she's decided to break in and—'

'Whoa, slow down,' Freddie says, holding his palms out. 'What letters? Who are you talking about?' His eyes widen. 'And what about the brakes?'

I'm pacing now, ignoring the stabbing pain in my ribs. 'Ingrid Kelly. She's been sending threatening notes for weeks. Nonsense about the truth coming out.'

He stiffens. 'What truth?'

'I don't know! About Sapphire, I suppose. But that's not the point. The point is, she's gunning for us, Freddie. You and me.'

He rubs his temple. 'I get that she might have me in her

sights, but why would she want to hurt you? What happened to Sapphire has nothing to do with you.'

'You were on your knees with exhaustion, remember? That's why you didn't diagnose her sepsis until it was too late. And that was down to me.' My voice wavers, the familiar guilt tightening in my chest, making it hard to breathe. 'If I'd held it together after Megan was born, maybe you wouldn't have been so exhausted, and maybe none of it would have happened.'

'It wasn't your fault, Al. I'm the doctor and I'm responsible for my patients. No one else.' He glances at the album. 'Maybe I should go and see her.'

I stare at him in horror. 'Are you mad?'

'Maybe if I explained the pressure I was under, she'll understand. Because this' – he waves a hand over the trashed photos – 'can't go on.' He frowns as a thought strikes him. 'What does Ingrid have to do with your brakes?'

I bite my lip, then fetch my bag, pulling out the severed brake lead. Freddie pales.

'The guy from the Volvo garage said it was cut deliberately.'

'Jesus.'

Dylan toddles over, clutching the little red car. Freddie picks him up and sets him on his knee. Dylan pushes the car back and forth across his thigh, babbling to himself.

Freddie looks at me. 'Show me the letters. I want to see them.'

I nod and make my way slowly up the stairs, pausing on the landing to catch my breath. If anything, the throbbing in my ribs is getting worse, not better. I want to crawl into bed and sleep for a week, but I can't, because I need to make Dylan's lunch and change the girls' sheets and tackle the mountain of ironing I've been ignoring for days.

I hobble over to the window on the landing and stare down onto the street. The cherry trees are in full blossom, the profusion of pink petals the colour of a ballerina's tutu. Normally, I

love this time of year. Everywhere is so fresh and full of promise. Objectively, I know it's beautiful, but I feel disconnected
from it. Numb.

I'm willing myself to feel something – *anything* – when a
movement on the other side of the road catches my eye.
Someone is staring up at our house. My skin prickles. It's Ingrid
Kelly. I tug at the sash window, but it's stuck fast. I clatter down
the stairs and into the kitchen.

'She's outside,' I cry breathlessly.

Freddie looks up, frowning. 'Who?'

'Ingrid Kelly! She's got a bloody nerve,' I hiss, making for
the front door.

'Wait, Alex – don't!' Freddie leaps up. 'We should call the
police.'

'The police?' I scoff. 'They already think I'm a neurotic
mess. They won't do anything.'

'In that case, I'll go. You stay here.'

'No!' I stop and turn back to face him, my hands on my
hips. 'I'm coming too, Freddie. I will not let that woman destroy
my family.'

56

FREDDIE

NOW

I stride along the hallway to the front door and pull it open. Alex follows, Dylan on her hip.

'She was over there.' Alex points at the pavement on the other side of the street. She's so close I can feel her breath on the back of my neck. She looks around her wildly. 'Where the hell has she gone?'

I check for cars and step out into the road, looking left and right. Apart from a ginger tom, who watches us with amber eyes from the top of a brick wall a couple of doors down, the street is empty. I glance at Alex.

'She was here,' she says, tilting her chin defensively. 'Right where you're standing.'

I look around. Roots from the nearest cherry tree have pushed the pavement slabs up, leaving a treacherous trip hazard for the unwary. The sweet, almost sickly scent of a lilac bush fills my nostrils. Dylan wriggles in Alex's arms and she deposits him on the pavement between us and grabs his hand.

'She was here,' she repeats, a little desperately.

I nod, scan the street again, then sneak a sideways glance at Alex. Her hair is dishevelled and there is a wary, almost fearful look in her eyes. She reminds me of a deer being stalked by a pride of lions in a David Attenborough nature documentary.

'You don't believe me, do you?'

'Of course I believe you, but she's long gone. She must have seen you watching her from the house. Come on, let's get you both inside.' Without even realising it, I've slipped into 'reassuring doctor' mode, my voice calm and steady. But far from soothing Alex, it seems to rile her.

'I'm going round there,' she announces.

'No, Alex, that's a really bad idea.'

'I don't care! I've had enough. D'you hear me? I. Have. Had. Enough. Take Dylan,' she instructs, picking the toddler up and thrusting him into my arms before striding off.

'Alex!' I cry, following her. 'Wait!'

She holds up a hand to silence me and quickens her step. For a second, I'm frozen to the spot. Dylan drives the Matchbox car along my shoulder and up my neck. 'Vroom vroom,' he says.

My heart pounds as I follow Alex down the street. She marches ahead, her shoulders rigid. I've seen that look in her eyes before, ten years ago. A closed-off, haunted expression that fills me with dread.

I'll never be able to forget the way she retreated into herself after Megan was born. Those head-spinning mood swings. I'd dismissed her volatility as the baby blues, too wrapped up in my job and weighed down by the crippling exhaustion of looking after a young family to step back and see what was really happening. It was weeks before I finally admitted to myself that Alex was barely functioning.

Even at that point I could have found her help. But then Sapphire Kelly was admitted onto Dolphin Ward and everything I thought I knew was turned on its head.

As if my culpability couldn't get any worse, my decision to

leave was based on a pathetic misunderstanding. *My* pathetic misunderstanding. If only I'd gone straight home that night instead of drowning my sorrows at the pub. If only I'd really listened to Alex. The one time she needed me, and I wasn't there for her. Everything that's happened since is down to me. I am to blame for it all.

A couple of paces ahead, Alex is muttering under her breath. I tune out Dylan's babbling and strain to hear.

'Bloody woman... I'm going to give her a piece of my mind... She can't just waltz into my house—'

A sick feeling rises in the back of my throat and for one awful moment I think I might actually vomit in the gutter. I want to believe Alex, of course I do. But I can't ignore the voice whispering in my ear. *It's happening all over again.*

If she is unravelling, I can't stand back and watch it play out. I have to do something, though I have no idea what. And there's something else: what if Ingrid *is* behind it all? The slashed brake cable, the ruined photos, the threatening notes? What if it was Ingrid who tipped off that reporter? What if Alex is right?

Alex stops outside a terraced house with a holly bush in the front garden, yanks open the gate and stomps up to the front door. She presses the buzzer and somewhere inside the house 'Let It Go' from *Frozen* plays. It's an odd choice for the humourless woman I remember from Dolphin Ward a decade ago and Alex must think so too, because she turns back to me with a perplexed expression. I pull a face and shrug, remembering one of Mum's favourite sayings: *It takes all sorts.*

There's no answer. Alex presses the buzzer again, and again, until the front door of the house next door opens and a slight, white-haired man wearing pebble glasses peers out.

'You looking for Ingrid?'

Alex nods.

'She's not in.'

'D'you know when she's likely to be back?'

'Hard to say.' He frowns. 'What day is it?'

'Thursday.'

'She works Thursdays.'

Alex exhales loudly. 'Where?'

'At the library.' He squints at Alex. 'I'll be seeing her later. Who shall I say was asking for her?'

'No one,' Alex mutters, turning and tramping back down the path.

I cup her elbow, encouraged when she doesn't shrug me off.

'Come on,' I say gently. 'Let's get you home.'

We retrace our steps in silence, but when we reach the cherry tree opposite the house, Alex stops.

'Just because Ingrid works on a Thursday doesn't mean it wasn't her. She must have slipped out in her lunch break. It's a ten-minute walk to the library from here. Don't look at me like that.' Her voice is almost pleading, and compassion for her washes over me. 'I know you think I'm paranoid, but I'm not.'

Alex gulps, her eyes filling with tears, and she grips my arm so hard I wince.

'She tried to kill me and Dylan, Freddie. Do you understand? We could have *died*.'

I watch the woman I swore to love forever falling apart before my eyes, and it wounds like the twist of a knife in my heart. Being here, in this house, surrounded by echoes of the past, has been bittersweet. Pleasure and pain. This life could have been mine if I hadn't walked away. Now it's Carter's. But that doesn't mean that Alex's happiness is no longer my responsibility. I have so much to make up for.

I reach a decision. I need to talk to Ingrid Kelly. It's clear we have unfinished business. I have no idea what kind of reception I'll get, but that doesn't matter. I'm not doing this for myself, I'm doing it for Alex, Erin and Megan.

I need to keep them safe, and if the only way of doing so is to confront my own demons, I will do it.

57

ALEX

NOW

I feel Freddie's gaze on me as I unlock the front door and step into the hallway. I know exactly what's going through his mind. He thinks I'm losing it; that I'm seeing dangers where there aren't any. But he's wrong. Ingrid is out to destroy us and God only knows where it'll end.

In the kitchen, I make an effort to keep busy, hoping small tasks will soothe me. I water the herbs on the windowsill and scrub at a dried crust of pasta sauce on the hob. I make Dylan scrambled eggs on toast and pop him in his highchair.

'Alex,' Freddie begins.

I shake my head. 'Not now, Freddie.'

'But—'

'I said, not now.'

'Fine.' He sighs. 'You know where I am when you're ready to talk about it.'

I make a non-committal noise. Dylan chunters away to himself as he demolishes his lunch, and I fetch him a yoghurt from the fridge.

My mobile rings, startling me. I feel anxious and jittery, my nerves so frayed they're barely holding me together. I grab the phone from the table, surprised to see Gemma's name on the screen.

'Hey,' I say. 'Aren't you at work?'

'Day off. Is Freddie with you?'

I glance at him. He's stacking Dylan's plate in the dishwasher. I step into the hall, pressing the phone against my ear. 'Yes, why?'

'D'you think he'd mind Dylan for a couple of hours? I thought we could take Fleming for a walk, just you and me.' She pauses. 'There's something I need to talk to you about.'

'Oh, yes?'

'I've had a call from Ingrid Kelly. She wants to meet me. I think she's trying to reopen the case against Freddie.'

'*What?*'

'I told you I'd heard she was sniffing around at work. She says she's found new evidence to prove gross negligence.'

'Christ.' I rub a hand across my face. Hasn't Ingrid already taken her pound of flesh? Freddie left his family and a career he loved – his whole life – because of what happened with Sapphire.

'Quite.' Gemma clears her throat. 'She says she's talking to everyone who worked on Dolphin Ward when Sapphire was there. Now it's my turn. The last thing I want to do is drop Freddie in it, so I want to run a few things past you before I speak to her.'

'Of course,' I say. 'Thank you.'

'Meet me at the café in the park at two. Just you and Fleming, OK? Don't tell Freddie what Ingrid's up to. It'll only stress him out.'

We end the call and I return to the kitchen. Freddie is wiping yoghurt from Dylan's face with a wet wipe.

'Everything OK?'

I plaster on a smile. 'It was Gemma, asking if I could meet her in the park for a coffee. I don't suppose you could mind Dylan for an hour?'

'Of course. It'll do you good. I'll pick Megan up from school and get the kids' tea sorted, so take your time.'

'Thanks.' I kiss Dylan goodbye, grab my bag and clip Fleming's lead on. Out of habit, I check the street for a glimpse of Ingrid as I leave the house, but, of course, she's nowhere to be seen.

Gemma is already seated at a table outside the small wooden café in the park, her head bent over her phone. As I approach, she places it face down and reaches across to scratch Fleming behind the ear. Her face is grim.

'We haven't had a council of war like this since Tina Dean stole Matt Stevens from you a week before the speech day disco in Year 12,' I say, trying – and failing – to raise a smile.

Gemma pushes a paper cup across the table. 'I ordered you a latte.'

'Thanks.' I prise the lid off and take a sip, even though the caffeine will be catnip for my anxiety.

'You didn't tell Freddie about Ingrid?' she checks.

I shake my head. 'He thinks I'm paranoid enough already.'

'Good.' Her gaze slides to her phone. 'Ingrid called again. She wants me to meet her at three.' Gemma bites her bottom lip. 'I know it's a big ask, Al, but I wondered if you'd come with me? I'd feel safer with you there. I don't want her twisting everything I say.'

I don't hesitate. Gemma is my best friend. I love her like a sister. 'Of course I'll come. Where are you meeting her?'

Gemma hands me a scrap of paper with an address scrawled on it.

'Twelve Millgate Close,' I read aloud. I feel a flicker of recognition. 'That's one of those cul-de-sacs that backs onto the river, isn't it?'

She nods. 'It's a friend's place, apparently. She thought it would be good to meet somewhere neutral.'

'I suppose it makes sense.' I frown, because something doesn't sit right. 'She must have pulled a sickie.'

'What d'you mean?'

'She works Thursdays.'

Gemma stares at me. 'How do you know that?'

My cheeks burn. 'I thought I saw her outside our house earlier and went round there to have it out with her but she wasn't in. Her neighbour said she works at the library every Thursday.'

'Oh, OK. I guess you're right.'

I'm about to tell Gemma about Ingrid sneaking into the house and defacing our wedding photos when she drains the last of her coffee and pushes her chair back.

'We should go,' she says. 'It'll take a while to get there.'

'Are you sure you want to do this?'

She nods. 'The woman's batshit crazy. We need to show her Freddie did nothing wrong or she'll take him down.'

'You're right.' Any misgivings I might have had that this was a bad idea melt away and I spring to my feet, gripped by a new energy. After days stuck in a limbo-like purgatory, having to deal with one blow after another, it feels good to be moving forward, doing something positive.

It's time I told Ingrid Kelly to stop her vendetta against us.

It's time she knew this ends here.

58

ALEX

NOW

Number twelve Millgate Close is a pebble-dashed, detached 1920s house with bay windows and a simple canopy jutting out above the peeling front door. The place has a neglected feel about it: weeds poke out from between the paving slabs on the front path, the roof is green with moss and the privet hedge behind the wooden perimeter fence has grown so high you can't see into the front windows.

I pause outside, one hand on the wrought-iron gate. The paint's flaking on that, too, its rusty metal core exposed. I can't shake the feeling I've been here before, though I suspect my mind's playing tricks on me. The cul-de-sac is identical to half a dozen others in this part of town; it's no surprise it feels familiar.

'What's wrong?' Gemma asks. She was monosyllabic on the walk over, shutting down every attempt at conversation. It's understandable: she's worried about talking to Ingrid. I am too. I know what the woman is capable of.

'I have a bad feeling about this, Gem. We shouldn't have come.'

'It'll be fine,' she says shortly, pushing open the gate. 'She said to use the back door.'

'The back door? Why?'

'How should I know? The woman's clearly unhinged. Who knows what's going on in her head?'

I trail after her, Fleming at my heels. The old dog looks around with interest, his tail wagging. His equanimity reassures me. Surely his doggy senses would be on high alert if we had anything to be worried about?

We walk through the gap between the garage and the house, past an old concrete coal bunker. I hold my breath as I stare up at the windows, watching for the tug of a curtain, or a flitting shadow, but the house is keeping its secrets, for now at least.

Fleming barks: once, twice. I jump a foot in the air, my hand clasping my chest with a cry when pain shoots around my ribcage.

'Fleming!' Gemma hisses. 'Button it, for Christ's sake.'

This strikes me as odd. Why would Gemma be worried about him making a noise when Ingrid must know we're on our way? Then a lightbulb pings. Ingrid may know Gemma's coming but she has no idea I'm with her. I stroke Fleming's head and tell him to shush.

Gemma raps on the back door. I hold my breath, slowly exhaling when there's no answer. I peer through the nearest window but heavy net curtains obscure my view.

'Perhaps we should wait round the front,' I whisper. Ignoring me, Gemma turns the handle. The door is unlocked. She gives it a shove and it swings open.

I tighten my grip on Fleming's collar and hang back. If Ingrid and her friend aren't here, surely we'll be trespassing the minute we step over the threshold – or worse: breaking and entering. Gemma glances back at me.

'Are you coming or not?'

I waver for a second, but I know I don't really have a choice.

I can't let her go in there on her own. Reluctantly, I follow my
best friend into the house.

* * *

The place smells damp; the air musty, like decaying leaves. My
gaze swivels this way and that. We are in a kitchen. It's like
something out of the 1950s, with grimy Formica units and a
dirty lino floor. It's also as creepy as hell.

'Ingrid!' Gemma calls as she walks through the kitchen to
the front of the house. 'Are you here? It's me, Gemma
Lawrence.' She turns back to me. 'You look down here. I'll try
upstairs.'

I nod, keen to get this over and done with. The sooner we're
out of here the better. I tramp through the kitchen to the hallway, then turn left into the living room. The curtains are closed
and dust sheets cover the three-piece suite and sideboard. I let
Fleming off his lead and he pads round the room, sniffing the
furniture.

'Come, boy,' I say, and we investigate the dining room on
the other side of the hallway. Again, the curtains are closed and
everything is covered in dust sheets. The damp smell is worse in
here, and faded floral wallpaper is peeling from a couple of the
walls. Ingrid's friend must have bought the place as a doer-
upper. It could be beautiful: the generously proportioned rooms
have high ceilings and the fireplaces are art deco gems. As I peer
through the curtains to the jungle-like front garden I get that
feeling again, that I've been here before.

Above me, a floorboard creaks, and I remember why we're
here. We're supposed to be looking for Ingrid. I make my way
back through the hallway, checking the downstairs loo and a
sun room at the back of the house that's filled with dead gera-
niums in terracotta pots.

'She's not here, Gem,' I call up the stairs. I can't wait to get out of this musty, damp house and breathe in fresh air. Anger at Ingrid for sending us on a wild goose chase ferments in my stomach. 'We should never have come,' I mutter to Fleming.

I rest one hand on the newel post and call, 'C'mon, Gem, let's go. There's no one here.'

Gemma appears. 'Did you check the cellar?'

'Cellar?'

'Didn't you see the door as we walked in? It's in the kitchen.'

I'm about to tell Gemma not to be ridiculous; there's no way Ingrid will be in the cellar, when I bite the words back. I will look in the damn cellar if that's what it takes to convince her the place is empty.

'Right,' I say, rolling my eyes. 'I'll check the cellar.'

It takes me a moment to spot the door, because it's wood-panelled and painted the same shade of yellowing magnolia as the rest of the kitchen. But there it is, next to the white cooker with an eye-level grill that looks so retro it should be in the Science Museum. I turn the doorknob, hoping it's locked, because if it is, we can put a stop to this nonsense and go home.

The door is not locked.

Fetid air hits me as the door swings open, and I pull a face. Wooden stairs lead down into a cavern-like darkness. I run a hand down the walls on either side of the door, hoping to find a light switch. Eventually, I locate the switch, but when I flick it, nothing happens.

I hover on the top step. The air behind me moves, so fleetingly I wonder if I imagined it. Then, out of nowhere, something slams into the back of my head. There's a blinding flash of pain as my vision blurs and the world spins.

Then everything goes black.

59

FREDDIE

NOW

I wait until Alex and Fleming have gone, then pack a drink and a snack for Dylan and strap him into his pushchair. I squat on my haunches and smile at the toddler.

'Want to go to the library?' I ask. 'We can find some books to read.'

'Yes!'

I ruffle Dylan's hair affectionately and check the time. It's just gone two. We have over an hour before we need to pick Megan up from school. Plenty of time to see Ingrid and find out what the hell she wants from me.

The library is a large, flat-roofed brick building next to the council offices at the top of the high street. I time the walk. Just under nine minutes. Alex was right: Ingrid could easily have had time to walk to the house, let herself in, damage the photos and walk back again. She had the means... but did she have the motive?

The children's section hasn't changed since I used to bring Erin here when she was Dylan's age. It's a colourful space, with bright rugs, a farmyard mural and kid-sized armchairs. A couple of mums with pre-schoolers are leafing through the shelves. I find Dylan some picture books, then scan the rest of the library looking for Ingrid.

Unable to see her, I push the buggy over to the main desk where a woman with an emerald-green scarf and reading glasses perched on her head is issuing a replacement library card to a man on a mobility scooter.

'Thanks, pet,' the man says, taking the card and placing it under his brown homburg hat, before trundling off.

'He wonders why he's always losing it,' the library assistant says, one eyebrow raised. 'How can I help?'

I clear my throat. 'Is Ingrid around? Ingrid Kelly?'

'She's in the workroom ordering books for the home library customers,' the woman says. 'I'll fetch her for you. Who shall I say wants her?'

'Freddie Harris.'

Both her eyebrows shoot up this time. She knows who I am, I think, rattled. Ingrid has told her what I did to Sapphire. My breathing quickens. It would be so easy to turn and walk right out of the library and forget all about the woman, but I can't. I have to do this for Alex and the girls.

The library assistant bustles off and I crouch down beside Dylan and look through the picture books with him, glad of the distraction. We're halfway through the second book when I hear footsteps. I take a deep breath and look up.

'Doctor Harris,' Ingrid says.

I spring to my feet, my throat tight with anxiety. She's a statuesque woman, almost as tall as me, with a strong jawline and piercing blue eyes. More handsome than beautiful, but undeniably imposing.

'Ms Kelly.' I extend a hand because I'm at a loss what else to do. 'How are you?'

'Me? I'm fine.' Her grip is firm. Of course it is. 'But I'm sure you didn't track me down to the library to ask how I am. What do you want?'

I squirm under her gaze. 'Is there somewhere we can talk?'

Ingrid assesses me for a moment, then nods. 'Come with me.'

I release the brake on Dylan's buggy and follow her past half a dozen book-lined shelving units to a fire door at the back of the building. Ingrid punches numbers into a keypad and pulls the door open and we step into a large room with piles of books on every surface.

She bends down to examine the two books Dylan is holding in his chubby fists.

'*Where's Spot?* and *The Very Hungry Caterpillar.*' She nods approvingly. 'You have excellent taste, young man.'

Dylan nods, suddenly shy. I can empathise. If I could crawl under a stone and hide, I wouldn't think twice. I lick my lips.

'I would like to start by saying how truly sorry I am for your loss.' I swallow down the lump in my throat. 'I will never forgive myself for what happened to Sapphire.'

Ingrid straightens. 'My loss?'

Words I've buried too deeply for too long find their way to the surface, and they tumble out of me before I can stop myself.

'I was supposed to be looking after her but I was so blinkered I couldn't see what was staring me in the face. It's my fault she died, and I don't care if I'm admitting liability by telling you that, because the fact is, if I'd spotted her sepsis sooner, she would still be here.'

Ingrid's expression is unreadable, though if I was a betting man I'd wager it falls somewhere between pity and anger. She glances at a wall clock to her left.

'Do you have to be anywhere for the next half hour?'

'I'm picking Dylan's sister up from school at a quarter past three. Why?'

'I want you to come to my house. It's on the way to your

daughter's school. I think it's probably easier to show you rather than explain.'

I frown. What does she want to show me? A dossier of papers proving my guilt? Sworn affidavits she's about to file? A shrine to her daughter? My grip on the handle of Dylan's buggy tightens as I picture a corner of Ingrid's sitting room dedicated to photos, candles, a threadbare teddy. I'm not sure I can...

'Shall we go?' Ingrid says, taking a jacket from the back of a chair and slipping it on. I swallow hard and nod, then follow her out of the stockroom, my movements torpid and mechanical. I wish I'd never come, even though I know it's too late to turn back the clock.

I have opened Pandora's box. Now, like it or not, I must deal with the fallout.

60

ALEX

NOW

When I come to, I am lying on a grubby pink candlewick bedspread in a small square room. The back of my head is pounding and my cracked ribs throb. I try to move into a more comfortable position and cry out in shock. My hands are tied behind my back. No. *No!*

How did I end up here? Memories shift like sand, in and out of my consciousness. Meeting Gemma at the park. Walking to this house to see Ingrid Kelly. Opening the door to the cellar and falling, falling.

I lift my head gingerly and look around. The walls glisten with moisture. The only light is from a narrow window near the ceiling. On the other side of the tiny room a flight of wooden stairs leads to the door at the top. Gemma is sitting on the bottom step. I sag with relief.

'Thank goodness. You're safe,' I say. My voice is raspy, my throat parched. 'Is there any water in here?'

Gemma looks up. 'Water?' She frowns, as if I'm talking in a foreign language.

'Or something else to drink.' With difficulty, I wriggle to a seated position. I've lost all sensation in my arms, which is almost worse than the pain in my head and my ribs. I scan the cellar looking for a water bottle, a cup, anything. But it is empty apart from the threadbare blanket. The bitch didn't even leave us any water.

'Where did she go?' I hiss.

Gemma looks at me blankly. 'Who?'

'Ingrid Kelly. Where is she?'

Gemma shrugs, as if Ingrid's whereabouts are of no consequence, when they so clearly are. The woman trapped us in this tiny room for a reason. I understand that she might want to hurt me to get at Freddie, but why take Gemma too? It doesn't make any sense.

'Did she tie you up too?' When she doesn't answer, I squint at her. She's clasping her hands round her knees. 'Gemma,' I say urgently. 'If you help me out of my ties we can see if we can kick down the door. If not, there's always the window—'

'Shut up,' Gemma says.

'With your help I might be able to—'

'I said shut the fuck up!'

I recoil as though she's slapped me in the face.

'I'm sorry. I know it's stressful, being locked up like this. But we need to stay calm.'

'How many times do I need to spell it out to you, you stupid cow? Shut up!'

I blink. Tears threaten. Why is Gemma being so horrible to me? Perhaps she blames me for walking straight into Ingrid's trap, but how was I supposed to know? And, after all, wasn't it Gemma who wanted to come here?

She picks something up from the floor beside her feet. I can't tell what it is from here. 'Gem, please, help untie me. We need to get out of here before Ingrid comes back.'

She laughs then, a brittle sound that pings off all four walls of the tiny room like a ricocheting bullet. 'Ingrid is not coming back.'

I'm hit by a wave of dizziness. 'But she has to. How else are we supposed to get out of here?'

Finally, Gemma turns to face me and I see that the thing she has in her hand is a kitchen knife. Her gaze is steady. 'You don't get it, do you?'

'Get what?'

'Ingrid's not coming back because she was never here in the first place.'

61

FREDDIE

NOW

Ingrid has a long stride and doesn't hang about. She's on a late lunch, she tells me, as we march along the pavement towards Church Lane. So much for Alex's theory that Ingrid broke into the house today.

If Ingrid didn't, who did?

I'm struck by an unwelcome thought. Alex's behaviour has become increasingly erratic over the past few days. She wouldn't have damaged the photos herself, would she? What about the anonymous letters, the tip-off to the *Daily Post* and the slashed brake cable? Could it be a twisted cry for help?

Even as I tell myself this is ridiculous, I can't help feeling I'm missing something crucial.

I stop and turn to Ingrid. 'Megan said a woman tried to talk to her at school the other day. Was it you?'

She stops, too, and fiddles with the strap of her handbag. 'I saw the story in the *Post* saying you were back and I wanted to check it was true.'

My eyes widen a fraction. I wouldn't have pegged Ingrid as a *Daily Post* reader. Reading my mind, she explains, 'I set up a Google alert for your name.' She frowns. 'I hope I didn't upset her.'

I shake my head. We set off again, and before long we're turning into Ingrid's street. She holds the gate open so I can push Dylan's buggy through, then darts round me to unlock the door.

'You can leave the buggy in the porch.'

I lift Dylan onto my hip. He looks around with wide eyes, grabbing a fistful of my jumper and holding on tight.

'Come with me,' Ingrid says. 'There's someone I want you to meet.'

I follow her along a wide hallway with grab rails on the whitewashed walls and light oak laminate flooring. The hallway leads into a kitchen at the back of the house. Sitting at the kitchen table, a laptop open in front of her, is a teenage girl with a silver nose ring and a pink pixie cut.

'Saffy, look who's come to see you.'

The girl looks up from her computer and smiles shyly. 'Hello, Doctor Harris. Mum texted to say you were on your way.'

Saffy? I gape. My brain is refusing to join the dots. I look to Ingrid for help.

'You look as though you've seen a ghost,' Ingrid remarks. 'I'll make us all a cup of tea, shall I? Would you like some juice and a biscuit?' she asks Dylan.

He nods, then, spotting an aquarium on the other side of the room, points and says, 'Fishes!'

'You can have a look at them if you like. See if you can find Nemo,' Ingrid tells him.

I set Dylan on the floor, pull out a chair and sit down heavily. Everything I thought I knew has been upended. The last time I saw Saffy – Sapphire – she was being wheeled into inten-sive care, her slender body in the grip of a deadly infection. Yet here she is, sitting across the table from me, watching me with a faint trace of amusement on her face.

'I... I thought you were dead,' I manage finally.

She grins. 'As you can see, I'm very much alive.'

62

ALEX

NOW

I frown uncertainly. Maybe Gemma hit her head on the way down to the cellar because she's not talking any sense. Of course Ingrid was here. Otherwise, who locked us in this hellhole?

Gemma flicks the knife with her wrist, then points it at me. 'Never satisfied, are you?'

'What?'

'Always moaning about your lot. Poor Alex, you're so hard done by I really don't know how you cope.'

Her voice oozes sarcasm. Gemma has always had a tendency to say what she thinks, but this is on another scale.

'Gemma, I—'

'It's not fair, you having both of them.'

'Both of who?'

'Freddie and Carter. One I could have handled, but not both. It's greedy, Alex. And greed is one of the seven deadly sins. D'you know how sinners were punished for their greed in biblical times?' She doesn't wait for an answer. 'They were boiled alive in oil for all eternity. Not very practical these days, though. Unfortunately.'

My head spins. What is she trying to say?

'All I ever wanted was a husband and a family. Why should you get to have two? It's selfish. *You're* selfish. And d'you know what pisses me off most of all? You wouldn't have met either of them if it wasn't for me.'

'I'm sorry, Gem. I had no idea you felt this way.'

'Of course you didn't.' She snorts with derision. 'Always too busy wrapped up in your own perfect life.'

'It isn't perfect! I was on my own for *seven years* after Freddie walked out.'

'You weren't on your own. You had the girls, you had your house and you had me at your beck and call. I was the one with nothing, no one.'

'You dated,' I remind her, because she was always having flings with men she met online. True, these affairs never lasted very long. Gemma would fall head over heels, talking about little else for weeks. Every text, phone call and date would be analysed for hours. She bought wedding magazines and scoured the property sites looking for her dream home. I once caught her looking at nursery schools. When I joked it was a bit premature – she'd only been dating this particular guy for a couple of weeks – she'd stormed out of the room.

Then, just as quickly as it had started, the relationship would go quiet. Gemma would voice misgivings. The guy was a workaholic or he was too controlling or too laid-back. Too needy or too high-handed. I could never work out whether Gemma's dates had lost their shine or they'd tired of her. Sometimes I wondered if they could smell her desperation and beat a hasty retreat before she could tie them down.

I was always there to pick up the pieces, and after a few days Gem would announce she was over men and happily single... until the next one came along and the cycle would start all over again.

'You mean I shagged them. But no one ever stuck around, did they? They took what they wanted and they fucked off, the bastards. Even Carter wouldn't give me the scraps from his table by the end.'

'Carter loves you. So does Freddie. We all do. You're our family.'

It's the wrong thing to say. Gemma's face twists in fury. 'Don't patronise me, Alex. You don't love me, you use me.' She puts on a sing-song voice, mimicking me. '"Oh, Gem, I don't suppose you could pick the girls up from school? Oh, and while you're at it, you wouldn't mind looking after them while I go to some fancy gastropub with your ex-boyfriend?" I'm not your unpaid babysitter, you self-serving bitch.'

Her words sting but it's the venom in her voice that hurts most.

'So why do it?' I ask her, dazed.

'Because I don't have anyone else.' For a second, a look of desolation sweeps across her face, but the fury is soon back and her eyes flash at me. 'I don't have anybody, thanks to *you*.'

I stare at her, lost for words.

'Carter was mine first. He wasn't yours to take,' Gemma spits.

'If anyone took him from you it was Elizabeth, not me.'

Her eyes narrow. 'I was happy to wait for him. But, oh no, as soon as he was back you were inviting him over for cosy Sunday lunches and dragging him along on family outings. You practically threw yourself at him. It was embarrassing.'

'Carter is Erin's godfather and my friend. Of course I invited him over.'

'You didn't have to make him fall in love with you.'

'I didn't mean to! And you were with that footballer, Ryan. You gave me your blessing.'

'And what about poor Freddie?' Gemma says, as if I haven't spoken. 'He worshipped the ground you walked on. How could you do that to him?'

'Poor Freddie?' Anger sparks deep inside me. Sparks, then flares. 'Freddie walked out on us, remember. He didn't love us. He wouldn't have left if he did.'

'There you go again, playing the victim. But it's your fault he went, Alex. You told him you were done.'

Just like that, the spark of anger flickers and dies and I stare at her with growing horror. 'How do you know that?'

She smirks. 'He told me.'

'When?'

'The night he left. He came straight to mine, you see. He was in a state because you'd all but kicked him out.' A smile creeps across her face and my stomach swoops, because I can tell from her expression what happened next.

How could she?

63

FREDDIE

NOW

'She's a fighter, is Saffy.'

Ingrid gives Dylan a beaker of juice and a couple of chocolate biscuits, then sets three mugs on the table and joins us.

She's a fighter, is Saffy. I can't tear my eyes away from the
girl who has haunted my thoughts for a decade. She is a fighter
– and she's *alive*. Why didn't anyone tell me? Of course, I know
the answer: no one knew where I was. If I hadn't fled to the Isle
of Lewis, I might have found out. But up there, I avoided the
news, ignored the papers and cut myself off from everyone and
everything. And, now that I'm back, Alex, Carter and Gemma
must have assumed I already knew.

The smile has slipped from Ingrid's face. 'Saffy spent over a
month in an induced coma in the paediatric intensive care unit.'

'Septic shock?'

Ingrid nods. 'Her doctors said it could have gone either way.
Her blood pressure was so low her kidneys and liver were
starting to fail.'

'But they didn't, Mum.' Saffy shoots me a worried look.

'No, they didn't,' Ingrid agrees. 'At the end of the fourth week she started showing signs of improvement, and two weeks after that, she was moved back onto Dolphin Ward.'

'I can't remember most of it,' Saffy says. 'And I wouldn't have Jake if it wasn't for the sepsis.'

'Who's Jake, a boy you met in hospital?'

Saffy peals with laughter and lifts the right leg of her jeans, revealing a prosthetic limb.

'You lost your leg?'

'Just below the knee.'

'I'm so, so sorry.'

'Don't be. You should have seen it. It was gross. All black and dried up like the leg of an Egyptian mummy. I was glad when they cut it off.'

'Saffy,' Ingrid chides. 'Doctor Harris doesn't want to hear about that.'

'Call me Freddie, please,' I say weakly.

'This isn't Jake, by the way,' Saffy says, tapping the prosthetic leg. She opens her laptop, types away, then swivels it round to face me. '*This* is Jake,' she says, pointing at the screen.

I stare at a photo of a lithe, pink-haired girl on a running track, arms pumping, her face stretched with exertion. On her right leg is a sleek prosthetic blade.

'That was the one hundred metres final at the English Championships,' Saffy tells me. 'I ran sub-thirteen seconds.'

'And picked up another gold medal,' her mum says, pointing to an old Welsh dresser I hadn't noticed when I came into the room. It is draped with trophies and medals. 'Saffy's hoping to make the team for the 2028 Paralympics.'

'That's... that's—' I'm momentarily lost for words. The girl I thought was dead, the girl I thought I had, through my own negligence, killed, is an elite athlete on course to compete in the Los Angeles Olympics. It's... it's blowing my mind. 'Amazing,' I finish lamely.

Saffy grins again, then collects her laptop and a couple of textbooks from the table. 'It was nice to see you, Doctor Harris, but my exams start in a couple of weeks and I need to squeeze in a couple of hours' revision before training later.'

'Saffy wants to be a doctor,' Ingrid says proudly. 'She's already looking at medical schools, aren't you, love?'

'Yeah, well, I wouldn't be here if it wasn't for you guys,' Saffy says, a blush creeping up her neck.

My own cheeks are burning. I didn't save Saffy's life. She probably wouldn't have lost her leg if I'd done my job properly. She turns at the door and gives me a little wave, then disappears into the hallway.

I drop my head into my hands and groan softly.

'I thought you'd be pleased to see her doing so well,' Ingrid says.

I look up. 'I am. Of course I am. I've spent the last ten years thinking she was dead.'

'Is that why you disappeared?'

'It was one of the reasons, yes. I blamed myself for not spotting the sepsis sooner.' I meet her eye. 'So did you, if you remember.'

'I did,' Ingrid says. 'I thought you were nice but incompetent. Sorry,' she adds.

'Don't be. With sepsis, every hour counts. If I'd recognised Saffy's symptoms and prescribed antibiotics sooner she wouldn't have ended up in intensive care.'

'I think you're being too hard on yourself. I know now you did your best.' Ingrid takes a sip of tea and regards me. 'Saffy organised a sponsored walk at school to raise money for Dolphin Ward at Easter. When we took the giant cheque to the hospital we presented it to Sister Adebayo.'

'Simi's still there?' I say, unable to hide my surprise. The senior staff nurse was in her mid-fifties when I worked on Dolphin Ward. I'd assumed she would have retired by now.

'She is. She was so pleased to see Saffy. We were about to leave when she asked if I had a minute. I presumed she was going to tell me what the money Saffy and her friends raised would be spent on, but it wasn't that. It wasn't that at all. She wanted to tell me what really happened to Saffy while she was on Dolphin Ward. There was another doctor, wasn't there? A registrar? I believe he's now the consultant on the ward.'

I nod. She's talking about Carter. 'Doctor Petersen.'

'That's right. He asked one of the nurses to take bloods the night Saffy was admitted. They were never done.'

'What?'

'Sister Adebayo says the nurse who was supposed to take them has a reputation for being lax.'

My head jerks up. 'Which nurse?'

'Gemma Lawrence,' Ingrid says. 'It wasn't the first time she hadn't done as she'd been asked, apparently.'

'Why was Simi telling you this now?'

'She's about to retire and said she wanted me to know the truth. She said it had been weighing on her mind. I'd made an official complaint about you and the care Saffy received on Dolphin Ward at the time, you see.'

I'm not surprised. I had thought as much.

'The trust investigated and my complaint wasn't upheld. I could have asked for an independent review but by then Saffy was out of the woods and I wanted to be able to concentrate on her rehabilitation. If Gemma Lawrence had done the blood tests when she was asked, Saffy would have been given antibiotics a whole twenty-four hours earlier. But that's not all. Doctor Petersen covered up for her.'

I frown. Carter always had a tendency to play fast and loose with the truth, especially where women were concerned. But his career meant everything to him. Why risk it for Gemma?

'Are you sure?'

'Simi said he didn't have a choice. They were having an

affair. Simi overheard Gemma threatening to tell HR if Doctor Petersen didn't help her out.'

'Simi told you that?'

Ingrid nods. 'If that had come out at the time they could have both lost their jobs. But Doctor Petersen was an experienced registrar and everyone deferred to him. And Saffy lived. Perhaps if she hadn't things might have been different. Someone might have spoken out. I've been trying to tell your wife this for the last few weeks, then when I heard you were back—'

'Wait,' I interject. 'Did you send Alex those anonymous letters?'

Ingrid grimaces. 'It was a bit cloak and dagger, I know, but I didn't want to alert Gemma. I know she and your wife are close friends. I hoped the letters might prompt your wife to look into everything that happened – or didn't happen – on Dolphin Ward when Saffy was there.'

'Are you going to take this new evidence to the trust?'

Ingrid stares out of the glazed patio doors to the small courtyard garden at the back of the house. 'I don't think so. I spent too long eaten up with anger when I have so much to be thankful for. It's the ward staff's responsibility to report her if they don't think she's doing her job properly, not mine. But there is something else,' Ingrid says. 'Something you can do for me.'

'Name it.'

'I want you to stop blaming yourself for what happened to Saffy. You've seen her. She's a happy, well-adjusted kid who embraces every moment, and that's because of what happened to her, not in spite of it. Do you see?'

I feel a lightness come over me, a lightness I haven't felt for years.

'Thank you. I think I do.'

64

ALEX

NOW

'Don't tell me,' I snarl. 'You found a way to console him.'

Gemma smirks. 'For a buttoned-up kinda guy he's pretty hot between the sheets.'

'Jesus, Gemma, how could you?'

'You didn't want him any more, remember?'

'I had postnatal depression! I was barely coping, and Freddie, he was always at work, too busy saving other children's lives when I needed him at home to help me look after ours. I might have had a go at him but that didn't mean I didn't love him! I didn't want him to leave!'

'Other women seem to manage,' Gemma says scornfully.

'Yes, well, I never claimed to be perfect.'

She jumps to her feet, clearly bored with the conversation.

'Get up,' she orders me.

'Where are we going?' I ask, my voice reedy.

'For a walk.' She waves the knife in my face. 'Come on, I haven't got all day.'

'Gemma, please, this is insane,' I plead, still rooted to the spot. 'Whatever happened between you and Freddie is water under the bridge. I forgive you. So can we please stop this?'

'Up the stairs,' Gemma barks.

Defeated, I struggle to my feet, arms and legs protesting. As I turn and hobble across the room, my hands still fastened behind me, I can feel the tip of the kitchen knife pressing into the small of my back. I itch to grab it, but what's the point? The blade would cut my fingers to shreds.

At the top of the stairs Gemma reaches past me and opens the door. It wasn't even locked. I step into the kitchen. Suddenly, I can smell freshly baked chocolate brownies. I turn to Gemma. 'I know this place. It's your Great-Auntie Heather's. Where is she?'

'In a home.'

I look around. I *knew* the house seemed familiar. Gemma brought me here once after school. We must have been about twelve. Heather baked a tray of brownies and gave us each a five-pound note. Then, she'd sent us to the end of her neatly tended garden to pick runner beans from the vegetable patch. She seemed ancient thirty years ago. She must be in her late nineties now.

'You didn't tell me,' I say. Gemma doesn't answer. She is pulling something from a carrier bag. It's a navy padded coat I bought in the sales a couple of years ago. Carter detested it on sight, said it made me look like the Marshmallow Man in *Ghostbusters*, but I didn't care. It kept me warm on the school run and when I walked Fleming.

'Put it on,' Gemma instructs.

'I can't. My hands are still tied.'

She grabs my shoulder and spins me round, then saws at the plastic ties around my wrists, releasing them. As blood flows back into my arms, the pins and needles return. I flex my fingers, wincing as the pain sharpens. Gemma thrusts the coat into my hands.

'Where are we going?' I ask again. My aching shoulders scream in agony as I shrug it on.

'For a walk. I told you.' She yanks something else from the bag. It's Fleming's ball launcher. She hands it to me, then opens the door to the hallway and Fleming pads out, his tail wagging.

'Hey, boy,' I cry, and he woofs with pleasure, his nails clicking on the lino floor as he lumbers over to me. Gemma watches dispassionately as I fall to my knees and bury my face in his fur. She slips her own coat on, clips Fleming's lead on his collar and hands it to me, before picking up the ball launcher and unlocking the back door.

I follow her out into the garden, surprised that the day has slipped into dusk. The grass in Heather's once-pristine lawn is now knee-high and through the gloom, I can just make out the overgrown borders and tangle of brambles where Gemma and I once picked runner beans. For some inexplicable reason, the sight of it makes me want to cry.

'Hurry up,' Gemma barks, and I clump after her. She opens the gate at the end of the garden and stands aside to let me through. She can't look me in the eye. Instead, she drums her fingers on the fence, agitation radiating from her in waves.

She sets off again, heading towards the river, and I follow obediently on wobbly legs. Running isn't an option – she's still clutching the knife – but maybe if I keep her calm, a chance to get away will present itself. It's all I can hope for.

The sound of the river is louder now. We can only be a few feet from the path, which is popular with joggers and dog walkers. I used to walk Fleming along here when he was younger. In summer the place is alive with dragonflies and moorhens. Once I even spied the metallic blue glint of a kingfisher in the branches of a tree on the other side of the bank.

A bramble catches my foot and I stumble, almost losing my balance. Fleming thrusts a wet nose into my hand. He was always Freddie's dog – until the day Freddie disappeared.

Then, he became my shadow, never leaving my side. Evenings were spent at my feet or resting his chin on my lap as I stared, mindlessly, at the TV. He slept sprawled across our bed, filling the space Freddie had left. It was as if he was telling me, by his constant presence, that he would never leave me.

It hits me with the force of a gut-punch that Fleming won't be here forever. He's twelve now, a good age for a retriever. His eyes are cloudy with cataracts and his hips are beginning to go, his creaky joints thickened by arthritis. Desolation sweeps through me. How will I cope without him? He doesn't care that my hair needs a wash or I haven't bothered with any make-up. He loves me unconditionally. I reach down to ruffle his ear.

'Good dog. Good boy,' I whisper.

We reach the path and Gemma stops. 'Peaceful, isn't it?' she says, waving an arm at the river. In summer, it takes its time as it meanders gently downstream, but after a wet spring it's swollen and impatient to reach the sea. A gushing, surging force of nature. It's about as far from peaceful as it's possible to get.

The wind whips my hair across my face and I shiver. 'Why did you bring me here, Gemma?'

65

FREDDIE

NOW

Megan seems unfazed to see me waiting for her at the school gates instead of Alex and she chatters about her day as we walk home.

'Bella's granny has bought her a hamster for her birthday and she's called it Taylor, because Bella is also a Swiftie, though not as big a Swiftie as me. She's never seen her live like I have, for example.' Megan hums a few bars of 'Look What You Made Me Do'. 'And I got ten out of ten in my spelling test and won a house point, which is cool, because it means we're now joint first with the Aztecs.' We've reached the bottom of our street when she tugs my sleeve. 'Daddy? I just remembered. Can we go past the Co-op? Mrs Bower says we need marshmallows for forest school tomorrow.'

By the time we've stopped off at the shop and bought marshmallows and some chocolate buttons for after tea, it's almost four o'clock and Erin is already home.

The two girls slouch in front of the TV and I take Dylan upstairs to change his nappy. 'Dadadadadada,' Dylan babbles as

I find wipes and cream. I haven't changed a nappy for a decade, but it's like riding a bike; once learnt, never forgotten.

I would have loved a son, but a decision made on the side of the bypass a decade ago put paid to that.

Before I'm gripped by sorrow for the life I have missed, I lift Dylan to his feet. 'There you go, kiddo.'

I'm in a strange mood. Seeing Saffy has thrown everything I thought I knew on its head. The guilt is still there, it always will be, because whatever Gemma and Carter did or didn't do, I know that if I'd acted sooner Saffy wouldn't have lost her leg. But to see her not just alive but thriving is making me re-examine every decision I've made in the last ten years.

I shouldn't have given up on my marriage without a fight. I know that now. I certainly should never have rocked up at Gemma's, drunk on beer and self-pity. And I should have listened to Tomas, the kind Lithuanian lorry driver who picked me up – both literally and metaphorically – when I was at rock bottom. Tomas told me not to stay away forever. Perhaps if I'd heeded his advice, I would be changing my own son's nappy.

My ancient Nokia pings and I pull it out of my back pocket. It's a text from Alex.

Can I take you up on your offer to make the kids' supper? Bumped into a friend on the way home from the park and she's talked me into going for a drink. Alex.

I raise an eyebrow. Alex always used to have a thing against calling dinner supper because she said it was pretentious. I didn't have her down as a social climber but a lot changes in ten years. The main thing is she's getting a well-deserved break. I tap back a reply.

Of course. You have fun. We'll see you later.

Back downstairs, I hunt through the fridge and kitchen cupboards, assembling a packet of macaroni, a block of cheese and a carton of milk. Macaroni cheese was one of my staple meals when I lived in Scotland. It was cheap, easy and carb-heavy; the perfect fuel for long days on the estate.

The kids have demolished their dinner and have disappeared upstairs when the front door clicks open and Carter arrives home from work. The smell of antiseptic clings to his clothes, transporting me straight back to Dolphin Ward.

'Where's Alex?' he asks.

'Having a drink with a friend.'

He frowns. 'What friend?'

'I don't know, she didn't say.'

'Why didn't she tell me?'

'Because she knew you'd be either at work or in the car. Don't sweat it. It'll do her good.'

Carter's eyes narrow to slits. 'You're not her husband any more, mate.'

'I know I'm not. I'm just saying she's had a tough week. And before you say anything, I know that's my fault.'

'You reckon?' He gives a hollow laugh. 'Tell me, did you ever stop to think how Alex would feel before you turned up on our doorstep after ten years like nothing happened? Did you not realise it would throw her for a loop?'

'I—'

'She's struggling, man. She's trying to hold it together for the kids, but she's hanging by a thread.'

'I know, I—'

'Do you? Do you really? Because I don't think you do. I picked up the pieces when you walked out. She was broken. You broke her. But she put herself back together and she's doing great. *We're* doing great.' He pauses, his lips compressed. 'Well, we were till you showed up again.'

'I know, and I'm sorry,' I begin, but Carter cuts across me.

'Another thing. How long exactly are you planning on staying?'

'Um, I don't know. But Alex said it was fine for me to be here.'

'Alex is a people pleaser,' Carter growls. 'She doesn't want to hurt your feelings. I, on the other hand, couldn't give a fuck. You've outstayed your welcome, mate. You need to go.'

'Now?' I run a hand through my hair, wondering if I can scrape together enough money for a night in a cheap hotel.

Carter looks as if he's about to say something, then exhales loudly. 'Not this minute. Alex would probably kill me for turfing you out behind her back. But you can't stay here forever, OK? You need an exit plan.'

I nod, then before I can stop myself, blurt, 'You didn't tell me Sapphire Kelly survived.'

Carter makes a beeline for the fridge, pulls out two bottles of Budweiser and offers me one. I shake my head.

He twists the top off his own bottle, drinks deeply, then regards me warily. 'I thought you knew.'

'How was I supposed to know? Telepathy?'

His grip on the neck of the beer bottle tightens. 'How, exactly, was I supposed to tell you? You'd fucked off, if you remember. Anyway, it was all over the news. I know Lewis is remote, but it's not a media blackout zone.'

'I never watched the news,' I say.

'So how did you find out?'

'I went to see her mother.'

'Ingrid Kelly?' Carter pulls a face. 'Why?'

'Because Alex is convinced she's behind the crazy stuff that's been happening.' I clear the table, slamming plates into the dishwasher with more force than necessary. But I'm just so damn *angry*. 'Turns out she did send those letters.' I meet Carter's eye. 'She knows you covered up for Gemma back then.'

Carter stiffens and his gaze flicks to the door, then back to me. 'What's she going to do about it?'

'Nothing,' I admit. 'But if Sapphire had died it would have been a different story. Why d'you do it, mate? Why put your career on the line for Gemma?'

Carter takes another slug of his beer, then rubs his chin. 'Because she threatened to tell HR that I'd covered up for her before.'

'Jesus, Carter. Does Alex know about this?'

He nods. 'Of course. We don't have secrets. And before you get on your high horse, it was for minor stuff. Sending over late blood samples and the odd medication that went unlogged. Gemma would blame it on the system and I let it slide because... well, you know how persuasive she can be.'

I do. And that's the problem. How can I take the moral high ground when I slept with my wife's best friend, then walked out on my family? I can't. I meet Carter's gaze and a flicker of understanding passes between us.

'Actually,' I say, 'I will have that beer.'

66

ALEX

NOW

'Did you know that falling into cold water causes an involuntary gasp reflex?' Gemma says conversationally, as if I haven't spoken. 'If you inhale water, you can drown in seconds. It's called cold water shock.' She still can't meet my eye. 'So, we should be careful, this close to the river.'

She takes something from her pocket and pulls it onto her head. At first I think it must be a hat, but then she fiddles with it and suddenly a light is shining right into my face, so bright I am momentarily blinded. As she turns back to the river the beam of the head torch picks out the muddy riverbank, which slopes steeply down to the water.

'Wouldn't it be awful if you were to slip into the river while you were taking dear old Fleming for a walk?' she continues. 'I can see the headlines now: *Body of tragic mum found in river.* Imagine how heartbroken both your husbands would be.'

Despite the gloom of the evening, I realise I'm seeing Gemma clearly for the first time in years, perhaps ever. Things are falling into place. The way she swans around my house like she owns it. The way she monopolises the girls, winning their affections with treats and days out. The way she flutters her eyelashes at Carter when she thinks I'm not looking. She is often sharp with me, but I've always brushed it off, telling myself she was a typical Virgo, only critical because she was a perfectionist.

Now I can see she has always wanted the one thing she didn't have. A husband. A family. *My* husband. *My* family.

Even so, I want her to spell it out.

'What are you going to do to me?'

She sighs. 'I want you out of the picture, Alex. You stole the life I was supposed to have. Now it's my turn to live it.'

'You're going to push me into the river and watch me drown?'

'Really, when you say it like that it sounds so... calculating. You're my best friend. I love you.'

'This isn't love,' I snap. 'You tricked me into coming here, then you locked me in a bloody cellar!'

'I needed you to listen to me.' Gemma's voice rises. 'No one ever listens to me. I'm just good old Gemma, always available, never appreciated. Admit it, Alex, you've been taking advantage of me for years.'

I'm seized by doubt. Is she right? Have I taken her for granted? It's true she kept me going when Freddie left. She had an uncanny knack of knowing when I was struggling with the demands of looking after two small children and would turn up on the doorstep with wine and a shoulder to cry on. She'd pour me a glass and run me a bath and when I emerged from the steam-filled bathroom, the girls would be fast asleep and she'd be fixing us something lovely to eat.

But I repaid her in kind, listening to her for hours as she moaned about work or her disastrous love life. I invited her over for family barbecues and Sunday lunches. It was an unwritten rule that she spent every Easter and Christmas with us. But that's what friends do, isn't it? They are there for each other through thick and thin.

No, I think, indignantly. She's lost her grip on reality. Our friendship was always a two-way street. I'm about to tell her as much when I realise she is already talking.

'You need to be taught a lesson. That's why we're here. Indulge me for a moment and picture the scene. You're taking Fleming for a walk when the poor old boy loses his footing and slips into the water. You pull off your coat and boots and dive in after him. You don't think twice, because you love that dog. Fleming clambers out a hundred yards downstream, whereas you...' She pauses. 'Well, you aren't so lucky. Such a shame you were never a strong swimmer.'

Gemma pats her leg and calls Fleming over. He trots towards her obediently, his lead slipping through my fingers. Before I can react, she grabs his collar and unclips the lead. I watch, horrified, as she shoves him towards the water. He teeters for a moment, his claws scrabbling in the mud as he desperately tries to find a foothold. But the bank is too steep, too slippery. I scream as my poor dog topples into the river and disappears from sight.

'You bitch!' I cry, turning to Gemma, but she is already walking away. I wheel back to the river. Fleming is trying to reach me but his frantic splashes are growing weaker. I freeze. I know it's madness to jump in after him and common sense yells at me to call for help. But Gemma must have my phone, and the riverbank is deserted. There is no one else. Just then, Fleming's head bobs beneath the surface and instinct takes over.

I yank off my coat and kick off my boots. The muddy bank squelches under my feet. Taking a deep breath, I jump into the river.

67

ALEX

NOW

The shock of the icy water takes my breath away, and I'm gripped by panic as I gasp and splutter. I concentrate every fibre of my being on keeping my head above water, letting the current pull me downstream towards Fleming. The sound of the river is deafening, a terrifying roar that blocks everything else out.

I kick out and, momentarily, the gap closes between us. But then Fleming is swept away again, and the brief hope I'd had that I might be able to save him disappears. In its place arrives the certainty that we are both going to die.

Cold. It is so cold. My teeth start to chatter, the sound like the staccato drumming of a woodpecker as it hammers its bill into an old tree. My limbs are heavy, dragging me down into the river's murky depths. Water rolls over my head and, panicking, I swallow a mouthful, gagging and spluttering as my lungs protest and my vision blurs.

For a second, my feet touch the riverbed. It gives me a

chance to catch my breath and I glance up. Through the gloom I can make out the shape of Gemma standing on the riverbank, watching me. She is as still as a pointer catching a scent. Not a pointer, I think. Dogs are loyal. Gemma has betrayed me in the worst way imaginable. She is a predator, ambushing its prey.

The water picks up momentum and, once again, I'm lifted off my feet and propelled downstream. I look for Fleming as I'm flung about like a piece of flotsam but I can't see him. I let out a howl of anguish, regretting it instantly when more water funnels into my mouth.

Thoughts whirl in my head, fractured and chaotic, as I cough and splutter, but I focus on one. Gemma wants me dead. I need her to think I've drowned.

I picture the river on a bright summer's day, kingfishers flitting through the low-hanging branches, their lapis lazuli plumage shimmering in the sun. There is a bend, I remember, its edges flanked by bulrushes. I can hide in them, play dead if I need to, until she leaves.

The water rushes in my ears as I let the river carry me towards the bend. As I near the looming shadow of the reed bed, I kick out desperately. At first it seems I'm making no progress and the river will sweep me all the way to the sea, but I keep kicking and kicking and then I am grabbing at the reeds' fibrous stalks like I'm clutching at straws.

The sharp tang of rotting vegetation fills my nostrils as I clamp my hands around the reeds and hold on for dear life. Gemma looks tiny from here, a diminutive figure gazing out across the water like a carved mermaid on the prow of a ship. I feel a cough building in my chest and I clap my hand over my mouth to suppress it. I can't risk making a sound. I watch Gemma until she turns and walks away. I'm filled with a cold rage. She is leaving because she thinks I'm dead. How could she do that to me, her oldest friend?

Inch by inch, I pull myself through the reeds, grimacing as the rough stalks cut into my palms. My arms feel like they've been pulled from their sockets when I finally drag myself, coughing and wheezing, onto solid ground.

Every part of my body aches and my lungs are burning, but I force myself to my feet and stumble along the bank, my eyes trained on the river, searching for Fleming. I've almost given up all hope of finding him when I spy his bedraggled form on a shallow beach ahead.

'Fleming!' I cry, and when he doesn't move, hatred burns inside me, raw and visceral. Gemma knew I would jump in after him. She knows me better than I know myself. And she used that knowledge against me so she could steal my life.

I reach the old dog and drop down to my knees beside him. 'Hey, boy.' I hold my breath as I give his shoulder a gentle shake. Tears of relief stream down my face as he lifts his head, his tail thumping weakly on the pebbles. 'Good boy,' I sob as I bury my face in his fur. 'Good boy, good boy, good boy.'

We stay like that until I start to shiver, then, teeth still chattering, I haul myself up and coax Fleming to his feet. At the riverside path I pause. If Gemma has any sense she'll have made herself scarce, but I don't want to take the chance that she's still at Heather's. I don't even want to risk going back for my coat and boots. Instead, I turn left. More houses back onto the river half a mile or so ahead. We can find help there.

Our progress is slow. Walking along the gravel path is like walking on a bed of nails, every stone sending a stab of pain through the soles of my feet. Fleming lumbers beside me, his head low and his tail between his legs.

As I walk, I try to make sense of everything. Gemma has been my best friend since we were eleven. I thought we were closer than sisters, yet I never knew she felt like this. Never realised how deeply she resented me for having a husband, children. A family.

Nor did I realise the lengths she would go to take it all away from me.

She loved Carter, I know that. She was obsessed with him for years. But she can't lay claim to him after giving me her blessing to date him. That's not fair. Anyway, to Carter, she was nothing more than a friend with benefits. I would never have married him otherwise.

I tackled him about it once, just before we got married. I was feeling insecure, worried I was his second choice, but he was quick to reassure me.

'I never led her on, Alex. It was all in her head. If we grabbed lunch in the canteen she considered it a date. If we hooked up she thought we were a couple. Maybe I behaved badly,' he'd said with a shrug. 'But I'm a guy and she was always there, always available.'

Gemma's revelation that she slept with Freddie the night he disappeared has blindsided me. I know he wasn't perfect but I'd always trusted him implicitly. Through his final years at med school, and later, at medical conferences, and even when Carter dragged him off on boozy boys' weekends, I never doubted him. Not once. I knew he would never cheat on me.

Yet he had. *Bastard.* And with Gemma. My best friend. The maid of honour at our wedding, for God's sake. How could he?

Hatred blooms inside me, hot and bitter, as images of them together flood my mind. Her face tilted up towards his, his eyes locked on hers, their limbs entwined... *No!* I push the images away, shocked by the depth of my pain. I thought I'd buried any feelings I had for Freddie years ago, but it's clear I was wrong. So, so wrong.

I still love him.

It shouldn't be possible, not after everything he put me through. But what else is this, this feeling, this sweeping desolation, if not the symptom of a broken heart?

And if I still love Freddie, where does that leave Carter?

Before I can examine this thought, two things happen: Fleming's head snaps up and he starts barking, just as a hooded figure steps out of the undergrowth, right into my path.

68

FREDDIE

NOW

Carter and I are on our fourth bottle of beer when Gemma turns up just after six.

'Look at the two of you, drowning your sorrows,' she chirps, hanging her bag on the back of a chair and looking around. 'Alex still not back?'

I set my bottle on the table. 'Not yet, no.'

'Have the kids been fed?' Gemma asks, rolling up her sleeves.

'Freddie gave them macaroni cheese,' Carter says.

'Where are they now?'

'The girls are upstairs doing their homework. Dylan's in the snug watching *In the Night Garden* before bed.'

Gemma nods. 'Want me to do his bath-time?'

'Yes,' Carter says.

'No,' I chime.

Gemma's laugh sounds forced. 'Make your minds up, guys.' She blows her hair out of her eyes. 'I'll do it. I've barely seen the kids all week. D'you know what Alex was planning for your supper?'

Supper. I frown. 'There's some stuff for a stir-fry in the fridge.'

'Stir-fry it is. Why don't you open a bottle of wine and I'll be as quick as I can.'

Carter pushes his chair back. 'There's a half-decent Rioja in the wine rack. I'm going to take a shower.' He follows Gemma out of the room, leaving me alone.

Before I can change my mind, I dart across to the other side of the table and unzip Gemma's handbag, rifling through the contents. I spy an iPhone lurking under a packet of tissues and pull it out. It's the same model as Alex's, but the screensaver is a picture of Gemma, Erin, Megan and Dylan, taken outside the entrance to London Zoo. Anyone who didn't know them could be forgiven for thinking she's their mum. It's the proprietary way she's gathered them in her arms. Alex probably took the photo. I wonder if she noticed too.

I continue to rummage through the lipsticks and hairbands, compacts and keys and I'm about to give up when I notice a zipped compartment. I give the zip a tug but it's stuck fast. It takes a moment before I realise the teeth have caught on the lining of the bag. Carefully, I tease the fabric free, pull the slider and feel inside the pocket. My fingers close around another phone. I pull it out and stare. This screensaver is a photo of Fleming on a pebbly beach, his tongue lolling and his eyes bright and full of life.

Alex's phone.

My stomach folds in on itself as I thumb the screen, unable to unlock it but knowing what it means: when the text from Alex arrived, Gemma had her phone.

There was no friend. Alex never planned to be late.

And I have no idea where she and Fleming are.

69

ALEX

NOW

My hand flies to my mouth as I stifle a small scream.

The figure steps towards me, one arm raised, and I shrink back. There is a rustle in the bushes and a small dog darts out. Beside me, Fleming's barks fade to a low growl.

'*There* you are!' a gravelly voice exclaims. 'Bloody dog.' The figure turns to me. 'It's my wife's mutt. She's just had a knee replacement so I'm having to walk him, and the damn thing keeps disappearing. Wilf, sit. SIT!' The dog, a chocolate-brown springer spaniel, ignores him and rushes up to Fleming, his plumy tail wagging. 'Sorry, I must have frightened the living daylights out of you, jumping out of the bushes in front of you like that.'

I keep my distance, one hand on Fleming's collar, aware there is no one else around. The man could be anyone. I force a smile, trying to hide my unease.

'It's all right. I'm fine,' I say, even though my heart is pounding and my legs are trembling. I try not to stare as he peels off the hood of his anorak to reveal a weather-beaten face, his bushy eyebrows raised in concern. He must be in his late eighties, but his back is ramrod straight, and his voice, though gruff, is kind.

He doesn't look dangerous, in fact he reminds me of my grandad, and my heart rate slowly returns to normal.

He looks me up and down and frowns.

'You're soaking wet. I know wild swimming's all the rage, but this part of the river really isn't safe.'

'I... I fell in,' I admit. 'Well, Fleming fell in, and I jumped in to rescue him.' I'm shivering again. 'I know you're not supposed to, but he's old and I... I—' I look down at the retriever, who is graciously tolerating a thorough inspection by Wilf the spaniel.

'You're going to freeze to death if you're not careful. I'll walk you to your car. Where are you parked?'

'I'm... I'm not. I was going to call my husband, but I've lost my phone.' I pat my pockets for effect and the man's gaze drops to my sock-clad feet, which are sodden and covered in mud.

'Right, Wilf,' the man says, clipping a lead onto the spaniel's collar, 'we are going to take this young lady home and get her warmed up.' He smiles. 'We're only round the corner. Peggy'll stick the kettle on while you phone your husband.'

I thank him, relieved when he sets off in the opposite direction to Gemma's Great-Auntie Heather's. He tells me his name is Bernard and he and Peggy moved to their bungalow when he retired from his job as a gas engineer twenty years ago. They have four sons, eleven grandchildren and four great-grandchildren. Christmas, he says with a chuckle, is mayhem.

'And you?' he asks. We've reached the outskirts of a village, the scrub to our right giving way to a long row of weathered fence panels. 'Do you have children?'

'Three. Two girls and a boy. Fourteen, ten and nearly two.'

'Grand,' Bernard says. He stops and points to a gate. 'This is us.'

A security light snaps on and I blink as I follow him through the gate and up a curved path to the back door of a chalet-style bungalow.

'Peggy!' he calls, as he kicks off his wellies and ushers me into the house. 'I've found a waif and stray.' I bend down to pull off my socks, and, not knowing what to do with them, shove them into the pockets of my jeans, and follow Bernard into the front room.

A white-haired woman – Peggy, I presume – is ensconced in an armchair in front of a gas fire, watching a quiz show on the television. One leg rests on a footstool, a wide bandage wrapped around her knee. She blips the remote control and the TV falls silent.

'Hello, love,' she says, bright eyes as sharp as a blackbird's. 'What happened to you?'

I try to imagine her reaction if I told her the truth: that my best friend has just attempted to kill me because she wants to steal my life. Why would she believe me when I can barely believe it myself?

'She fell into the river trying to rescue her dog. She needs to call her husband for a lift home.' Bernard hands me a towel, then fetches the phone from a dark oak sideboard. I give my hair a quick dry, then squat down and do my best to dry Fleming. The smell of wet dog pervades the small room and I apologise.

'Don't be silly, love.' Peggy swings her leg off the stool and slowly pulls herself to her feet. She picks up the sticks propped against her armchair. 'You sit here by the fire and I'll make a cuppa.'

Alone in the room, I debate who to call: Carter, or Freddie?

Suddenly, it is so much more than a simple phone call. It's about who I want to spend the rest of my life with. Who I want to grow old with.

Freddie, my first love. Funny, steadfast, patient. A kind man who never cared if my hair needed a wash or my jeans were too tight. Loyal and loving. Safe. But safe hadn't kept me company during those long years I was on my own. And he betrayed me...

Carter gave me a second chance at happiness. Driven, impatient, exciting. Being with him is like riding a roller coaster, and I'm not sure I'm ready to step off. But does he really love me?

Who should I choose?

Think. *Think.*

I stare at the keypad, unconsciously weighing the phone in the palm of my hand. Along the hallway a kettle whistles. Peggy and Bernard will be back soon. I don't have long.

Freddie or Carter?

I reach a decision and dial.

70

FREDDIE

NOW

I grip Alex's phone and tramp upstairs, clutching the banister with my other hand because my legs feel oddly weak. Megan's door is ajar and I poke my head around it. She's sitting cross-legged on the floor, reading her school copy of *The Railway Children*.

'Everything OK?' I ask.

Her face is stricken. 'Their daddy's disappeared.'

Oh, the irony, I think. 'Keep reading, poppet.'

'Does he come home in the end?'

'We all come home in the end.' I force a smile. 'Another half an hour, then it's time to get ready for bed, OK?'

'OK, Daddy.'

'Sleep tight, angel.'

Megan nods and goes back to her book.

Erin is bent over her desk, her head buried in a maths textbook. She looks up when she hears the door open. 'How do you make seven an even number?' she asks.

'Um, I don't know.' I scratch my chin, realising she's feeding me a line. 'How *do* you make seven an even number?'

'Just take away the "s"!' She giggles, then sighs. 'Seriously, though, I'd like to give the guy who invented algebra a piece of my mind. It does my head in.'

'Erin,' I begin. I want to ask her if Gemma ever oversteps the mark, if she is aware her mum's best friend has been winding her way into their lives like bindweed for years, but I don't because it wouldn't be fair. I sigh. 'Doesn't matter. Don't stay up too late, OK?'

She nods and turns back to her homework. I cross the landing to the bathroom. I hesitate outside, cocking my head to listen. Gemma is singing to Dylan. It's a lullaby, one I haven't heard for years and, inexplicably, the words make my skin crawl.

'Hush, little baby, don't say a word. Mama's going to buy you a mockingbird.'

I steel myself and open the door. Dylan is sitting in the bubble-filled bath, banging two plastic ducks together while Gemma, kneeling beside him, wipes his face with a sponge.

'And if that mockingbird won't sing, Mama's gonna buy you a diamond ring.'

She stops singing and looks round.

'Look who's come to see you, Dyls. Uncle Freddie!'

I hold Alex's phone towards her.

'Why do you have Alex's phone, Gemma?'

'What?'

'I found it in your bag.'

'What were you doing in my bag?'

'Why do you have it?' I repeat.

'She asked me to look after it.'

'Why would she do that?'

Her gaze darts to the door. 'Because she didn't want Carter looking for her on Find My iPhone.'

I frown. 'Why not?'

'Because she was meeting someone.'

'Who?'

'A man, if you must know.' She sits back on her haunches, watching for a reaction.

My eyes bulge. Alex was meeting a *man*?

'I know, right?' Gemma says. 'As if two husbands weren't enough, she's out there chasing another. Never satisfied, is she? Never bloody satisfied.' The bitterness in her voice is unmistakable and something in my brain clicks.

'I don't believe you.'

'Believe what you like.' She turns back to Dylan, her movements slow and deliberate as she runs the sponge over him, but her fingers are trembling and I know I'm right.

'I think you're lying. I think you texted me pretending to be Alex, and you know damn well where she is.'

Gemma's eyes narrow. 'Who cares where she is? We don't need her, do we, Dyls?' She tickles the toddler under the chin and he gurgles with laughter. She starts to talk, her tone conversational but her words are laced with vitriol.

'D'you know, she left Dylan at home alone when he was a baby?' She glances at me with a spiteful smile. 'I came over one morning to find him in his cot and Alex was nowhere to be seen. He was crying his little eyes out, weren't you, darling?' She squeezes Dylan's shoulders and I realise how easily she could push him under the water. I inch closer. 'She'd pissed off and left him. I couldn't believe it. But you'd know all about that, wouldn't you? Runs in the family, doesn't it?'

Dylan has stopped chuckling and he's staring at Gemma with round eyes.

'By the way, I told her we fucked the night you left. Went down like the proverbial lead balloon. She never did like me playing with her toys.' Gemma gives a brittle bark of laughter.

'Where is she, Gemma?' I edge closer still. Dylan's face is

scrunched up. Any minute now he's going to start crying, and I'm worried it might push Gemma over the edge.

'Who cares where the selfish bitch is? She got herself in too deep, didn't she? In more ways than one.' This time Gemma's laugh tips into hysteria. She tightens her grip on Dylan, who whimpers, arching his back as he tries to wriggle away. Before I can reach him, his head clouts the hot tap and he lets out a cry before slipping out of her grasp into the water.

A red bloom unfurls in the bathwater, spiralling out like the petals of a scarlet rose. I lunge forward, pushing Gemma to one side as I reach for Dylan. The toddler is heavy and as slippery as a fish but I pull him from the tub, cradling him in my arms as he coughs and splutters.

'Give me a towel,' I snap at Gemma. After a moment's hesitation, she grabs one from the rail and hands it to me, averting her gaze from the blood seeping into my jeans.

I wrap Dylan in it and gently examine the wound. It's not deep, I see with relief. Head wounds bleed a lot. It's all those blood vessels close to the surface of the skin. He'll be fine.

The floorboards on the landing creak and Carter appears in the doorway, his hair still damp from the shower. His expression shifts from confusion to horror as he takes in the scene: me clasping Dylan, both of us covered in blood; Gemma frozen in the corner; the crimson bathwater.

'What the hell?' he cries, just as my phone rings. I pull it from my pocket and stare at the screen. I don't recognise the number.

I hand Dylan to Carter and answer.

'Who is this?'

'Freddie?' Alex's voice is scratchy. In the background, Fleming barks.

I grip the phone tightly, relief mingled with apprehension. 'Are you all right?'

A muffled sob on the other end of the line is like a skewer through my heart. 'C-can you come and g-get me?'

71

ALEX

FOUR WEEKS LATER

The dreams are always the same. I'm back in the swirling river, the weight of the muddy water dragging me down into its murky depths, filling my mouth, my nostrils. My lungs are burning as the current pushes and pulls me, tossing me about like a piece of driftwood. I don't know which way is up and which way is down. All I know is that I am going to die.

I wake from these dreams gasping for air. Even though I tell myself it's just a dream, the fear is suffocating.

Sleep is impossible afterwards, and I lie awake staring at the ceiling and replaying the moment my best friend tried to kill me.

The police arrested Gemma that night. Freddie phoned them as soon as he ended the call to me and Carter locked her in the bathroom until they turned up, sirens blaring. She was being led from our house in handcuffs as we arrived home from Bernard and Peggy's bungalow. I willed her to look at me, to acknowledge what she'd done, but she kept her eyes firmly on the ground.

Coward.

She was arrested for attempted murder. Not for the incident in the river – she may have pushed Fleming in but I jumped after him of my own accord – but for cutting my brake cable. Police found footage from a doorbell camera across the street showing her kneeling by the front wheel of my car using wire cutters to slice through the line.

'She probably looked up how to do it on YouTube,' the officer in the case, a shrewd detective sergeant called Tony Flynn, said. 'That's how all the scrotes find out how to break the law these days. That and ChatGPT.'

'She wouldn't have needed to – her dad's a mechanic,' I told him. 'Gemma used to spend Saturday mornings in his workshop while her mum was at work. She could change a spark plug before she was twelve.'

During the police interview, Gemma admitted cutting the Volvo's brake cable but blamed it on a mental breakdown triggered by stress at work. She also admitted telling *Daily Post* reporter Tess Brown that Freddie was back.

'Why?' I asked the detective, bemused.

'Seems she wanted to draw Ingrid out of the woodwork to ramp up your paranoia and, more importantly, to frame Ingrid for your death.'

'And Ingrid isn't in any trouble for sending those notes?'

The police had taken away the pile of anonymous letters as part of their investigation. Ingrid's fingerprints were all over them.

'As they weren't explicitly threatening and Ingrid is of previously good character, the Crown Prosecution Service is of a view that it's not in the public interest to charge her with any offences,' he said.

I'm glad about that. Ingrid had only been trying to get me to look into what had happened while Saffy was on Dolphin Ward. It was a ham-fisted attempt but made with good intentions. Freddie took me to meet Ingrid and Saffy a week or so after Gemma's arrest. I wanted to say sorry for accusing her of taking Megan, and was relieved when she accepted my apology with good grace. She's nothing like the bitter, vengeful woman I'd painted her as. She's actually a lot of fun, with a wicked sense of humour, and Saffy is a little superstar.

I suppose I should have told Freddie that Saffy survived the sepsis. I'd just assumed he knew. Silly of me, but it was such a crazy few days I didn't think. Ingrid and I have met for coffee a couple of times since and we all went to watch Saffy compete at a track and field event last weekend. She and her prosthetic blade, Jake, ran a personal best in the hundred metres, beating a pack of able-bodied kids to the finish line. Erin and Megan were in awe and have been pestering me to take them along to Saffy's athletics club ever since.

Gemma's mental health will be a mitigating factor if she pleads guilty. She's still looking at a sentence of between fifteen and thirty years, according to DS Tony Flynn. Even though she'll probably only serve half of that before she's released on licence, she'll be in her late forties before she's out.

The irony is, she'll have run out of time to start her own family because she tried to steal mine.

I'm a long way from coming to terms with the fact that my best friend wanted me dead. It's like something from one of those true crime shows on Netflix. The jealous friend who steals your life. I don't know how long Gemma has coveted mine. Perhaps it began when Freddie and I got married, or when Erin was born. Maybe it goes back way longer than that.

I'll probably never know.

One thing's for sure: the damage she has done to our family can never be repaired.

'You awake?' Carter whispers.

'Mmm.'

'Me too.'

I turn on my side to face him, and he reaches out a hand to stroke my cheek.

'Another bad dream?'

I sigh. 'Yes.'

'I'm sorry.'

'Not your fault.' I wiggle closer to him, nestling into his chest. Our bodies fit together like two halves of a whole; they always have. He runs his fingertips along the curve of my hip and I shiver with pleasure; I always do.

As I stood in Bernard and Peggy's house debating which of my husbands to call that terrible night, the answer came to me as clearly as if I'd known it all along.

Carter is the axis my world spins on. He is my everything. It was him I rang. I had no idea he was in the shower and couldn't answer. I had to call Freddie to come and pick me up instead.

'Are you cold?' Carter asks, concerned.

I shake my head and roll on top of him. He groans with pleasure and I shower his face with kisses. The tears wetting his cheeks mingle with my own.

We make love slowly, tenderly, as if it's the last time.

'I love you, Alex,' he whispers into the darkness.

'I love you too,' I whisper back.

72

FOUR WEEKS LATER

To: Gemma Lawrence
C/o HMP Bronzefield
Ashford
Surrey

Gemma,

I expect you're surprised to receive this letter, but my coun-
sellor suggested it might be cathartic to write and tell you how I
feel.

That's right, I'm seeing a counsellor. Her name's Alison
and she reminds me of Mrs Fairweather, our old English
teacher. D'you remember her? Half-moon specs, droopy cardi-
gans and even droopier breasts? Sorry, I'm going off on a
tangent. Alison said that might happen, but she also said that
writing to you would help me process everything. Put pen to
paper, she said. Tell Gemma exactly how you feel, and I
thought, why the hell not?

Mostly, I feel sad. Sad that my life meant so little to you that you were prepared to rob me of it. In the early hours, when I can't sleep, I go over and over things, trying to work out if there was anything I could have done differently, anything that would have changed what happened.

If only I hadn't gone to that damn student party. If only Freddie hadn't walked out. If only Carter hadn't come back. Alison says I shouldn't think like that, because it's where madness lies. She's probably right. Besides, if I hadn't, Erin, Megan and Dylan wouldn't be here.

What were you thinking as you cut through my brake cable? When you pushed Fleming into the river? Did you think about my kids? You claim to love them, but you don't, not really. You are selfish, Gemma, always looking out for number one. They'd have seen that eventually, and they'd have despised you for it. It would've served you right.

I've been thinking about our friendship a lot, re-examining it under the harsh light of hindsight, and d'you know what? I don't think you ever truly loved me. You always wanted what I had, whether it was a snazzy new pencil case or a different haircut. The next day I'd come into school, and you had the same pencil case, the same hairstyle. They say imitation is the best form of flattery, but what you were doing wasn't flattering, it was parasitic. You were sucking me dry.

Yes, I feel sad. But I'm angry, too. How dare you think you can help yourself to my husband and children?

I get the feeling you hoped Freddie and I would pick up where we left off when he came home, leaving Carter free for you to sink your claws back into. Maybe you imagined cosy foursomes at the pub, double dates at the cinema.

Not a chance.

I've forgiven Freddie for sleeping with you, but I can never forgive him for walking out on Erin and Megan. Too much has happened for us to go back to the life we once had. Besides, *there's nothing like a near-death experience to sharpen the mind. And after I almost drowned it hit me who I wanted to spend the rest of my life with.*

Carter.

You were wrong that day on the riverbank when you called me greedy. I never wanted two husbands. One was plenty.

It's Carter I choose to grow old with. Neither of us claims to be perfect, but we love each other.

Carter is my future, Gemma. And if you can't deal with it, you can go to hell.

Alex

73

GEMMA

FOUR WEEKS LATER

I sit on the edge of my narrow bed in my suffocating prison cell and reread Alex's letter, my nostrils flaring.

> *Carter is my future, Gemma. And if you can't deal with it, you can go to hell.*

My fingers twitch. I long to crumple the letter into a ball and hurl it into the bin or tear it into a hundred tiny pieces and flush them down the toilet, but I stop myself. I will keep it as a reminder, not that I need one, of Alex's duplicity.

How dare the treacherous bitch tell me to go to hell, as if she hasn't put me there already? I scan the tiny room, the bars on the window, the heavy steel door, the graffiti-covered desk and plastic chair, and my lips curl. Most animals are treated better.

A white-hot fury pounds through my veins with a ferocity that takes me by surprise. I want to smash things up, to punch the wall. Most of all I want to see Alex's face tight with fear in the moment she realises she is about to die.

Because I've had a lot of time to think while I've been on remand. Let's face it, there's sod-all else to do. And I've had an epiphany. I've realised my life can't begin until Alex's life is over. We negate each other. We can't both have Carter and the children. Like two queens on a chess board, one of us must eliminate the other to survive.

I have pleaded guilty and my sentencing is in a few weeks' time. My solicitor has told me that I shouldn't get more than fifteen years if I play the mental illness card, in which case I'll be out in under eight. I'll be forty-seven, too late to start my own family, but not too late to slip into the life that should have been mine. Erin and Megan will be twenty and eighteen, but Dylan'll only be ten. He'll still need a mother when his own is out of the picture.

While I wait, I will hatch my plan. It'll be like a game of chess, I think, liking the analogy. I'll need to plot several moves ahead while predicting Alex's next steps. I'll have to retain control so I have room to deflect and attack. Most of all, I'll need to stay calm and focused. One rushed move could cost me the game.

But that's all right, because time is the one thing I do have. Seven years to pore over the minutiae, to anticipate the risks and come up with answers. Seven years to get every detail just right.

Two things are clear. I'm in this for the long game, and it's a game I fully intend to win.

74

ALEX

TWO MONTHS LATER

I stand on the deck of the ferry and breathe in deep lungfuls of salty air. Above, seagulls ride the thermals, squawking like a gang of playground gossips. Below, the Minch – the stretch of water separating the west coast of Scotland from the Outer Hebrides – rises and falls, the gentle swell as hypnotic as a rocking cradle.

Apparently, it's common to see dolphins and porpoises along the Minch and, if you're really lucky, you might even catch a minke whale's dorsal fin slicing through the water before it arcs its back and dives. So far, the only marine life I've seen are some plump grey seals just outside the harbour at Ullapool, but I shield my eyes against the sun and scan the horizon, nonetheless.

Gemma and I caught the ferry from Dover to France the summer we left school, bound for a month-long Interrailing trip around Europe. Our itinerary sounded so glamorous and grown up when we planned it: Paris, Amsterdam, Berlin, Prague, Vienna, Venice, Rome and Nice. The reality was crowded trains and cramped hostels, arguments and tears. We were mugged in Paris and lost our passports in Vienna. Our backs ached from carting our oversized backpacks around and we ran out of money a week before we were due to travel home.

I used to joke that if our friendship could survive the holiday from hell, it could survive anything. I was wrong about that. But then I was wrong about so many things...

Gemma was sentenced at crown court last week. By pleading guilty, she saved us from having to take to the witness stand to give evidence. Some might see that as a good thing, but I wanted my day in court. I wanted to see her punished for what she did to my family. If I'm honest, I wanted to see the guilt written across her face as she stood in the dock and got her just deserts. I wanted her to look up at where I was sitting in the public gallery and mouth 'I'm sorry, Al.'

I wanted justice.

But when Gemma was escorted into the courtroom by two security officers, she didn't meet my eye, she just stared straight ahead, her face curiously indifferent as the prosecution barrister summarised the case. I thought I caught the corners of her mouth twitching when our victim impact statements were read out, as if she found the whole circus faintly amusing. I told myself I must have imagined it because no one, *no one*, could be that callous.

Gemma was jailed for sixteen years for the attempted murders of Dylan and me. Summing up, the judge said she'd taken into account Gemma's fragile mental health and her early guilty plea. She'll serve eight years before she's released on licence. We'll both be forty-eight. Middle-aged.

I wrote to her while she was on remand, hoping I'd find it cathartic. She didn't bother to reply, which is probably just as well. I never want to see or hear from her again.

'Mum!' a voice calls, and I turn to see Megan skipping towards me, Erin and Dylan at her heels. 'Guess what?'

I smile, pushing all thoughts of Gemma away. She takes up far too much space in my head. 'What?' I ask my quirky middle child.

'We saw puffins, just floating about in the sea like Dylan's plastic ducks in the bath. They're so cute! Come on, we'll show you.'

I allow her to lead me along the deck to the stern of the ferry. Sure enough, a dozen puffins are bobbing about, their distinctive orange parrot-like beaks giving them a comical air. We watch them until an announcement on the tannoy says we're twenty minutes from Stornoway.

'I'd better text your dad,' I say, pulling my phone from my bag.

I thumb a message to Freddie.

Ferry's on time. See you soon x

Two blue ticks appear so quickly he must have been watching his phone.

On my way x

I smile. Freddie's been as excited about our visit as we have. He moved back to Lewis a few weeks ago, saying island life suited him. He's planning to retrain as a GP and join a local practice. He's already looking for rental properties big enough for the girls to come and stay.

After Gemma was arrested, I asked Freddie what he meant when he said I'd be a fool to trust Carter.

He'd looked a little shamefaced. 'He was always such a player back in the day. I didn't want you to get hurt.'

'People change, Freddie.'

'I know that.'

'Carter loves me,' I said.

'I know he does.' He pinched the bridge of his nose. 'Sorry if I made you doubt him.'

Had I doubted Carter? Maybe, for a while, in those fraught days after Freddie's return, when emotions were running high and we were all struggling to keep a level head. But deep down I'd always known Carter loved me. Freddie's opinion didn't matter. I trusted myself – and my instincts were right.

Now, I turn to Erin and Megan, suddenly keen to be with my husband. 'Girls, can you keep an eye on your brother while I see how Carter's doing?'

'Course,' Erin says. 'We'll see if we can see any dolphins, shall we, Dyls?'

'Dolphins,' Dylan repeats, nodding furiously as he slips his hand into hers.

I find Carter in the observation lounge, his normally tanned face tinged with green and a glass of water in his hand.

I sit next to him and squeeze his knee. 'Feeling any better?'

He grimaces and shakes his head.

'We'll get you some seasickness tablets for the journey home. You'll be fine. Just keep sipping the water.'

'Whose idea was this anyway?' Carter grumbles.

'Yours, if you remember.'

When Erin and Megan decided they wanted to spend a couple of weeks of the school summer holidays with their dad, Carter had said, 'Hey, why don't we all go?'

I'd found it impossible to hide my surprise. 'Do you think that's a good idea? You couldn't get rid of Freddie fast enough before.'

'I know, but that was when I thought he was going to steal you away from me. Now I know I've won, it's fine.'

'You're incorrigible,' I told him, batting him lightly on the arm.

'I know, but you can't resist me, can you?' he'd said, pulling me close and kissing me till I was dizzy with desire.

He's right. I can't resist him. So here I am with my second husband and kids, about to arrive on the Isle of Lewis to spend two weeks in an Airbnb with my first husband. It might not be everyone's idea of fun, but, after everything that's happened over the past crazy few months, I can't wait to make happy memories with the people I love.

We watch the pretty harbour town draw closer. Somewhere on the quay, Freddie is waiting. My thoughts drift to Gemma, as they so often do. Eight years is a long time to hold a grudge, but I know there's a chance she'll come after me when she leaves prison.

When she does, I'll be ready. Because no one's going to take my beautiful, messy family away from me.

No one.

A LETTER FROM A J MCDINE

Dear Reader

Thank you so much for reading *The Husband Before You*. I do hope you enjoyed this twisty love triangle as much as I enjoyed writing it. If this is the first of my books you've read, welcome, and thanks for giving me a try. If you've been around from the start, a million thank yous. Your support means everything.

If you would like to be the first to hear about my new releases, you can sign up to my newsletter using the link below. Your email address will never be shared and you can unsubscribe at any time.

www.bookouture.com/a-j-mcdine

The Husband Before You is my ninth psychological thriller, although it wasn't supposed to be. I was working up another idea entirely when I met my editor, Natasha Harding, for lunch in London last summer. I'd spent the train journey up from Kent jotting down ideas for stories and, as the train trundled along, a premise popped into my head: what if a husband who disappeared ten years ago suddenly turned up on the doorstep, only to find his wife had remarried and her second husband was upstairs, and none too pleased about his return?

I mentioned the idea to Natasha at lunch, and she loved it. I worked up a rough synopsis and that was that. The other idea was shelved for the time being, and *The Husband Before You* began to take shape.

My books tend to be more character-driven than plot-driven, and so one of my priorities is always to make sure the people I'm writing about feel real and relatable. The kind of people in your own family or friendship circle. The kind of people you love... or love to hate.

Alex was an enigma to me for a while, while I felt I knew Freddie and Carter from the get-go. Gemma, well, what can I say? I think we've probably all come across a Gemma at least once in our lives. I just hope your Gemma didn't wreak as much havoc as mine!

I try to push boundaries with every book, and this is the first time I've written from a male point of view. I adored writing Freddie's chapters and I hope I did the male voice justice, though I'll let my male readers be the judge of that!

If you enjoyed Alex and Freddie's story, I would be so grateful if you could leave a review on Amazon or Goodreads. Not only would I love to hear what you think, but reviews help new readers discover my books.

But, please, no spoilers!

Please feel free to drop me a line at amanda@ajmc dine.com, visit my website or come and say hello over on Facebook or Instagram.

All the best,

Amanda x

www.ajmcdine.com

facebook.com/ajmcdineauthor

instagram.com/ajmcdineauthor

ACKNOWLEDGEMENTS

First of all, I would like to thank my editor, Natasha Harding, whose eyes lit up when I first mentioned the nub of an idea I'd had for this book. Natasha, not only did you have so many good ideas along the way, you wrested my first draft into some kind of order when I couldn't see the wood for the trees. You deserve a medal!

Thank you to my copy editor, Jane Eastgate, and proof-reader, Jenny Page, for their eagle eyes and expertise, and my publicist, Noelle Holten, for spreading the word about *The Husband Before You*. I appreciate everything you do.

My heartfelt thanks go to the wider Bookouture team for helping launch my books and audiobooks out into the world. I feel so privileged to be published by Bookouture, truly the most friendly and forward-thinking publisher in the business.

I would like to thank my lovely friends Harriet Monday for the final, final read-through and Dr Barbara Beats for checking the hospital scenes for accuracy. Any mistakes are my own.

Book bloggers are the lifeblood of the reading community, and I'm so grateful for every review, recommendation and shout-out. You are the best!

The biggest thank you of all goes to you, dear reader, for choosing this book. I hope you enjoyed it!

PUBLISHING TEAM

Turning a manuscript into a book requires the efforts of many people. The publishing team at Bookouture would like to acknowledge everyone who contributed to this publication.

Audio
Alba Proko
Sinead O'Connor
Melissa Tran

Commercial
Lauren Morrissette
Hannah Richmond
Imogen Allport

Cover design
The Brewster Project

Data and analysis
Mark Alder
Mohamed Bussuri

Editorial
Natasha Harding
Lizzie Brien

Made in the USA
Columbia, SC
07 May 2025